All That We Say Or Seem

Cole Delacour

All That We Say Or Seem

Chapter One

Brown shag rug - musty and moldy and spread out from one room into the next. Cobwebs clung, hanging from the ceiling. Rust covered every hinge. Doors hung askew. The air smelled stale and itched the back of my throat. Layer upon layer of dust caked the molding, leaving them a dingy brownish-gray which only minutely improved when I ran my finger through them. If this represented something of import, my mind stood underwhelming blank. I'd never been here before. None of the houses back home had wall-to-wall carpeting. Creaky wood floors and area rugs from one side of the town to the next.

This must've been a nightmare. An amalgamation of everything I loathed. A house haunted by disrepair instead of ghosts. Even the chandelier in the foyer hung dull. Missing half its crystals, the fixtured crumbled beneath the weight of the greasy air. Too still. Too heavy. Moist enough to make the fabric on the furniture sag under more than the weight of time. I hadn't even taken a step onto the angled stairwell, but the creaks echoed in my ears, sending a shiver down my spine. Darkness and a haze of dust loomed above. Some light refracted of floating specks.

"Why am I here?" I grumbled.

Every single night, I ended up in this same stupid house. One night, sure. Maybe I failed at lucid dreaming. Wandering into a nightmare sounded my speed, but this? A dingy house I'd never seen before irked me. Room came after grimy room without anyone there. Nobody showed up, but the weight remained. Eyes followed me from somewhere like two lasers burrowing into my back. If any of the walls had paintings, I would've checked them, but only random nails and hooks where things used to hang covered the walls.

Some nights, if I tilted my head just right - turned around quick enough - squinted until I had a headache, on those nights, the grime faded. The floors became rich mahogany, shining as if newly polished. Above my head, the chandelier gleamed and sparkled as if the house wanted to impress me. Floorboards creaked then. Footsteps running, and an ominous knocking preceded smoke curling around my nose, and I woke up certain my roommate had set something on fire.

If this was supposed to be a doorway into my subconscious, my subconscious was embarrassingly dull.

"I know you're there," I called when the watching returned.

A weight fell across my shoulder blades. As loudly as my voice echoed, the leaky sink in the kitchen toward the back dripped louder. Upstairs, the doors rattled.

Only one door on the second floor ever unlocked - a narrow room with a bed and little else save an old Ted Williams baseball card. The same dingy carpet lined that room underneath the metal-framed bed with an uncomfortably thin mattress. In those few moments when my squinting brought about some semblance of old elegance, only the Ted Williams card remained the same.

Shoving my hands into my pockets, I huffed. "I'm not going to hurt you."

Who would even personify somebody to watch them in their subconscious? Did this mean I was a narcissist?

Before I drove myself mad with self-analysis, a shuttered hiss rebounded back. "I know I'm not supposed to ask, but why are you here?" No one answered. Rolling my eyes, I grumbled, "Not like I thought this was real anyway."

"It is real." The voice whispered, but for the silence I expected beyond my own movements, I startled, spinning in a circle and almost falling to the ground like an idiot. Stumbling, I stared. My eyes scanned up and down. Why was I dreaming about some random guy?

Pale enough to scare the crypt keeper, a teen around my age - maybe a bit younger - cocked a brow. His large gray eyes flickered between the floor - entirely mahogany beneath his feet - and me. Lashes like a china doll curled, and for all his pallor, a rosiness colored his cheeks. If it wasn't for his mousy brown hair, I might've thought him a creepy doll come to life. A doll would've made more sense. Those high cheekbones weren't something I would've forgotten. Neither the white button-up shirt with lace at the cuffs nor his tailcoat and the rest of his black suit, more fit for a funeral than for the dusty mess of a room we stood in together, matched anything I remembered. Despite his strangeness, he blended right into the walls.

"Great!" I exclaimed, clapping my hands together. "What are you?"

"What am I?" he echoed. His nose wrinkled.

"Fine. Whatever. Who are you?"

Nobody said I had to be polite to myself. Everything about him left my skin itching and muscles twitching. The urge to push him back nearly overwhelmed me. His heavy-lidded eyes looked like those baby dolls as if I could tilt him back and put him to sleep. If I did, would he collapse back until I stood him up again?

"I-I am..." he stuttered and then gaped as if the answer would walk out of his mouth if he kept his lips parted long enough. But after thirty seconds or so, he closed his mouth and took a shuddering breath before saying, "I fear that I am not quite certain."

Of course. I had to name the idiot in my own head. What even was he supposed to represent? Was he my Id? My Superego? Did anybody still care about Freud?

"How can you not know your name?"

When he stepped back, the mahogany moved with him. "I do not have an answer for that either." A slight accent curled his vowels, but I couldn't place it. "But you may call me Gray; everyone here does."

"Everyone?" Who else was crawling around in my subconscious? Shaking my head, I rubbed the bridge of my nose. I could deal with the rest of them

4

later. "So...Gray...as in the color?" He nodded. "Wonderful. I'm stuck in who-knows-where with a loony bonker named after a color."

"If you prefer you could think of me as Gray as in the city." He hummed softly, shifting his weight to his heels and then back to his toes before adding, "Or is it cities? I can never remember how many Gray towns and cities there are."

Of course - he didn't protest 'loony.' Nope - that wasn't the problem. The problem was his name. Seriously, what part of me was this unstable? "So...you live here."

"I do," the pale teen replied and rocked backward, almost hovering like a ghost. "And you are the boarder?"

"No." I shook my head and leaned against the doorway. "This is a dream for me."

A frown tugged at his lips. "A dream?"

"Yeah, this," I gestured to the room, "is a dream. Cause, I mean seriously, I go to Harvard College and live in Straus. Not in this weird house of mirrors."

His voice tightened, growing clipped when he spoke, "This is my home, and it is quite rude of you to insult it. A dream, it is not! It is as real as you or me."

"As you are a part of my dream, the majority of that sentence is just a little flimsy." With a huff, he deflated. "Anyway, nobody should live in this place. I feel like I'm going to get lockjaw just walking around."

"The house is perfectly liveable, thank you," came his sharp reply.

"I just mean - usually it is...uh..." Even my own psyche couldn't give me a break. All the floors transformed into rich mahogany from one blink of the eye to the next. Every speck of dust vanished from the intricate molding. No amount of squinting made the place look as good. "Just forget it."

"Think it forgotten."

As I searched for some sign the dream would end soon, I sighed. "So...you're a Red Sox fan."

"I do enjoy a good game now and then."

"So it's yours?" I pointed upwards, but his eyes simply narrowed. "The card? The Ted Williams trading card?"

"Oh! Yes, yes it is..." He pressed the knuckle of his forefinger against his bottom lip. "I didn't realize I left my door open. If you would kindly not enter my room again, I would be grateful."

"Sure. Just thought the card stuck out. It was the only thing in there, so it kind of..."

"My father sent it to me while I was staying here..." Gray's eyes jumped toward the stairs, and his posture crumbled as his shoulders rose. "I mean, he sent it to me because I am staying here."

Seeing fear in Gray's eyes made me uneasy. Leaning so I could look up the stairwell easier, I had no idea what I expected. Some sort of nonsense monster maybe. Something more exciting than a large-eyed nobody with bow-lips. There was nothing there.

Glancing back at Gray, I raised an eyebrow, but he was not paying attention to me anymore. Gray seemed completely distracted with inching slowly away from the stairwell and toward the kitchen hall leading off the side of the front parlor. After another glance at the stairs, I crossed to Gray's side. Without really thinking, I lifted my hand and reached out to touch him. The moment before it landed, Gray looked away from the stairs and straight at me, shocking us both, and leaving my hand to fall when he practically jumped back.

"She would scold me if she heard that," Gray whispered. "I am still staying here, and she hates..." he trailed off and moved closer, almost unconsciously, to me.

"Who will? What are you talking about?"

"My governess," he meekly replied.

A tingly feeling started in the pit of my stomach. All the dreams ended that way. A sinking feeling and then a snap, and I would wake up back in Strauss in my own bed. Normally, I welcomed it. Nothing made sense here, but this time, I didn't want to go.

Gray trembled. His teeth chewed on his bottom lip. I just wanted to stay with him, to keep him safe, and to figure out who he was and why he was floating around in my head. Was he a symbol of my childhood innocence? A friend I forgot who disappeared? A story on the news? His vulnerability flipped a switch inside me. I wanted to protect him.

Which made no sense. Gray wasn't real. When I woke up, he ceased to exist. He never showed up in my dreams before, so after tonight, I might never see him again. Because he wasn't real - so I shouldn't care.

Like a huff from a punch to the gut, I exclaimed, "I'm James."

Then I woke up, staring unseeing at my roommate's *Fight Club* poster. The click of heels echoed in my ears. Probably just tinnitus. Rubbing the side of my head, I groaned, rolling over to glare at my alarm clock. Three minutes until it sounded. Not enough time to sleep. Great.

Chapter Two

Exhausted, I trudged the length back to my room. My bag weighed heavily on my shoulders, and when the door swung open to reveal Tom missing, I wasted no time, throwing the weight aside to jump into the warmth of my bed. I planned only to close my eyes. A quick nap seemed a safe bet with the alarm set on my phone, but I sunk deeper quicker than intended, snapping to awareness on the stiff cushions of the coach in that decrepit manor.

Face pressed into the rough fabric, I groaned. Sad brown carpet covered the floors. Even before I flipped onto my back, cobwebs and fluffy clouds of dust gathered in corners. Knots of hair - who knows whose - gathered under the feet of the couch and the rest of the furniture. Wet and rotten, the scent stuffed itself up my nose. Eau de wet dog and moldy toast.

The floorboards groaned, creaking when I sat up to count my fingers. All ten stood in a row. Two hands, five fingers on each - just the way I remembered every single time. Crossing the room, I tugged a dusty book from the shelf. Each page detailed the same murder mystery as the last time I'd picked it up.

Not much remained to read in the place. A book with half its pages missing lurked on the lowest shelf in the far corner of the room. In the kitchen, I had found an index card with nearly indecipherable cursive. I almost cheered when I found it, but the more I stared at the curling loops, the more I recognized I could still read the notes on how Heather Proust couldn't have dairy of any sort and refused anything with the slightly bit of green. The third and last bit of text required me to climb the stairs and invade Gray's room. While the notecard and book left my hands itching with grime and threatened to crumble at my touch, the Ted Williams baseball card never aged.

THEODORE FRANCIS WILLIAMS
Outfielder - Boston Red Sox

I could name all the stats. Born in San Diego, California. October 20th, 1918. Bats Left. Throws Right. Ridiculous - because I learned his actual middle name was Samuel.

Gray hadn't popped up, and he'd asked me not to invade his room, but this was my dream, so why should I listen to a figment of my own imagination? If I did, Cheyenne and Chad would have a field day.

"Hey?" I called out. "Gray?"

No response. Maybe my brain deleted him.

As I stepped off the stairs, crossing to the second floor landing, sweat poured down my face. My eyes stung. Everything itched. Rubbing my palms against my jeans, I glared at the card. Same words. Wiping my face across my upper arm, I looked back. Same words. Ten fingers and I could read. Recognizing a dream without a trigger? Priceless. Every speck of data from my experiences undermined our group project. This early in the semester, my grades could recover, but I'd never hear the end of it from Cheyenne.

"You're in my room." Gray hovered by the door. His large eyes avoided mine, bouncing from one end of his tiny room to the other.

Frowning, I sat down on his bed - because taking my frustration out on a figure of my subconscious felt like some self-flagellation, and honestly, I hated when my body betrayed me. Lucid dreaming shouldn't have been this hard.

When his fingers curled into fists, I pointed at the card. "That's a 1940s card."

"It is."

"You're dressed like it's the 1800s."

His eyes narrowed. "I am dressed how I like to dress."

"Lie." Before he could argue, I grinned and continued, "You're overly controlled. I assumed you were a representation of my subconscious, but I'm giving you too much credit, right? I'm not a control freak, but I have some obsessive tendencies. I don't like being wrong. That's you."

Tilting his head, Gray scoffed, "Disassociation. And here I thought your psychosis would be more interesting."

"What?"

"You think reality is a dream. Your perception is flawed. This house, me, everything around you - you're just seeing what you want," Gray said.

I rolled my eyes, clucking my tongue. "Dream-reality confusion? Seriously?"

"If that's what you'd like to call it." He glided into the room to stand over me. His thin lips twisted into a smirk. "You often fall asleep at random and in strange places. Narcoleptics are more likely to confuse reality and dreams..."

"Paraphrasing my psych textbook? Yeah, sure, you're your own person," I sneered. Grabbing his wrist, I tugged him down onto the bed beside me. "If this is a boarding house, where is everyone else?"

A wrinkle formed between his brows as they tugged together, furrowing as he studied me. "I never said it was a boarding house."

He stared up at me. Like an owl, Gray blinked ridiculously slowly. My hand, which still encircled his wrist, slid up his arm to press against his shoulder. The urge to push - to send him tumbling backwards onto the sheets itched, causing my fingers to twitch against the coarse fabric of his jacket. Would he close his eyes if I did? Fall asleep and be unable to wake until I brought him back up again?

Biting my lip, I tugged my hand away. "Then what is it?"

A flash of white teeth - his eyes softened and laughter echoed through the room. A chill ran up my spine. The sweat - sticky and warm, causing my shirt to stick to my back - itched against my skin. Nails dragged down my spine, and the explosive rush of heat slammed into me like leaning too close to a gas grill when it caught, but the moment that I blinked, Gray frowned up at me the same as he had moments ago. Then the world blurred.

Back to the *Fight Club* poster. No answers.

Rubbing my hands over my face, I groaned, "Great."

Chapter Three

"Hands up if you've successfully recognized you were dreaming," Cheyenne called out before most of our group had even settled in their seats.

On the plus side, I didn't have to be the group parent - rushing everyone else to actually do their parts, but on the down side, nobody wanted Cheyenne to be the one in charge. Her dream journal inspired the project, so it made sense; however, her end goal was astral projection and reaching enlightenment. The rest of us just wanted a passing grade - preferably an A.

Her hand remained up, and she glared about the group until two others - myself and Tom - joined her. Reluctant - it seemed - on Tom's part as he weighed his hand in a weird tilted climb as if to say almost. Cheyenne skipped any questions and focused on the stragglers.

"What are you doing wrong?" she demanded.

Marie crossed her arms over her chest. "Who says we're doing anything wrong?"

"Well, you aren't lucid dreaming, so obviously, you did something wrong."

Drumming his pen in an off-beat on his notebook, Tom hummed. "Yeah, but I recognized I was dreaming, but it wasn't like I could do anything but keep going. Like - yeah, totally not actually taking a test with no pants on but 'oh well, where's my number two pencil?' Ya know?"

A slight wriggle of Cheyenne's jaw followed. Her eyes, however, remained on Marie. "Recognizing you're dreaming is step one. If you can't do that, we've halved our sample size for step two."

"Failure to obtain data is data in and of itself," Marie retorted.

Now, her - I wanted in charge. No nonsense and the least talkative out of everybody - she would get work done. Even better, she'd probably do it herself rather than ask any of us. Not the best for learning, but it wasn't like Psych 101 had anything useful in it that wouldn't be repeated a thousand times in every subsequent class.

Leaning back in his chair with his hands behind his head, Alexander sighed and grumbled, "Pretty sure I don't dream."

"Pretty sure you've been black-out drunk every night since we started this project," his roommate, Chad, snapped though the second his voice jumped in volume - almost cracking on 'drunk,' he winced. "I hate you so much right now."

Without missing a beat, Alexander laughed and kicked Chad's chair. "Nah, man, you love me."

"It won't work if you're drunk!" Cheyenne shrieked.

Rolling her eyes, Marie clucked her tongue. "Forget about the project. How are you getting alcohol already? It's barely a month into the first semester. You want to be kicked out?"

"Legacy baby!" Alexander cheered.

"God, can't you be quiet?" Chad growled.

Cocking one brow, Alexander grinned. "For a smoothie."

"Fine. I'll buy you a smoothie if you shut up."

"Two smoothies."

"What?" Chad's head snapped up, and he rocked in his chair, putting a hand to his head to steady himself. "I'm not negotiating on this - one smoothie."

"Two. One for coming to this dumb meeting like you promised me this morning. Another one for being quiet. Two smoothies," Alexander counted them on his fingers, wiggling the two digits in front of Chad's face.

"Fine, whatever! Shut up!" Chad snapped. If Chad didn't kill Alexander by the end of term, it'd be a miracle.

Cheyenne gave one last glare before tossing her pale blond curls over her shoulder to focus on Tom and me. "So?"

Tom wiggled his fingers. "Extra digits then - BAM! I'm awake."

"That's good," she cooed. "It's a start. Now, you just need to stay in the dream."

Her eyes shifted to me. Immediately, everyone else focused on me too. Great. Just what I didn't want. Psychoanalyzing Gray and the bullshit manor seemed like a literal nightmare, so I leaned back in my chair and focused on the minimum. They needed basics. Nothing fancy. Nothing that might lead to some weird diagnosis because when didn't new wanna-be psychologists offer unsolicited and ego-destroying analysis.

"I know I'm dreaming, but not like how it says in those articles - my fingers are all there. I can read fine. It's just the same weird house every night, so - not really useful, right?" I reported, scrolling to my notes in the shared online document. "Did find out that I apparently paid more attention to my Granddad's Red Sox golden age rants than I thought."

"What do ya mean?" Alexander prompted.

I shrugged. "There's this card in the dream - Ted Williams. Don't remember ever seeing one, but I looked it up online, and it's exactly the same in the dream as it was in real life, so I must have at some point."

Focused on the card. Honed into the almost normal - the things I had already traced and connected in my life to something understandable and not controversial. No talk about my sexuality personified into a nerdy, Victorian twink. Nobody needed to know my kinks. I wasn't out and proud about being gay, and dealing with tastes that would make Oscar Wilde preen could be left for my future self - my rich, independently successful, impossible to otherwise critique future self who had a hot Victorian-cosplaying gothic twink boyfriend.

"Like Tris."

All eyes jumped to Marie. I blinked. "What?"

"Like Tris," she repeated. "From *Divergent*. She just knew it was fake. No tells or anything. Just - not real."

"Lucid dreaming isn't like the fear simulations," Cheyenne argued, but Alexander slammed back in his seat.

"Whoa! You're right!" he cheered, causing Chad to groan at the exclamation. "Dude! You didn't tell me I could lucid dream myself into a movie!"

"That's not what I was dreaming..."

"I'm gonna be Bruce Wayne!" Alexander mimed driving a car, leaning back to bounce from side to side in his seat. "Hit the town in my batmobile and kick some bad guy -"

"Great," Cheyenne interjected. "So you're actually going to try to do the project now?"

The wild smile across Alexander's face grew even larger. His enthusiasm would have been more endearing if he wasn't such a cocky dick most of the time, but chasing after straight guys led to heartbreak. Plus, getting close to him would mean dealing with his partying, and I wasn't a legacy. Scandals got guys like me kicked out of Harvard.

Chad gurgled as he sunk his face into his forearms on the desk. "Can we be done?"

"Seconded," Marie called, already dropping her pen and notebook back into her bag.

"We barely started," Cheyenne complained.

Leaping from his desk quickly enough to almost knock it over, Alexander crowed, "Thirded!" He swiped an arm over Chad's desk, dumping everything into his roommate's backpack - even his own notebook. No pen or pencil though. I could spot a weak link in a group project when I saw one, but he was really hitting it home. "Smoothie time! Smoothie time!" he chanted, pulling Chad out of his seat.

"I still hate you," Chad spat, but he allowed his roommate to carry his bag and drag him off.

Cheyenne continued to complain, stalking Marie out of the study room as Tom leaned over to me. "Odds on Chad killing him versus them boning by Christmas?"

"Not everyone's gay, Tom."

Slinging his bag over his shoulder, he scoffed. "Who said gay? My bet is Alexander is bi, and Chad...maybe pan?"

"Bi-curious at most, and if Chad isn't already in a serious relationship, he's ace. Cheyenne and Alexander in our group - and not a single glance at chest or butt on either one," I explained then shook my head. "I can't believe we're even having this discussion. We're majoring in psychology."

"And my goal is to be a sex therapist."

"Well, if those who can't do -" I began, but the floor went out from under me as I exited the room, and my eyes caught on a lean form stretching up to pull a book from a high shelf. Standing on his toes, he shimmered like a beacon, and the second my eyes caught on him, I couldn't look away. All around me, the world faded. Every shelf and person disappeared. Only he and I remained.

Was I dreaming? Had I slipped into sleep without noticing it? I traced the hours back from the moment I rolled out of bed until now, but there wasn't anything to suggest I'd stumbled into a dream, yet there he stood. Completely out of place. Dressed in black slacks and a white dress shirt - his jacket folded over one arm as the other stretched upward. His skin so pallid it nearly made the shirt cream in comparison.

My world narrowed, and his name slipped from me - a summons or a curse, I couldn't be certain. "Gray."

Then, like an elastic snapping back, he was gone.

"Yeah, yeah," Tom drawled, smacking me on the back. "You're real funny."

"Funnier than you," I retorted and kept walking.

Chapter Four

Even as I drifted off to sleep, the glare of my computer screen ached, reflecting in the back of my eyelids. Nothing helped. Every post I read contradicted the last. Half of them said I had some psychotic break. Divided personalities or disassociation as a result of trauma - something I never had. My life was boring. Wake up. Eat. Study. Repeat until sleep.

Yet I woke up tired. Embroidery pressed against my skin, indenting paisley on my cheek when I turned to glower at the ceiling. Clean molding tonight.

"You should sleep in your own room," Gray drawled. Sitting rigid and too far forward in a nearby seat, he held his book down upon his knees. A thumb marked his pages. "The sofa isn't terribly comfortable." His eyes scanned down the length of my body. Heat followed in their wake until his eyes narrowed. Frowning when his gaze reached my feet, he clucked his tongue. "Your shoes will sully it!"

I rubbed my hands over my face. "Can't help it. It's too short."

"You're simply too tall."

"If I were under six foot, I'd still be too big for this dumb couch," I grumbled.

I don't want to be here, I thought. Every ounce of me focused on my college-issued mattress. Old and plastic-wrapped, it had at least two inches more padding to its worn surface than the tight-stitched padding on the old sofa, but willing myself away didn't work. For worse, I remained.

Despite scolding, Gray did nothing to get my feet off the fabric. He, instead, returned his attention to his reading. Some foreign language book with a black cover and inlaid scrawl on the front. Probably something fancy and out of time. Victorian clothes - Victorian mansion - 1940s brat beneath it all. Beautiful - not handsome. Pointed chin and large eyes like a china doll. The creepy sort that I wouldn't want in the same room as me when I slept. Lips - too thin. Not the kissable kind. Too thin and tightly pouting with a downward curve at the edges which marked all dour pessimists.

Shit, he'd look good flushed and upset at his own desperate cries. The quiet ones broke like a rushing crescendo, didn't they? All the notes falling over and on top of each other in a desperate thrumming.

"I'm horny," I declared, drawing one knee to my chest as I sat up.

Glancing over his book, Gray glared. "If you are not going to be quiet, vacate."

I slid closer until our knees brushed. Along his jaw, the muscles twitched, but he didn't move his leg. Probably didn't want to screw up his perfect posture. Leaning forward, I set my hand on his thigh. He was impossibly warm. The heat leaked up my arm, leaving my fingertips feeling burnt, but I edged up and up as his large eyes stared into mine.

"You know what horny means, right?" If I was backed up and needed to give my repressed sexuality a bit of care, then I would. No progress meant dealing with Cheyenne. Sooner this ended, the better.

"You have a room and a hand."

My breath caught in my lungs as my ribs squeezed tight. This ended here. "Sure I do, but I like you more." I pushed forward, brushing my fingers against his inner thigh.

The full weight of his book slammed into my face. Rearing back, I blinked as blood dripped down my front. Wide eyes stared at me. Tears lined his long, dark lashes, and everything in me withered at his terror, but before I could apologize, he flew out of his chair and ran back toward the kitchen. Any hope I had to follow him and try to set things right regardless that he was a figment of my subconscious fell to the wayside as the air thickened around me. Time slowed as he fled. With each step, the grandeur faded. Cobwebs gathered, and carpet rolled into place until nothing of the original house remained. Through its ruination, I sat alone.

But I didn't feel it.

Stones fell into water. Marching *one-two, one-two* with a sliding scratch across the rug. A presence loomed behind me, casting shadows over the decrepitude. Just like the song, my mind raced, but my heart beat slurred in a slow pulse - sticking to the skip between the beat as my neck broke out into a cold sweat.

Weight dropped onto my shoulders. Two long-fingered hands with sharp, well-maintained nails pressed me down, holding me in place, but for

26

all the weight of their grip, the heat was worse. Wherever the hands touched, my skin blistered and burned as if someone had swept up the still glowing embers from a fireplace and dumped them over me. No matter how painful, my body wouldn't move to scream.

In the vacuum of time, a single syllable stretched out. It bounced around my ears. Slipping through the sludge of what used to be air, the word - whatever it was - just made the hands burn more. Spots danced in my vision. I was waking up. I had to be. Passing out in my dream might send me straight into another, but the way my gut rebelled, I knew this nightmare would be over like how a stomach ache sometimes gets better right after puking.

Only when the blackness right before waking turned to bright white light, the heat and thick air remained. Sweat painted my skin. Up and down had no meaning. Just bright white light. My stomach threatened to go inside out. A molasses mumbling.

Then two new hands grabbed me. They pushed me down, back against sweat-soaked sheets as a shadowy figure loomed above me. "James!" a voice cried out through the murkiness.

"I'm sorry," I gurgled.

Everything hurt. Why did everything hurt?

Words faded in and out. Half-formed sentences: "...no! Mack get the...blow...James, you idiot!"

Like electricity, the pain overtook me, and my spine snapped, sending me half off the bed, rolling as I nearly projectile vomited into a well-placed trash bin.

Patting my back, Tom sighed. "What the hell did you take?"

With bile embittering my tongue and a new kind of frustration itching across my skin, I couldn't answer him as I vomited again. There was no relief. Everything hurt. Gray didn't want me. A figment of my imagination ran away from me. That shouldn't hurt. He wasn't even a well-fleshed out delusion. I could count the facts I knew about him on one hand and have fingers left over. Nightmares happened. I feared rejection like any sane person, so this was just a personification of my fear that even if I did come out, nobody would want me. Just another stupid paranoia.

But it hurt so bad.

Chapter Five

A week passed without a single dream. Rejection - even private, even by my own mind - curdled in my gut like a sore. Internalization. I had that. Though I intended to take it to my grave or to wherever I needed to be to feel untouchable, I recognized the issue and its source. Worse still - when I spiraled, my mind wandered back. Some kids pulled on pigtails when they were little. They saw something they liked and wanted to wreck it. A desperate urge to do whatever it took to get attention at an age where attention - positive and negative - all felt the same. Many people never grew out of that urge. Probably they just never had to.

I never cared to pull pigtails. Everybody whose attention I wanted already looked at me. They were my friends, so I played with them whenever I wanted, and by some lucky fluke, I was the kid who everybody thought was their best friend, which meant I never had to worry about a friend liking another friend more than me.

Until middle school. Middle school was a nightmare. I wasn't into girls. Everybody else started to consider the possibilities, and I just stayed the same. I wanted to hang with my friends. Which was fine. I joked, taunting crushes. Desperately trying to figure out why I would hate how much time so-and-so spent thinking of whatever girl had caught their attention. Luckily, my friends had short attention spans, so I could talk myself down without getting too nasty.

Until I couldn't. Until I realized exactly what I wanted. When my own feelings focused entirely on a single boy - Simon. Everybody loved Simon. He smiled all the time with two perfect dimples. With chestnut brown hair and a constant bronze tan - even in winter. Made him practically glow like a demigod. I hated him for it.

We weren't best friends. By middle school, the everybody's best friend became a generally good friend with everybody, but it seemed they had all paired off, having given up on me since I reveled in the attention rather than sticking to any one of them. I hadn't really minded before Simon. Then I realized I liked Simon. Woke up having dreamt about Simon in the way the health class teacher talked about, and I got sick in the pit of my stomach every time I saw him - especially when I saw that unlike me, who hadn't picked anybody, he had used his everybody's best friend time to pick the dorkiest kid in school - Reggie Huberman.

Dark haired and pale - the flushed red to burning to white lily sort of pale. He wore overalls more than jeans in elementary school, and for some reason, we all thought that was the dumbest thing ever, so most of the boys bullied him. I hadn't. Overalls seemed dumb - inconvenient really - but Reggie Huberman could wear whatever he wanted. Small and skinny and more into books than actually playing on the playground, he had other problems besides his clothes.

Simon hadn't thought that though. He always tried to get Reggie to play with us, and if the other guys were a bit too harsh, he ditched them for Reggie. Nobody knew why. It wasn't like Reggie lived next door or the two of them had known each other before school. Reggie hadn't even gone to our school until fifth grade, but in a single year, he won over Simon and became best friends with one of the most popular guys in school.

It didn't matter to me until seventh. In seventh grade, I wanted Reggie to just fuck off. Still into books. Even more into his debate club and Model UN. And wherever Reggie went, Simon followed like a puppy. Even before I realized what that meant for the two of them, I hated it.

Despite that, I tried to join in. Between practices, I hit up debate club. Reggie could twist words like he breathed air, and whenever he won, Simon beamed, so of course, I studied and got friendly with the rest of the debate team. Eventually, I started winning against everybody else - even Reggie sometimes. Simon went on beaming. After one particularly frustrating afternoon in our sophomore year, in which I won against Reggie in a mock debate, I caught Simon frowning. But it wasn't at me.

He frowned at Reggie. If his best friend noticed, the dark haired kid didn't say anything. Reggie smiled up at me, congratulating me for victory, and it felt like he was handing Simon over to me. Like he was saying: "*Well done, James. You're obviously the better choice for best friend.*

Here's the guy you've been wanting to kiss on a platter."

Then Suzanne Gleason caught Simon and Reggie kissing behind the gym. From popular to plague-ridden, Simon fell right off the popularity chart. People ignored him. Picked last for gym - last of the athletic boys at least, people still wanted to win. Otherwise, a few guys called him names, and his general friend group became distant, but ignoring seemed the punishment for him.

Reggie got it worse. Everyone blamed him for turning Simon gay. They wrote words all over his locker. Spat it in half-whispers in the halls. Snickered and pointed whenever Reggie showed the least bit of discomfort. Girls talked about how ugly he was - how they couldn't possibly see why someone like Simon wanted to be his friend let alone his boyfriend. They turned it around, saying Suzanne said Reggie kissed Simon and not that they were just kissing in general. It was horrible.

The school stepped in on the locker part, but they didn't really see everything else. Two months into this, Reggie broke down crying in the debate team room - to me. Internally, I panicked, but I patted him on the back awkwardly, hoping nobody would see us because if these two months taught me anything, it was that being gay - liking boys like I did - was unacceptable. Especially for dorky guys like Reggie Huberman.

I wasn't a Reggie. I liked to think myself a Simon, but that meant I didn't have friends to support me like Reggie did. The whole debate team

- all six of them in a school well over two hundred - supported Reggie. But they couldn't do much besides be there for him, and maybe knowing they were there for him is why he thought that I - a part of the debate team - was also on his side.

"I don't know if I can take it," he had cried, hidden behind the teacher's desk.

Sitting right beside him - happy he'd picked somewhere out of view but nervous that if someone saw us they'd think we were out of view for a different reason, I had leaned my elbows on my knees and shrugged. "They'll forget about it after summer vacation. That's like a month and a half away. Six weeks, right? You can survive until then."

"But what if they don't? What if it gets worse?"

I couldn't imagine it getting worse. Back then, I had no idea how naive I was, but Reggie wasn't, so when I said, "How can it get worse?" like an utter tool, Reggie had told me just exactly how.

And he'd ended a whirlwind speech which gave me nightmares and a desperate desire to never **ever** let anyone know I was gay - for fear of death and dismemberment - with: "Simon and I aren't even dating anyway!"

My brain had come up short. "What?"

His dark eyes - bright with tears - focused on me as he repeated, "Simon and I aren't even dating. We were. But I-I wanted to break up with him, and I told him that the night before, but he dragged me behind the gym and then - then..."

34

Reggie cried so much I thought he would drown himself, but I could only robotically pat him on the back and let him soak my shoulder as my brain stumbled over what I had just heard. Simon and Reggie weren't dating. They weren't even dating, and Reggie got put through all this.

"Why didn't you tell everyone?"

"I did!" Reggie exclaimed then ducked down, burying his face in his own arms. "I told them we weren't dating, but Simon just - he just wouldn't say anything. Just confirmed we were kissing. Told everybody we kissed a lot - that he liked me and that was it. Nobody cared what I thought. And I couldn't say I wasn't gay."

"You could've," I had contested.

It was true. He could've lied, and it would have saved him a lot of trouble, but Reggie wasn't a liar. If anything, he was too honest, which was why it was strange nobody believed him when he had spent the first week denying they were dating despite not denying they had been kissing and everything else, which made me an utter idiot.

A week later, I showed up early for the next debate team meeting as well. Reggie huddled behind the desk again, waiting for the rest to come. Everybody knew where the debate team held their meetings, so it made no sense why he was hiding if he wasn't crying this time - until I realized the bag and soda sitting on one of the desks were not Reggie's. Simon strolled into the room just as I set my bag down and headed to see how Reggie was. His bright eyes half-lidded. When I offered him an awkward smile and opened my mouth to say hello, he glared. Even when he was being ignored and sneered at, he never glared at those guys, but he looked at me like he wanted to punch my throat.

"Hey," I ended up saying then pushed on toward Reggie, but the second I sat down with a: "Hey, Reggie, how's things?" Simon sat down on the teacher's desk, letting his feet fall right between Reggie and me.

I inched back, but after over two months, Reggie reached his limit. He jumped up, clenching his fists at his sides as he glowered at Simon like he wanted to set him on fire. Honestly, after everything he had gone through - maybe he really did.

"What is your problem?" Reggie cried.

Leaning back, Simon tilted up his chin. "What? Can't I be part of the conversation?"

"No! No, you can't. You gave up any right to be part of any conversation when you screwed me over," Reggie railed, and Simon's face remained blank - almost holier-than-thou. I had never seen such an ugly expression.

"Funny. When we were screwing, you said that was because we were boyfriends," Simon retorted. My brain completely shutdown.

Growling, Reggie spat, "We aren't dating! We aren't anything!"

And that had gotten Simon pissed. He slid off the desk, using every inch he had on Reggie though there were only two. "And why is that? I love you! If you're going to dump somebody, you should give them a reason." In his rage, Reggie sputtered, but Simon plowed right on, "It's cause you like James, isn't it? Well?" His glare shifted to me. "Well?" he demanded again. "What about you, huh?"

And holding up my hands, I waved the whole affair off with a pointed, "Hey, we're just friends. I'm not gay."

Even though he looked like he was going to cry again, Reggie had pointed at me as he stared Simon down. "See? You stupid, jealous asshole - friends. This is why I didn't want to be with you."

Reggie made it to the end of the year, but he hadn't come back for the next. He had moved to live with his aunt out in California. Simon could've started dating girls if he had wanted to get back to where he'd been, but he just ignored everybody - quit debate, quit soccer for a year. Practically went silent in our junior year - then came back determined in our senior year. Some college in California ended up recruiting him for their soccer team. I didn't keep track of him after that. Maybe he went there because they offered. California seemed more open about guys like us, but knowing Simon, he probably went there because he still hadn't completely given up on Reggie. I always hoped he never found him. Reggie deserved better.

That year had cemented two facts: 1) nobody could know I was gay, and 2) people who say they love you can (and will) betray you. And somehow, though I started with a crush on Simon, it was Reggie - dark and pale and clever - who set the mold for every guy I'd like after. Wherever he

37

ended up, I always hoped he was happier, but some part of me will always wonder if he had actually liked me.

Wondering never helped. For all I yearned to know if Reggie had made it out completely or if California wasn't the golden land of acceptance I once dreamed it to be, I made my choices. I could have gone there. Applied to a school out west - Berkley even, but I hadn't dared. My father's sneering words, joking that we'd all be better if they'd just fall off the map, haunted me. No matter how good the school, the east coast remained safest. Ivy League gentled my sports abandonment. Intelligence only mattered in my house if it was a death blow at the water cooler. Scholarships to a lesser school withered when my dad could lean and talk about my full ride to Harvard. First in my family to attend college. A doctor in the making. Not that he'd tell anyone my major was psychology. Psychologists and dentists - the lesser doctors.

"Man, come on!" Tom threw his pillow across the room.

Hitting me square in the face, I left it where it fell. Gray rejected me. Must mean I hated myself. Rejection of self and the possibility of romantic fulfillment, right?

Chad huffed. Why he even came to our room, I would never know. Maybe to hide from his group project admirer. "What's his problem?" he demanded.

A sigh came from Tom. "Beats me. Been weird since he almost overdosed."

"I didn't almost overdose. I didn't take anything," I grumbled.

Lifting the pillow, Tom cocked a brow - or at least tried to. His forehead muscles jerked on one side, but the eyebrow stayed pretty level with the other. "You woke up in a cold sweat, vomited repeatedly, and couldn't handle us turning on the lights."

Chad furrowed his brows. Arms across his chest, he leaned over me. "Migraines can do that too."

And what could I say? Nightmare caused it. I rejected myself completely and wrecked even my ability to verbalize and consider a future where I was anything but so deep in the closet Marie Kondo couldn't find me? Even if she did, what would she say? *Does this bring you joy?* Fuck no. This useless sack of human flesh brought nothing but misery, existential panic, and lies. Couldn't even donate it.

"He still looks like shit," Chad said. "Maybe we should take him to emergency care?"

"It's been two days. I'm fine. I'm just depressed. Repressed memories. Lucid dreaming can bring them up, and I had a particularly unpleasant experience," I informed them, sitting up and swinging my legs over the side of the mattress. "Give me ten. I smell like shit."

Even if I wanted to spend my days in half-purposeful starvation, Tom wouldn't let me. I knew I shouldn't have made friends with my roommate. Rookie mistake. He clapped me on the back. "That's the spirit!"

As I mulled about the room, grabbing a change of clothes and my bathroom kit, Chad leaned closer to Tom. If Chad intended to whisper, he failed when he said, "Is he always this much work?"

Tom - bless his heart - shrugged. "Nah. My stupid's outweighed his moody so far."

I didn't deserve Tom. Sure, I helped him with assignments in our shared classes, but he wasn't stupid. When I screwed up on an assignment, I suffered from laziness. He had ADD and dyslexia. Stuff took him longer, but he still had high Bs in everything. Hardworking, loyal - I'd only drag him down.

"Keep it moving!" Tom pushed me toward the showers.

***

Cleaned up, I looked better than I felt when Tom and Chad finally dragged me to the dining hall. Food only made me nauseous. My stomach churned, and an ache - bone deep - haunted my body. Not a new feeling. Muscles and skin - I had hurt those time and again, but bone deep without the other two, the kind of in the chest want-to-cry-but-can't sort of hurt was one I tried to push down more often than I cared to think. Eventually, pushed down long enough, the pain would go away or add another layer to the self-loathing suffocating at my core.

Reggie leaving - the accusations and everything unsaid - that still hurt. The moment they argued in front of me - probably the moment I realized what was going on between them - I knew it would be the lasting sort of pain. Gray felt like that. I rejected myself consciously more often than I liked, but to have it so literally spelled out for me? *Nobody's going to love you* - the ache whispered. *Especially not yourself.*

"Hey!" Tom bumped his shoulder into mine. "Grab a seat. I'll get you a plate."

Chad glanced between us. His nose wrinkled, but he held his tongue. Probably holding back another comment about how much more Tom put into our relationship than I did.

"I can get my own plate," I argued, but he shoved me toward a table.

"And then we won't get a table because your lazy butt couldn't get up in time." Tom didn't wait for me to agree. He marched off. A man on a mission. It would be so easy to like a guy like him. Smarter than most but ridiculously nice and self-deprecating. Sincerely self-deprecating. If he were -

No. Not a chance. Tom had Sydney - his high school sweetheart, and monogamous could've been his middle name. As long as they dated, nobody else registered for him.

I slouched down at the nearest free table, glaring at anyone who dared approach until Chad returned with two plates. One was a salad - piled high. The other was a mix of roast chicken, some kind of beef casserole, and hamburgers with those soggy fries everybody says they hate, but they all still ate.

"What's your deal?" he demanded, shoving both in my direction. "Tom's worried."

"Just having an off day."

"You depressed?"

I shrugged. "Probably just need to go for a run or something. Get my endorphins back up."

"That'd be the healthiest way. But I'm pretty sure Tom's grabbing every dessert he can find, so sugar could help too. Not like you couldn't use the freshman fifteen," Chad informed me, which was dumb. I had worked out in high school. Under my loose shirt, there was muscle. Chad - well, sparklers had more muscle than him. "Eat."

"Where's your food?" I deflected.

Rolling his eyes, he scoffed. "You're gonna wait until Tom's back, so you can eat the least amount possible to get him off your back."

"If you knew that, why'd you bother asking?"

"Because I sometimes forget how useless most people are. Eat," he demanded, shoving the plates into my elbows until I slid them off the table.

"I'm not Alexander. I don't need you to tell me when to eat."

I definitely didn't need the smarmy look on his face. Crossed arms, cocky smirk - Chad leaned back in his chair. "If you think I'm the one reminding him to eat, you're dumber than I thought."

"Seriously? I'm having a shit couple days. I just want to be left alone, and I get Tom needs everyone around him to be peppy, but I thought you'd appreciate the value of a little sulking."

Sometimes, I amazed myself with how much cruelty I kept buried inside. Tearing him apart would be so easy. Instead of telling him just how co-dependent the two of them were and beating down his hypocritical ass verbally, I grabbed one of the burgers and stuffed my mouth. Couldn't be a dick through half-chewed food. For once, all the rapped knuckles at the dining table had a point.

Tom came around, shoving a plate of desserts my way before settling with a salad and burger. He picked off a few fries from the plate Chad had shoved my way before glancing between us.

"What'd I miss?"

"Drinks," Chad retorted.

Popping right up, Tom rushed off with a quick: "Crap!"

Rolling his eyes, Chad shook his head. "Idiots. All of you." Another bite of hamburger - shovel the vitriol back with too much ketchup and an almost sweaty bun. "So you got dumped?"

Only my etiquette training kept me from spewing bits of hamburger across the table. "I'm not dating anyone."

"Sorry. Right." He waited until I had another bite like a dick. "So you got rejected then?"

"I'm not some one-dimensional human. I can be upset about more than a girl."

43

"Never said girl," he pointed out. "Just asked if you got rejected. You're moping. Top three reasons to mope: rejected, screwed up, jealous." He counted them out on his fingers, holding them up to my face. "I know your friends. You aren't dating. Jealousy doesn't fit." One finger dropped. "While you and Tom argued, I looked through your desk."

"What the hell, man? You don't just - "

But Chad plowed right on. "No failed grades. You aren't in any clubs or teams, so screwing up doesn't make sense either unless it was a personal screw-up, which you'd talk about unless you were embarrassed."

"Or maybe we're just not that close," I retorted, but he snorted and lowered a second finger.

"Leaves one thing. You got rejected."

Focusing on my food, I ignored him. No matter what I said, he'd think what he wanted, and I didn't have the energy to talk about it anymore. If he pushed when Tom got back, I'd just say it was the nightmare and talk about that time my uncle brought over a deer and left its skinless corpse draining in our garage. Neither Chad nor Tom were hunters. They didn't come from families who did that, and based on their political leanings, the idea of a defenseless animal's corpse being somebody's first memories would be horrifying enough. I never had to tell them how the next memory I had involved discovering how delicious it was.

44

Chapter Six

"I'm not angry," Cheyenne informed us in our final group meeting. "Just disappointed."

"Good. You should be disappointed in yourself," Marie retorted.

Chad sat rigid in his chair. Pulled up close beside him, Alexander had one arm wrapped around the back of his chair while resting his face in the other with his elbow on his own desk. Thank god he had his own problems. Tom, I could run in circles. Chad, when sober and not hung over, had the best chance of finding me out of anyone in our group. Which made the upcoming end of this project all the sweeter.

"Powerpoint looks good. Our runtime is smooth as long as Cheyenne goes last, so the teacher can cut her off...I think we're set," I said, grinning at Marie when Cheyenne scoffed.

"Perfect. Presentation's Wednesday." And without anything else, she packed up and left.

Cheyenne clicked her nails against her desk. "I can't believe you people."

"Go complain to your psychic. I'm out," Chad announced, but he remained where he was, glaring at Alexander for a good ten seconds before his roommate blinked owlishly at him.

"Oh...I gotta move, right?" But he didn't.

"Five bucks?" Tom whispered.

The muscles in Chad's jaw tensed. In a flash, he punched Alexander right below his ribs. "Move, dumbass."

Shoving his chair back, Alexander let Chad go as Tom leaned over and repeated, "Five bucks?"

Rolling my eyes, I stood. "I'm not betting on somebody's sexuality."

"Me or Chad?" Alexander asked. Like a puppy, he perked up almost immediately even as Chad flinched before storming out the door even faster, making his getaway while he still could. It wasn't often he left without Alexander right behind, but then again, they shared a room. It wasn't like he could avoid him forever. "Or both?"

"Both!" Tom replied, bouncing over to Alexander. If Tom didn't have a girlfriend, he probably would've gone after Alexander. It would've been terrible. Two high energy, low common sense guys. Thank goodness for Sydney.

"Sadly, we're both straight," Alexander confessed. He stretched, not having bothered to even fake being useful today. Not a notebook or text in sight. "But he's pretty cute when he's flustered."

Tom's shoulders sagged. "Damn. Guess I'm glad you didn't take the bet."

"Yeah - but now I'm suspicious."

Nose scrunching up, Alexander bounced out of his seat. "Huh?"

"'He's pretty cute when he's flustered,'" I repeated, and he shrugged.

"Yep! Goes all pink."

God, he was thick. Skipping off without a care in the world, Alexander probably planned to forget the conversation as soon as he turned his back to us. Must've been nice to be so secure in your identity. Well, not that Alexander knew what that was like, but Tom did. Tom had a blunt appreciation for good looks and easy smiles. Supportive family and a happy childhood left him without reason to question who he had those feelings toward, and as envious as I was of him, I respected his decision as much as I was determined to keep my own. But - as a liar, I'd gotten good at spotting others. If Alexander wanted to pretend he wasn't getting his heartbroken on the regular by Chad, that was his prerogative. He decided on being the straight jock frat boy. It wasn't my place to say anything else, and I hoped that if Alexander looked at me and saw the same that he'd keep his peace too.

And maybe it was the calm of recognizing part of myself in another that did it, but that night, I woke up back in the house. Mahogany beneath my feet. The smell of something savory baking. Mostly just the scent of onions caramelizing. I didn't have a nose good enough to discern anything else though the scent being anything besides smoke or mothballs was pretty weird.

Gray sat in his regular seat, but his book was nowhere to be found. His lips pressed into a tight line. A slight pink tinged his sharp cheekbones, and the small dread in my heart that he was some sort of mental projection of my emotions toward the incident with Reggie came back full force. The two looked nothing alike. Gray had angles Reggie didn't. Too thin - too pale - too fragile. More like a work of art than a human had any right to be. Which made sense. He wasn't real after all.

"I am sorry if I made you uncomfortable."

I blinked, sitting up to stare at him. "Me? Uncomfortable?"

"I know that I've been - been sheltered," he told me. "No one has ever...I mean, that is to say...I am not the sort who is unused to attracting such attention; however, I do not share such inclinations."

Scratching the back of my head, I sighed. "You're a shit liar."

"Excuse you!?"

Not real. Unlike Alexander, confronting Gray didn't negatively affect him. I couldn't out him. He wasn't real, so slouching back into the couch, I sighed. "I'm a good liar. I've grown up lying, and maybe it's because I'm always afraid somebody will find out despite that - maybe that's why you're so horrible at it, but whatever you say - you're..." and I couldn't. Even in my head - even in my dream, I couldn't call him out in full. This was a delusion. A figment of my imagination, but I couldn't out him. Somebody cooked in the kitchen. That governess seemed like a nightmare. I couldn't do it. "Sorry - I'm...I'm projecting. I've never told anyone about me, and I - I guess I just wanted somebody else like me to talk to about...things."

His lips trembled for a moment before he bit them. "I may not understand or share your...habits, but I would not be adverse to being a kind ear."

No clicking. No stones through water. Nothing but the warm smell of something cooking. Somehow - it formed safety around the room. As if a good dinner could make all the world better. Wash away all the terror. The fear.

What would it hurt? A traitorous whisper wrapped around my head. *This isn't real. You could say it - say it here if nowhere else. What would it hurt?*

But my mother cooked. We ate dinner around a table after saying grace. Onions and garlic - gravy in a pot - those scents reminded me of home and being fed - being cared for, but they bound up my tongue too. I couldn't tell my dad. I would've been dead to him. He would've thrown me out. Disowned me. Beaten me - but my mom...she would have tried to fix me.

I didn't know when I hunched over, head in my hands and elbows on my knees. My brain sputtered in confusion. A black out with a tight chest feeling. Then Gray touched my shoulder, and my body convulsed, flinching as he held out a handkerchief toward me. When had I started crying?

51

Chapter Seven

"How have you never had pizza?"

Day to day, the question sounded reasonable. Surrounded by early days electricity, it tasted weird in my mouth the second it came out. I honestly had never seen Gray eat, so the question gained a whole new level of ridiculousness.

Since our awkwardly emotional reunion, the manor hadn't shifted. Everything stayed pristine. Perfectly glowing floors. Additional blankets and pillows on the sofas - which were still stupidly hard and uncomfortable Victorian statement pieces. Every time I woke up there, a new scent tickled my nose, luring me into a weird state of comfort before I even opened my eyes. Obviously, my brain was taking it easy on me.

Gray shrugged, but he rubbed his palms across his knees. Always did that when I used words he didn't think he should understand. Which was ridiculous. Pizza had been in Boston since the early 1900s. If he knew about Ted Williams, there was no reason for him not to at least have heard of pizza.

"I enjoy Mrs. Hayward's cooking," he told me.

He dropped names as if I should know them. I had a list going on my bedside table whenever he mentioned someone new. Governess (heel-wearing, horrifying), Mrs. Hayward (apparently the cook, a motherly woman akin to Mrs. Weasley or every plump, happy motherly woman I'd ever seen on TV or in film), Mr. Cohen (never leaves his room, a soldier from 'the Great War'), Helena Graham (cries a lot, has a doll she considers her daughter, likely suffered multiple miscarriages (guess on my part)).

They had to mean something, but I wasn't ready to look into them seriously. More than likely, my brain pulled from my textbooks. Which meant my psych degree turned the manor into an insane asylum. Not exactly a fun thought. Seemed like something better suited to the Joker, but it wasn't like I had Cheyenne breathing down my neck asking me questions anymore.

Curled up under the blankets, I clucked my tongue. "What if we brought a slice back for her? I'm sure she'd like getting someone else to cook for her."

His fingers drummed for a moment before he shook his head. "My governess would not give me permission - "

"How old are you?" I asked, and when he didn't immediately answer, I sighed. "There's no way you're young enough that you need to listen to what your governess says all the time."

"Even if that were true, she isn't the only one I'd need permission from if I wanted to leave," Gray said.

His voice fell low and gentle. Whenever he spoke like that, the timbre of his voice dropped almost as deep as my voice, but it carried the posh English clip which set my heart to flutter like a nerdy school girl. The urge to ruffle his hair had my hand moving, but I shifted, keeping my fingers knotted in the soft woven fabric of the blanket. If I touched him, this would all shatter again.

Which was stupid. This wasn't real. Everything here was in my head. Gray wasn't real.

"What if I made pizza for you?" I offered.

He blinked, tilting his head. "You can cook?"

"A bit, yeah."

How hard could pizza be? I could find a recipe, memorize and make it in real life enough that I could walk through the steps in a dream. It would be worth it. I loved pizza. Gray was part of my mind - a very horny yet prudish part of my mind, so he would likely love pizza too. Nobody would be hurt if I wanted to see him happy. Honestly, it was like self-care.

Before he could answer, the manor shifted as if someone had pinched one end of the room and pulled it like taffy. Peddles plopped into water. Gray paled. The growing calm which seemed to reveal his true age - closer to mine than I had first believed - vanished, and the youth-inducing terror returned, widening his eyes.

She wanted him dead. The Governess was going to kill him. I knew it. His face screamed he knew it too, but he didn't move. Gray remained in his seat, tensing but waiting as if he had just come to accept that there was nothing he could do.

I couldn't say what made me do it. Or even how I did it. Everything inside me had frozen with fear last time she interrupted us, but this time, all I could think about was how scared Gray looked. He shrunk into himself. A sort of horror I never allowed myself to imagine. The face I envisioned as a child taking over my face if my father ever learned what I was - who I loved, so I couldn't stay still this time. Darkness loomed. Crawling in at the corners, waking threatened, but I moved. I stretched with the taffy pull, leaping forward toward Gray.

His eyes remained beyond me. Focused on the stairs. I dove. His knuckles whitened. I grabbed his hand, and -

And I woke up.

Chapter Eight

No matter how many showers I took, a cold sweat enveloped my body. A layer formed like lamination upon my skin. No scrubbing rid me of it. Three days without dreams - my skin red and raw, I sequestered myself in my dorm room.

"He's not on drugs," Tom hissed. Whether he spoke with Chad, Alexander, or our R.A., I had no idea, but I wasn't so sure he was right.

Sure - I hadn't taken any drugs, but something had happened. Maybe Cheyenne got pissed enough to poison us. But then again, Alexander ate the cookies she baked as an end-of-project celebration too. If he had the same symptoms, Chad would've caught on, right?

Knees pulled to my chest, I huddled in the corner of my bed, hidden behind the height of my desk which abutted the end of my bed and the wall. My stomach churned. Sick. Not hunger. I ate recently. Didn't I? I remember eating. Maybe thirst?

My water bottle sat on one of the bedposts. All I had to do was reach out, but my arm wouldn't move. Somewhere inside of me, I tore myself apart. Beat all honesty out of me. Wrecked the terrified reality of who I am, and nothing I did could stop that, and it was me, so I shouldn't have felt guilt, but like a bitter coating on my tongue - nauseating and thick to swallow - guilt settled about my shoulders, weighing me down until I became a stone. Unable to move. Unable to think. Just staring at my blankets - gathered around my feet.

When my eyes fluttered closed, I expected blackness. Empty space. A vast abyss like the last few nights, and there it stood. Cold and stretching like death - unfathomable. Untouchable. A stark reality which threatened to drown me. Discomfort and unsettled, I broke beneath the tidal wave of helplessness. My mind was not my own. My body - exhausted. His hand on my forehead, a welcome chilling relief.

"You've got a fever," he whispered, sitting down beside me.

The sheets scratched at my bare chest, but I didn't have the energy to fling them off. All I could manage was to cling to him, burying my face into his side as my arms wound around his hips, keeping him planted at my side.

His hands brushed through my hair. Nails scratched across my scalp, and under his touch, I melted even as my body ached. Tears gathered in my eyes. Liquid I didn't have to spare seeking release. I held tight.

"Don't leave me. I'm sorry - don't leave me." My lips moved. The words vomited out without my consent.

He shushed me. "Mrs. Hayward says I'm to take care of you. I'm not going anywhere."

And like a demon - a snake in the garden - he shifted, and the smell of soup - chicken broth and something more which I couldn't concentrate on enough to name - curled around my nose. Forcing my eyes to open, I pushed beyond the blur until Gray's face came into focus. His pale features and

57

calm countenance soothed my soul - a poisonous balm.

"You need to eat something," he insisted.

At that moment, the pomegranate seeds made sense to me. Trapped in phantasmagoria, I lost sight of all sense, and with an indescribable hunger building beneath my skin, I could only open my mouth and take what was presented before me regardless of how it might later haunt me. Each spoonful of broth coated my tongue. Swallow by swallow, the bitter taste faded, but the weight of it remained as my sight cleared, and my focus - lost for longer than I cared to admit - honed in on every nuance of Gray's movements.

"You're hurt."

Wincing as I shifted, wrapping my arms tighter around him, Gray bit his lip. When I refused the next spoonful, he sighed. "It is only a bruise."

"You're lying," I insisted.

My fingers slid over his sides, tracing his ribs - too defined beneath his shirt. Though he didn't seem keen on my exploration, Gray remained seated. Perhaps my pitiable state forced him to indulge me. For all my concentration on him, sense hadn't returned to me, so I shifted, unbuttoning his shirt until his undershirt could be tugged up, and all the bitter nausea returned. His flat stomach remained untouched, but his back - visible from where I clung to his side, had raised red lines. Welts crisscrossed.

Again, he shushed me, thumbing away the tears which rolled down my cheeks before I even realized they were there. Somewhere in my exploration, he had placed the bowl aside, and seeing his arms empty, I lunged upward, wrapping a hand around the back of his neck - the only bare spot on his back that I could see and dragged him down atop me.

A delicate pink highlighted the sharp cut of his cheeks. The warmth of him leaked down into me from where he straddled my thighs, sending my pulse racing. He was incredibly close, and every bit of me ached. Not to kiss him. Not even to touch him. Just an incredible churning of my body. Too tired, too desperately lonely for me to exactly intend where my lower brain immediately ventured, but his prior discomfort should have put me off it.

"I'm sorry," I whispered, trying to find some way to build distance between us without letting him go. "I...I don't know what I'm doing."

His fingers ran through my hair. The soft drag of his nails over my scalp sent me sinking down into the sheets of the strange bed in the strange room in that shadowy room where only he practically glowed in the dim light. When I laid far enough to lay my head upon the pillow, he slid off to the side and gently removed my hands from his sides.

"You need to sleep," he told me.

A joke. Funny man. If I weren't sleeping, the two of us wouldn't be here - in this strange room - wait, I've thought that before. I've never fallen asleep in a dream, but darkness - friendly and warm - crawled into my vision. All the while, Gray

59

remained beside me. His hand, holding mine, kept me grounded in a dream, sending me deeper into sleep.

Chapter Nine

"Man, you're a stressful roommate," Tom complained as we headed to class. "Do you always get sick this often?"

Chad snorted. "Or he's doing drugs."

"Come on," Alexander urged, bumping shoulders with me. He meant the gesture to be friendly, but it nearly knocked me off my feet. "You can tell us. No judgment."

"Sure. Safe space," I drawled.

And my stomach sank. Chad - rested for once - blinked. I could hear the gears between his ears turning. Any other day, and he would've been too tired to realize, but leaving the air charged with possibility was dangerous. He would only read into it if I acted weird, but my heart buzzed like a hummingbird's wings. Frozen - though still walking in pace with them, I swallowed, but Alexander just bumped into me again.

"Yeah. Totally," he declared, and like that, the spell broke.

"I'm fine. No drugs." I drew an X over my chest with my finger. "Promise."

Tom hummed. His steps bounced as he declared, "It must be the air. Like Heidi, right?"

"What?" I asked.

Nodding along as if someone else were already agreeing with him rather than asking for an explanation, Tom said, "You're from back town nowhere, right? This is - like - your first winter in the big city."

"Not exactly winter yet," Chad argued, shoving his hands in his pockets where Alexander's swung too close.

"Still cold," Alexander retorted.

Brilliant Tom. He had to be the ideal mix of well-intentioned and gullible. Anyone else - like Chad - would've been suspicious. Hell, Chad had called their RA on Alexander even when he had been drinking too. Unfortunately, their RA was like a larger, slower-talking Tom, so there were way more 'next-times' and second changes than anyone deserved. Maybe that's why Chad always ended up drinking too.

"Yeah," I said. "Probably. Must've been the flu."

Chad scoffed, but he only grumbled, "You better not get me sick."

We shuffled into our seats. Professor Haggard hadn't arrived, but his teaching assistants all sat in their perches, waiting to shut the doors and take names of any stragglers. As we settled in our usual Wednesday sprawl, my eyes caught on a huddle down front. Cheyenne sat with her things, taking up two spots, but that wasn't new. What was, however, was Maddix standing in front of her. He hissed, speaking way too low for me to hear, but the way he glared at anyone who walked by and stopped talking, whatever he was saying had to be interested. Not for the first time, I wished I could read lips.

"Not that it'd help," a familiar voice drawled. "He's purposefully minimizing his movements."

A cold sweat beaded on the back of my neck. In dreams, Gray's soft voice had grown more comforting the longer I spent with him. However, while I was awake, his presence set me off kilter. My stomach churned, yet I dared not turn around. As if to torment me further, he ran his fingers through the short hairs at the back of my neck. He leaned forward. His cheek hovered only inches from mine as his indecently pretty profile came into view.

Not many people had good profiles. But his nose tilted slightly up at the end. It wasn't terribly noticeable from the front, but from the side, it gave him a spritely appearance. His long dark lashes curled up, and the worried pink of his lips parted like petals. With a pointed chin, he went from Victorian dandy to ethereal fairy in profile, and I didn't need to think about Gray in a loincloth or with flowers crowning his hair.

Like a victim in a horror movie, I closed my eyes, taking a deep breath. Building my courage, I leaned to the side, turning to look, but he was always gone.

At my side, Chad grumbled, "What's with you?"

"Just trying to figure out why Maddix is reaming out Cheyenne," I admitted.

He frowned, glaring down at them. "Probably because she stole his essay topic."

"But she's doing a paper on sleep disorders and waking hallucinations," I said. "Isn't Maddix doing something on sanitariums? Like pre-World War II psych?"

"Yeah, but he's focusing on a local place. It turns out a patient claimed to see ghosts. Cheyenne wants to argue something about him subconsciously deducing what he knew about the doctors and everybody from a dream-state. He was pretty famous - Theodore Thompson..." Chad paused as if waiting for a response, but the name wasn't familiar at all.

"I have no idea who you're talking about."

Tom piped in, "Me either."

"He only knows 'cause he's doing his project on him too," Alexander said, and Chad punched him in the arm. "Ow! What? That's the truth."

"Yeah, and I don't want Maddix knowing. Thompson's just one guy. I'm looking into the practice of institutionalizing queer children and how it led to acquired psychoses. They go in healthy and end up getting their heads fucked up - sometimes literally. Like Thompson - went in a ridiculously intelligent, brutally honest kid and two years - two years into it, he's seeing ghosts," Chad explained, never looking away from Maddix as if discussing the topic would draw the other's ire onto him. "Anyway - it's what Maddix gets for ranting during his part of the group presentations."

"Seems like you're all coming at it from different sides. Why would Professor Haggard have a problem with it?" I wondered aloud, but Chad only shrugged.

As if he felt the weight of our gaze on him, Maddix suddenly snapped his glower in our direction; we all startled, but the professor barreled down the stairs beside us, waving his briefcase.

"Sorry, I'm late - had a bit of a coffee catastrophe. For anyone who enjoys whole milk in their coffee, avoid the cart closest to William Jones Hall. Absolute disaster. Had to run across campus," he complained as he held his usual large brew aloft. "If I'm under caffeinated, blame them."

Chapter Ten

"Do I have a tumor?"

Gray's eyes narrowed. "How would I know?"

We sat side by side on the bed where he had cared for me. He leaned against the wall. His legs stretched out before him, hanging off the bed at the ankles while I had my knees against my chest. The bed seemed strangely large. A gap stretched between us though I could knock my foot against his thigh.

"Then how did you show up in my classroom - and that time in the library," I murmured, running a hand through my hair.

He licked his bottom lip. The slight movement drew my eye, and panic fluttered in my stomach. Maybe I should submit myself to Cheyenne. She could take data, studying first hand someone losing touch with reality - seeing waking dreams.

God, I had to be losing my mind to consider going to Cheyenne for anything.

"What are you saying?" Gray whispered. His hand shifted - a half-aborted gesture to rest in comfortable companionship on my knee, but perhaps the desperation in my gaze kept him from closing the gap. "Maybe you should go see one of the doctors."

"Yeah - probably."

I wanted to close the distance between us. To knot my hands in his soft, smooth hair. Tangle them there as I pulled his pale face close to mine. Press kisses against his bitten pink lips. He had pushed me away before, but a tenderness ached between us when I was sick. If this was my dream, was it so terrible to push? To make another move? Nobody was around. No heels in the hall or sweet smelling fragrances rising from the kitchen. Only the two of us. Side by side, together in this strange place.

Inhaling slowly, I reached out. My hand fell over his own. We sat like that. Side by side with my hand on top of his own for several minutes before he shifted, turning his hand over to entwine our fingers. In my chest, my heart raced. I wanted to pull him closer, but this - just his touch was enough. I stretched out my legs, shifting to tap our knees together briefly.

Gray stayed by my side. His eyes stared blankly ahead, but a pink dusted his cheeks, and when his gaze shifted to me - it quickly fled again as the blush deepened.

I had never had the chance to endure such innocent affection. Though I had kissed a girl before - more than once to keep the rumors at bay, I hadn't ever held hands. Never sat close and thrilled in the distance being breached with something as chaste as our fingers entwined. In that instant, it seemed as if I could be content for the rest of time with just the soft warmth of his skin against my mine. I wanted this moment to never end.

"Where are we?" I asked when no other words but almost sycophantic praise leapt to my mind.

I couldn't call him sweet. Whisper how beautiful he looked. How I wanted to kiss him. Tell him there was no sight more beautiful in the world - no touch as sweet - nothing in all the world but him and me in the unknown stretched between. Not knowing had never been less daunting.

Gray hummed, and as if he wished to drive me mad, he leaned, resting his head against my shoulder. "Crables Manor."

The name itched in my mind. Familiar. Maybe he had mentioned it before. I rested my cheek against the top of his head. "Do you like it here?"

I could feel him shrug against me, and like a warning, he squeezed my hand, but Gray remained against me - his cheek against my shoulder - his hand within mine, so I let that topic fade. Silence gave me enough. Companionable and warm - I didn't fear myself at his side. He knew what I was - who I was in a way no one else in the world knew. Each new memory with him erased a bit of self-loathing from me, and whether he was real or a figment of my imagination, it didn't seem to matter. If he made me better, I couldn't be going insane, right?

Chapter Eleven

Suddenly, I chased sleep like a dog after a rabbit. Any moments I could sneak away, I did. I found the corners in the library where no one went. The abandoned lecture halls, study rooms set aside for the graduate students in the library, anything and everywhere became my nap place, so I could spend time with Gray.

We didn't do anything particularly exciting. Curled up in my room in Crables Manor, we talked about books and baseball. The strangest bits of facts and ridiculousness became our background chatter. An utterly dull soundtrack to cover for the way my heart raced, drumming in my chest as his fingers entwined in mine.

Sometimes, I couldn't help but toe the line. "Do you ever realize we never eat?"

Gray blinked, lifting his head from the pillow beside me to stare down at me. "What do you mean?"

"When was the last time you ate?" I asked.

"This morning," he replied, laying back down beside me. As he wiggled closer, he grumbled, "Just because you go out to eat every day doesn't mean they let the rest of us."

The 'us' always bothered me. Who else was here? I hadn't seen the Governess before though I had heard the click of her heels. Scents from the kitchen suggested a cook - but I couldn't remember what Gray called her. There were other doors. Bedrooms, I guessed, which were locked. No sounds suggested anyone had them. I hadn't passed them in the hall when I wandered - before I got sick. Before this strange possibility bloomed between us, I had explored the manor. Nobody else was here.

"Do you want to come with me? To lunch?"

Leaning his head against me, I could feel him smile into my shoulder. Electricity sparked wherever he touched. Sharp and sudden and overwhelming at first before turning into a strange dull heat. A warm reassurance that he was here. Somehow - he was with me. Impossible and beautiful and I wanted to roll over and wrap my arms around him. Keep him with me. Find a way to drag him back to Harvard. Or maybe find a way to sleep forever. Whatever would keep me at his side.

And I couldn't help the want, but I had enough experience with self-loathing to recognize a dangerous thought when it circled around my head like a shark. But I couldn't stop it. I wanted to be with him. I just had to find out how to keep him permanently. Make sense out of the recklessness which threatened to pull me under.

"I don't think the doctors will let me," he said, his hand squeezing mine. Another topic not to press. Another boundary found.

"But if I'm accompanying you..." I offered, pressing just a little - just a bit more.

Gray's hand tightened around mine. Trembling, he whispered - low and quiet, "Where would we go?"

His voice was so quiet - delicate and shy and the anxiety there - the hope almost killed me. I would have done anything for him in that moment. Climbed Everest. Killed a bear. Started a war. Helen could eat her heart out. I might not have had a thousand ships, but if he'd asked me to sack Troy, I would've torn it down in a heartbeat. Achilles would've understood.

"I could take you around Harvard. Show you my classes. Maybe introduce you to my friends?" I offered, starting small. Starting where most people wouldn't be scared away. "We could find a place to eat along the way. There's so many restaurants in Boston." He listened, remaining quiet, so I kept speaking. "I could take you to Fenway."

That caught his attention. His eyes sparkled as he smiled up at me. "Fenway? Are you sure? Isn't it expensive."

"I have some money," I told him.

The seats would be cheap. Nosebleeds, but I could get us two at least once. I'd work myself to the bone if I had to - taking notes or tutoring or in the back of a kitchen somewhere scrubbing dishes. Anything if it kept him smiling like that.

He hummed against my shoulder, sleepily curling up against me, but I dared not close my eyes for fear that I'd wake back up where I'd left myself. I held onto the feeling of him. The heat of his breath against my shoulder as he murmured, "That sounds lovely."

And then I snapped awake, falling out of the chair and onto the floor as Chad cackled. He stood over me with his hands in his hoodie pockets and a bag tossed over one shoulder. The jerk had dark circles under his eyes. Likely, he had only woken me out of jealousy that he hadn't been getting enough sleep, but as he stole my chair, kicking his feet over one of the arms, any pity I had evaporated.

"What the heck man?" I demanded, brushing off my pants.

He shrugged. "I wondered where you went between classes. This is awesome. Does nobody come back here?"

"Yeah - which is why I was sleeping!"

Where did Gray think I went when I woke up suddenly? Where did he think I went at all? I rarely got to say goodbye. I tried. When everything went fuzzy, I attempted to tell him goodbye. To walk out of the room or something as if I should start hiding I vanished randomly, but what if I didn't? What if I wasn't actually in my own body? Had I ever seen my own reflection in the dream? What if I became someone else? Someone who hurt him? Or didn't understand why they woke up randomly cuddling with another man?

"Sleep in your dorm room." Despite that, he jumped up and dug into his backpack. "Even better, take this."

He tossed a book at my head. I barely managed to catch it in time. "What the heck?"

"You need to check that out. When you return it - make sure Tom checks it out next. It's not allowed to be reserved, but we can take it out," he explained, zipping back up his backpack. "But only for a week each. I need it for my project, and I don't want Cheyenne or Maddix to get it."

75

"You're kidding me," I grumbled. But sure enough: *The Sanitariums of 1900s Boston* by Michael O'Reilly. Ridiculous. But the sooner I gave in, the sooner I could get away and get back to sleep. "Fine. Come on."

Chad smirked, following close behind as I headed to the front desk. When we got close, he took the book and did a quick return before passing it over for me to take it out. I carried it just beyond the library doors before handing it over, and the text disappeared into his backpack once more.

"Thanks."

"Yeah, whatever," I grumbled, adjusting my own bag as I headed toward my dorm hall.

Ruining any hope I had to get away from him, Chad fell into step beside me. "A group of us is going to go on a local murder tour. Are you coming?"

"Why would I want to come? It sounds morbid."

Why would I waste hours I could spend with Gray walking around Boston with a group of stupid college students? I lost time in classes and doing work and eating to avoid drawing negative attention. The balance wrecked me. Sensible enough to keep doing what I had to do. Desperate enough to hate myself about it.

However, Chad narrowed his eyes. The glare reminded me of our last longer interaction, and Tom wasn't around to save me this time, so when Chad pushed, saying, "You've got to hang out with friends, man. If you aren't relaxing, you're going to burn out."

I had no choice but to say: "Yeah, I guess you're right."

Ridiculous. The idiot had bags under his eyes. He looked exhausted, but I was the one who was going to burn out? I had two lives going - one in the waking world and one in the sleeping, and in both, I was well-rested. It was the best. Practically magical, but at least this trip meant I didn't have to deal with Chad bothering me about hanging out elsewhere. I still didn't know why he thought we were friends. Alexander, I got. That idiot was like a dog. Everybody was a friend, but Chad stuck around me for no reason.

Or maybe for a really not great reason. I hated people who hung around because they wanted to see someone screw up. People who treated others like walking, talking car crashes waiting to happen. I knew I was a wreck. I had issues - hidden and threatening to pop out when I least wanted them to do so, but I didn't need people like Chad pretending they cared while bubbling from excitement to see me burn.

Whatever. He ditched me part way back to our dorm, and I opened the door to another big middle finger from the universe. Tom sat at his desk, legs bouncing up and down as he studied. Even if I wanted to sleep, my body was so well rested, I couldn't nap unless I was almost completely undisturbed. I fell into my chair, tugging out my work. If I could get further ahead, I could sleep more later. Time didn't pass the same for Gray. I could do it. Find a way to make it work. I just needed time.

Chapter Twelve

Halloween loomed. Drawing closer like a hangman's rope. A few hours on a single night, yet the idea of giving up any time at all to anything that wasn't with Gray left me raging. Frustrated. Clawing against my own rationality. No good excuse came. Everything would draw more attention. Offering only a short respite if it didn't simply drive my roommate and the rest to bother me into submission.

A week before then, I sat in class - drumming my pen against my notebook, watching the coils shake and the twitch of the guy in front of me. Nobody else heard the noise. Not with me in the far back corner of the room. They all wanted to pass. Their eyes trained to a lesson on basic grammar. I'd read the chapter before, and if it hadn't been for the pop quiz which the professor put at the end of the class every other week, I wouldn't have bothered coming except to hand in my homework.

My skin itched. The longer the professor droned on, the worse it became. I probably could nod off. This wasn't a main course. Just my mandatory English component. It would be fine. One class where I fell asleep. It wasn't like I snored. I hadn't made any friends in this section yet. Professor Nawotka had an old school every man for himself approach to education, so he probably wouldn't even care if I slept. Any dip in my grade would be my own fault.

That thinking led to disaster. First, it was one class. Napping a bit. Just a quick visit. Just to see him. Then it would grow. Sprinklings of a class here and there until I stopped going at all to any of them. My grades would drop to barely passing - just enough work to keep enrolled, and then - when I got the first letter warning about my scholarships - I would throw up my hands entirely and do everything I could to never wake up. I already noticed my eating and drinking habits changed. My stomach used to growl in protest as I skipped lunch for a nap, but now - now the emptiness inside waved a white flag. This was a slippery slope, and I could see myself tumbling toward the edge - wide and deep and endless. Once I passed the event horizon, I wouldn't be able to escape. The gravity - the desperation to spend every moment with Gray would consume me.

Maybe life was better that way. Better spent dreaming. Spent unconscious. My parents couldn't hate me if I slipped into an unexplained coma.

Shit. I ground my teeth, clenching my fists as I struggled - pulled between my survival instincts and my addiction. I had never cared about anything but getting away from home as much as I obsessed about Gray. Even thinking about not spending the break between my classes with him had me panicking. My chest tightened. The air in my lungs locked down -refusing to move as I stared straight ahead. Trembling. Helpless. How had this happened? He wasn't even real. *He wasn't even real.*

But he was. Nothing in my life left me aching like Gray did. When awake - attending school, I walked around half-dead. Emotionally distant and exhausted - terrified someone might catch me in my lies. Might realize and out me. I hadn't even spoken to my parents more than once since I packed my suitcases and took a bus to Boston. Dad couldn't afford to take off work, and we only had the one car.

Gray left me desperate. Electricity surged through my body - like taking a breath after holding it too long. Waking up after falling in a dream. A sudden kick and jolt. When I had I last felt that way? Nobody ever made me want to the point of desperation. To dangerous obsession.

No. That's a lie. I had wanted. Before I realized how dangerous wanting could be. Secret and held back in my throat. Then he had loved somebody else, and what was I supposed to do? Join in the torment? He had thrown the person he loved on the fire because he wanted to isolate them. Keep them to himself. Selfish - greedy - destroying any beauty I had seen in him. Leaving me hating myself for what I was - for who I had risked my life to love.

Everyone around me rose. Standing and shuffling - shoving away their notebooks as I sat frozen. A scream caught in my throat.

"Ah, James, good of you to stay behind," Professor Nawotka sauntered over to me after everyone had filed out. "This short story you did for last week's creative assignment - tremendous job! A bit overly descriptive of the front parlor, but I truly felt I was there - in that room with that poor young girl, Gray."

"You wrote about me."

My mind chanted - a repeat of: *No, no, no - this is not happening - not now!*

But sure enough, Gray sat on the desk beside me. His legs crossed as he observed the professor and myself. He didn't seem upset. Maybe he hadn't heard that I'd made him a woman in my short. I couldn't exactly share what had happened between us any other way. I never had a creative bone in my body. Writing about the dreams and Gray had gotten me through the more artsy parts of the course, and from the beginning - when he made my stomach churn with want and confusion - I knew I had to give myself an out - just in case.

"Really? Uh, thanks," I pushed out. My tongue sat heavy in my mouth, refusing to offer anything more intelligible.

Smiling, Professor Nawotka studied me with a twinkle in his pale blue eyes. "Would I be correct in saying the young lady was based on someone in your real life?"

When my mouth wouldn't work, I nodded. Why did I nod? Gray wasn't real. He was a hallucination. He was sitting right there. A phantom - still somewhat translucent about the edges, but clearly there - and if nobody else could see him, that meant something was wrong with me, and I shouldn't have been pleased by that, but it sent a thrill up my spine to think he was just mine. That no one else seeing him meant I never had to share. Never had the risk that someone would find out and destroy me. Can't out a guy when his boyfriend was a delusion.

Were we boyfriends?

"Well then, I wish you luck, young man. Go forth! Win the day!" and off he went with a little grin on his tan face beneath that snow white goatee of his.

Gray, however, remained. "Rather sprightly for a man of his age."

"I think it's the no longer giving a damn," I replied as I put my things away. My eyes never left him, but I moved slowly. Drawing it out as I stood and reached for him.

He blushed. A flair of pink across his cheeks when my fingers slid over the cold, smooth skin of his neck. I could feel him. Without thought to what someone else might see, I curled my fingers, wrapping my hand around the back of his head and leaned in - desperate. My heart raced. My breath caught in my lungs, and when our lips touched - his slightly chapped from biting lips to my own, I wanted to weep.

The kiss stayed chaste. A pressing - a peck. Just enough to taste him then I drew back, resting our foreheads together. His eyes had closed. Dark lashes fluttered against his high cheekbones. God, he was beautiful. And here. He was here.

"How did you get here?"

The question slipped out before I could think. Then my brain caught up. I was in the middle of a classroom - empty, sure, but anyone could've walked in at any time. Would they have seen me kissing air? Or would they have seen me kissing another man?

I'm not sure which would have been worse.

"Oh, shit, you're here!" I pulled back, and he opened his eyes, blinking as if startled out of a daze. "Gray, can you see where you are?"

"What? Of course, I can. You asked if I wanted to spend a day with you, so I came," Gray retorted, huffing as he brushed off his jacket. "Honestly, James, do you even listen to yourself speak?"

"But - but you're at Harvard. How did you get here?"

He shrugged, stepping forward to hold my hand. "I walked. It wasn't that far."

He had walked. My dream guy had just walked right out of my head to show up. With the amount I slept, I couldn't be sleep deprived, and I ate. Not probably enough. But not little enough to explain hallucinations. It had to be a tumor. I had brain cancer. Any moment, it would block a vessel, and I'd be in a comatose state. Or dead.

I wonder if I'd still get to see Gray if I was unconscious because I was dead.

Probably not.

"I have another class - but I could ditch it," I offered. "We could walk around Boston together..."

"Certainly not. I'd love to sit in on a class with you since I missed this one," he told me. His lips curled in a cherubic smile.

Tense - my movements stiff and my heart accelerating to hummingbird levels, I led him to my next class. We walked the whole way. Hand in hand. Nobody glanced my way. Gray took everything in silently. He shifted around groups, pressing up against my arm from time to time, but otherwise, he remained just close enough to casually hold my hand as our arms hung by our sides. It was perfect.

It was nerve-wracking. By the time we reached the lecture hall, my head spun. Worse still - Chad was in this lecture with me. A statistics course aimed at social science majors. I sat down in the back. Gray took the inner seat, so I sat between him and whoever else might come. And there came Chad.

"Sup," he greeted with a tilt of his chin.

"Hey," I returned then my stomach churned. I had to introduce Gray, didn't I? Turning to look at him, relief and frustration compounded when his chair sat empty. Of course, it was empty. He had never been there at all.

Chapter Thirteen

Every habit I made, I struggled to break. No more sleeping between classes. I avoided sitting down in anything but hardback chairs whenever necessary. Any comfort went out the window, but on the plus side, I'd never spent more time with my friends. Tom took full advantage.

"Hey, the guys and I are gonna play a pick-up game of soccer at the park, you wanna come?" he asked.

My brush with obsessive organization meant I'd gotten far enough ahead that I had no legitimate excuse to say no. I wanted to refuse. Wanted to curl up in my bed and sink into the manor. Sink into the dream. I could almost see him. His silhouette formed a beacon in my mind. There - in the dreams - he radiated warmth. Not like the chill when he came around at school.

"Yeah, course."

My mouth moved ahead of me. An instinct to run built from years of holding back. Of suppressing every impulse I had. They came in useful now at least. Might just be saving my life. Yet as I changed and followed him out the door, the distance clawed at my chest - threatening to drag me under. Didn't matter what I thought. Everything turned topsy-turvy.

***

Exercise helped. Sweating and hot in the late October chill, I finally managed an honest smile as I scored. If I just kept running, maybe I could outpace this. Tire myself out until all I saw was black. Poke at the holes again and again. I could do this. Gray wasn't real. It was all in my head.

Then like a curse brought on when someone finally forgets it, Gray stood at the edge of the field where we played. All in black - he stood out. A high-contrast grayscale in a colored world. Shifting about from foot to foot, he watched with a wrinkle between his brow. His arms wrapped around his waist. Biting his lip, he seemed somehow smaller. As if the paper-thin slip of him could shrink down and fade to nothing underneath the spots of sunlight filtering through the clouds which hung over Boston.

One of Tom's friends, Mikey, smacked me on the shoulder. "Come on! Just 'cause you scored doesn't mean you can stay off-side!"

An apology on my lips, I glanced back, but Gray had disappeared. Which didn't make my heart clench. Didn't send a chill down my spine, and didn't make my stomach do flips. Because he wasn't ever there to begin with, so of course he was gone. Because he wasn't real.

Just breathe. Run. Dribble. Pass. Scream and interact. Focus on right now. Focus on this - the cool air. The way my feet thudded across the ground. A body colliding with mine, the ball going the opposite way. Turn and run. I could do this.

As we played, the clouds darkened. The glimpses of sun waned until the gray blanket overhead rumbled. Rain - wet and plopping down against the leaves. Plinking at first. Just one drop here and there. Large, fat raindrops - one-two one-two - almost like the phantom of clicking heels.

One second, I stood on a field. The next - only blackness. The manor never came. Neither polished mahogany nor cobwebs greeted me. Heat - unbearable heat flared up along my legs. Rising, curling smoke choked my lungs, and paralyzed in the empty abyss, I couldn't even scream. No doors. Though something creaked on its hinges. A lock - turned and clicked. Not a single glimpse of light though I heard the glass panes rattling in a window. Just claustrophobia. Invisible walls closing in around me.

And a scream. Long and blood-curdling only to fall away into coughing. They didn't even beg. Didn't call out for help. Though I heard fists pounding against the door, they didn't say anything as they burned in that darkness beside me. Cold hands brushed along my face. A cold palm against my forehead. Quick. There and gone.

I'm going to die here.

The thought invaded my mind. Macabre and softer in tone than my usual morbid insertions - it curled around everything until the fear and panic dimmed beneath a dark acceptance. Over and over, the single sentence repeated. A mantra of death as the heat grew.

Then another followed it. A sharp cry: *I don't want to die.*

Jolting up, I almost slammed heads with Tom. Paler than normal, tears streamed down his face, and he deflated with a long sigh.

"He woke up!" Tom called. His hands pressed against my shoulders, encouraging me to sink back down. "Lie down. We've got an ambulance coming."

"Shit - I can't afford that," I told him.

His nose wrinkled. "You completely just blacked out dude. Went down like somebody shot you."

"And I can walk to the clinic."

His lips squirmed, but he helped me get to my feet. "Danny? Cancel the ambulance. We'll take him."

"What the - ? Can you cancel an ambulance?" Danny asked. A woman's voice interrupted his confusion. "Huh? Oh - yeah...yeah...I mean, he looks like shit."

"I'm fine," I growled, pushing away from Tom. "Just haven't been sleeping well lately."

Nobody argued. They didn't know my habits - except for Tom. He stared at me. Just this endless unblinking stare. His mind obsessed on facts. Given a second - when he wasn't concerned, I probably would get a lot of shit for it, but for now, I focused on putting one foot in front of another. Any weakness risked more attention than I could afford. If Gray was a delusion, there was a chance I had something wrong with me - something not so easily

91

fixed, and anything that would send me back to my family - away from Boston - wasn't something I wanted discovered, so I kept my head high and headed back toward campus.

Most of the guys - Tom's friends - headed out, assuming Tom had it handled, but Danny followed. "I don't want to have lied to a 9-1-1 operator," he informed us, and I honestly didn't try to push him away. As long as he was here, I could put off dealing with whatever questions Tom had planned to volley my way.

When the nurse available to see me looked me over, she diagnosed dehydration and stress. Relieved of his self-imposed responsibility, Danny ditched us; however, Tom stayed silent. Even when we got back to our dorm, he didn't say anything until I had drunk two water bottles and headed to bed with a book in hand. Resting didn't mean I had to sleep.

"Who's Gray?" he asked, sitting on his bed across from mine. I had every plan to lie, and he held up his hand, shaking his head. "Forget it. I'm sure it's not something you're going to talk to me about. You just kept saying that over and over after you first went down. I thought it had to be a name."

He didn't give me time to consider telling him anything - not that I planned to anyway. Grabbing his shower caddy and pajamas, he left without further prying. Leaving me alone to think. About Gray. About what I wanted out of life. It had seemed so clear. Become independent. Find a good job where I could make money where I could come out without it causing me trouble. Come out. Lose my family. Find a guy.

But my brain was impatient. If it had been sex, I might've thought it all libido driven, but everything with Gray remained staunchly sweet. Romantic even. Had I starved myself for affection? People touched me. High-fives and shoulder bumps. Checks on the field. Repression out loud didn't do this. I could keep a secret without it killing me.

Right?

Chapter Fourteen

Tom watched me from across the room - likely still suspicious though I hadn't had another black out since the day on the field. Not a single sick spell. Every single day, I spent surrounded by his friends or my friends or whoever. Anyone and everyone - even those I disliked - to ensure I wouldn't nod off unexpectedly. I spent hours in the gym, practically beating myself into shape, so that when my head hit that pillow, only blackness followed.

Because if Gray looked at me - with those large eyes of his, I'd break. Fold like undercooked bacon. Even the thought of him made me waver.

Thankfully, Gray hadn't popped up again since that day on the field. Maybe my brain finally got the message. Healthy eating. Working out. I could do this. Keep on the straight and narrow like I always had. My life - planned out perfectly in front of me. If I strayed, it would fall apart. Without success, I couldn't come out. If I did, my dad would feel vindicated in how much he hated me. Mom would cry, blaming herself for failing me, drawing upon whatever stupid mistake she could tie to it. Guilting me into saying it was a mistake - a joke - a lie.

So I couldn't think about Gray. I had to look ahead. To a future with a doctorate and a comfortable practice. A house in Nantucket or wherever was the right place for people like me to have houses when they got a lot of money but were still down to earth. Not bragging kind of house. A house which said - 'I've done everything right in my life, and anyone who hates me should probably be my patient.'

That future. With me and the real guy - the guy who I'd find when I was ready. When I wasn't still pretending. He deserved me not to be hung up on a delusion. Because he would be amazing. Even better than Gray. Someone successful too. Probably still slim but with darker hair - more like Reggie's maybe. Maybe a guy with those pale eyes - like ice for most people, but they'd warm right up for me. Smile at me when everyone else just got a frown.

But like a traitor, my hands itched. My mind wondered if the exhilaration would be the same. Would this future man make my stomach flutter and my heart race just by holding my hand? Would he smile shyly up at me as he leaned against my shoulder, trusting me to keep him up - to keep talking about everything and nothing? Would I be the rock for them?

No. Because successful people weren't codependent. They didn't huddle, hidden in a corner of their mind desperately relying on a figment of their imaginations, and successful people weren't as broken as Gray. They didn't have that hard fragility. Speak through glances and bitten lips.

"We going?" I asked, focusing on the night ahead. Halloween and Chad's murder tour. "Come on - the guys are probably waiting."

"We're gonna be fifteen minutes early," my roommate informed me, but he didn't argue.

I couldn't handle the silence. Any gaps had my mind careening to Gray, but I didn't have anything to say, so like an idiot, I asked, "How are the Red Sox doing?"

Tom's nose wrinkled. "The season's been over for a while. You sure you're okay?"

I knew that, or I should have. Would have. I used to keep track for Gray. Not that we ever talked about it because after hearing the Curse of the Bambino was broken, he seemed to deflate a bit, knowing he hadn't gotten the chance to see it. But I kept an eye on it in case he ever changed his mind.

Grasping for something that wouldn't remind me of Gray, I said, "You think Cheyenne knows Chad planned this?"

"Sheesh, I hope not. Chad's paying for Maddix's ticket to get him off his back about the topic, but if Cheyenne comes along, I think I'll tear my eyeballs out," he complained, miming the action and resulting blood spurts.

A flash of blond caught my eyes, and sure enough, Cheyenne flounced up with a girl I didn't know at her side. The unknown girl had perfectly curled black hair that stopped at her shoulders. With golden skin and full lips, she swayed with each step. Slanted, almond-shaped brown eyes scanned us, and both of them wore runic pendants and loose flowing blouses with jackets with swaying fringe.

They came from behind Tom, so while he waved to Maddix, Chad, and Alexander, he couldn't see who else was on their way. There was a chance - however small - that Cheyenne and her friend intended to go somewhere as 1960s witches, but from Chad's bland expression and Maddix's squirming, she had weaseled her way into the group - probably with the promise of bringing her pretty friend.

"Well...tear out your eyes."

Tom blinked, glancing around before his shoulders sank. "Seriously?"

"Hi, boys," Cheyenne greeted. "Leilani, you know Maddix. That's Chad, Alexander, Tom, and James."

"Thanks for letting me come along," Leilani said - her voice low and a twinkle in her eye.

When Maddix flushed a bright red, stumbling to say we were more than happy to have her, Chad and Tom groaned in unison. Cheyenne smirked, but Leilani focused entirely on Maddix. Hopefully, she wasn't just messing with him, but from the curious blinking from Alexander, he knew something I didn't.

Dumb college drama - the perfect distraction. Sidling up to the football player, I walked with him as Tom and Chad grumbled back and forth over the invasion while Cheyenne and Leilani sandwiched Maddix between them. If nothing else, he'd gain some cred as something besides an anal retentive nerd.

"What do you know?" I asked, nodding at the trio.

Alexander shoved his hands in his jacket pockets. "Huh? Know about what?"

"Leilani."

He glanced down at me with wide eyes. "You interested? Didn't think you -"

"Yeah - but not if you know a reason I shouldn't be," I grumbled, cutting him off. I didn't want to think about how he was going to end that sentence. "She actually interested in Maddix? Or is she dating somebody else?"

He couldn't have known. Even caught up in Gray with all the pretending forgotten though the silence remained, everybody assumed. But Alexander wasn't everyone. He roomed with Chad. Chad who noticed my slip-up. Who was looking for it. Just cause he might be something too - some other flag - that didn't mean he had any right to look for it in me. Secrets made mysteries didn't last. I had to make it disappear entirely. Even if that meant dating a girl again.

Scratching the back of his head, Alexander shrugged. "Man, you've been sick every other day. Maybe now isn't the time to be trolling for a girlfriend."

"Be straight with me." Bad phrasing. Shit - really crap phrasing. "She free? Or not?"

Chad scoffed - somehow always managing to listen in when I least wanted his opinion. "If you go after her, you're getting a Cheyenne. Only difference - she's a bit quieter, majors in children's lit, and a different coloring. Still demanding, annoying, a know-it-all -"

"A strong woman, you mean?" Cheyenne returned, crossing her arms over her chest.

Her and Chad - always listening. Rolling his eyes, Chad sighed. "Leilani - maybe. You? A hundred percent annoying."

Flipping her hair, Cheyenne sneered, but Leilani asked her something I couldn't hear, and - to Maddix's seeming frustration - Cheyenne returned to her original group.

"Leilani's actually really nice," Tom piped up.

Chad scoffed. "You're only thinking that because you've got cow eyes for Nina."

"Or cause she's actually okay. Cheyenne's not athlete's foot. You aren't contaminated by proximity," Tom retorted, knocking elbows with me. "If you date her, you could be my in."

"That's dumb. And he's not even flirting with her. If you like her so much, maybe you should go up there." Chad shoved me, but I stayed between him and Alexander.

"No chance."

Alexander chuckled. "He's no idiot. Better chances once Cheyenne's distracted."

Chad hummed, glaring a bit more before focusing up ahead where a woman not that much older than us held up a sign for the tour.

"Seven for the tour? Harvard crew, right?" the woman asked with a bright smile. Her purple lips shimmered beneath the streetlamp she had picked as our gathering spot. "I'm Teresa. We'll just wait a bit longer. Got a couple from Germany that should be here soon."

Putting on my smarmiest grin, I left the rest of the group to their small talk. "So - you live in Boston?"

"Yep," our tour guide replied. Her eyebrows rose.

"This your main job?"

Her lips squirmed like worms. Laughter or disgust kept at bay beneath the movement. "Nah, I'm a crime analyst. I moonlight as a tour guide." She paused, just long enough for me to open my mouth with a planned one liner when she stepped away. "You must be the Gersts. Hope you're ready for a great night!"

"And he's struck out!" Chad pitched his voice low and drawling, mimicking a sports broadcaster. When I rolled my eyes, his hand darted out to smack me. "Come on, man. Nobody's on your case."

I scoffed, blocking his next attempt to elbow me. "Whatever."

Off we went, stopping on dark corners and taking turns down dark alleys which we'd all avoid most nights. Every once and awhile, a gaggle of kids or party-goers would pop up. Frankly, the kids were more startling. Teresa got into the stories, so when she was mid-stabbing and a group of preteens charged around with pillowcases full of candy, the contrast resonated eerily.

I followed along, watching as Cheyenne started bouncing. She practically vibrated when we walked up to this old house. I might've written it off, but Maddix and Chad had joined her up at the front, waiting for her to push open the iron gate, but she didn't.

"And as our eager beaver Harvard students already know - this here is an old sanitarium from the 20th century. In 1942, a fire starting in the widow's watch almost resulted in it being shut down; however, it reopened with a focus on drug rehab until a patient started a second fire in 1987," Teresa explained. "The second patient from 1987 survived the fire; however, the first burned alive in the watch."

Burned alive. I fought against the urge to cringe. The structure looked sound. New roof. Older foundations. Sure. But up on top, they had reconstructed the widow's watch. A single rectangle standing on the high roof, looking out toward the sea. Which was stupid because if it had ever been able to see the sea, it had been wrecked by a line of residential houses build up along the waterfront. Plus, the whole thing was marked for demolition. A red sign and yellow tape screamed caution and condemned.

"The patient, Theodore Thompson, was a famous medium who had been institutionalized since he was seven years old - dying at eighteen. A week after his father had signed the papers to remove him from the facility." Teresa exaggerated a shiver. "Some have speculated that a group of nurses trapped Theodore in the watch in hopes of hurting him enough to keep him in their institute as they had been using his renowned abilities to see the dead to make money under the table. Several arrests were made for negligence as a result of suits posed by Theodore's father regarding his son's forced labor."

"Don't we get to go in?" Cheyenne demanded.

Maddix nodded fervently. "Yeah - the description said the tour goes into the manor."

Pulling out a key, Teresa smirked. "You guys are lucky. This'll be the last year we get to do this. They're tearing it down next spring."

Filing through the gate, we all headed toward the house, which Teresa unlocked. The door creaked, swinging open as she said, "Welcome to Crables Manor."

Bile churned in my stomach. Dull and bitter in my throat. I stepped inside, following my friends who had already raced ahead, studying every bit they could. Not that it could help their projects. This was just some sick horror show to them. The rug - shaggy and brown. Cobwebs in the ornately carved corners. No shimmering mahogany. Out of place light bulbs instead of the chandelier which hung in the hall when it was Gray's home.

It was real. Crables Manor was real.

"Hey - uh - Maddix, you showed some photos of this place in your project, right?" I asked, trying to breathe.

Maddix shook his head. "My group didn't let me."

"Chad - didn't you -"

"What? Show you pictures on my phone? What's wrong with you?" Chad traced his eyes up and down me. "You gonna puke."

Cheyenne hadn't. This was the first time I spoke with her since the group presentation. Teresa walked through, pointing out features - talking about the restoration and subsequent abandonment when a patient tried - and failed - to mimic the fire in the eighties but started it in the kitchen, distracting the doctors as he took a hatchet to the locked door of the widow's watch.

But her voice faded. Facts droning as the group moved toward the kitchen, but my feet took me up the stairs. The same path. Right to Gray's room. It didn't look the same. None of the furniture remained in the house, so I shouldn't have been surprised that the desk and bed were gone, but my eyes went right to the wall. Right where Gray's room had a line of wood which separated the bland tan wallpaper from the painted white slats below. The band remained.

My fingers moved of their own accord. Running across the lip there. Testing the give. Maybe I went mad. One minute, I tested the give, and the next, I ripped a slat off the wall then another. At the base of the second, a small rectangle caught my attention. I wanted it to not be what I thought it was. I should've stood. Left it there. Forgotten all about it. But I didn't. I picked up the Ted Williams baseball card.

He was real. Crables Manor was real. Gray was real. I had abandoned him, and he wasn't in my head. A chill came over me then. The world tilted, and blinking to try to get my bearings, I almost missed the noise echoing in the back of my skull - like stones dropping into water. A tugging sensation - like when I used to snap out of the dream - followed. It was all real.

Or this was all in my head.

Shoving the card into my pocket, I ducked back downstairs. Finding the kitchen was easy enough. Everything in the places I remembered as the basic structure hadn't been changed that much. Tom gave me a once over, but I shook my head before he could say anything. At least until we got back out onto the street.

"Hey." I sidled up to him. "Look what I found."

I flashed the card, and his brows jumped. "Shit, man! Where was that? Is it an original?"

"Found it in room three. Right off the main staircase," I told him, tucking it into my pocket before he could touch it. My mind just kept screaming - *it's real. He sees it too. It's real.*

Maddix fell back. "You went upstairs?"

"Just to room three."

"That was Thompson's room! What did it look like? Could you feel a presence?" Cheyenne demanded, joining us.

"No," I lied. "It was just a room."

They grumbled, banding together to chat about what they'd seen and how they thought the use of a private home for a sanitarium had affected the mental health of the patients.

I kept pace, forcing my face to not show any emotion. A bland smile. Keep the eyes bright. Look interested. No thinking about how the card feels like a lead weight. Not a word about how it radiated heat. Kept the lie going all the way back to our dorm room.

Gray was real. Gray was dead. But he was real. He had been real. I wasn't crazy. He was real. Just a ghost.

That stopped me short. Believing hadn't been easy. I used to believe. Then our pastor lectured on how people like me were a sin. The Devil's work. Couldn't take it seriously after that, but now there were ghosts. Were ghosts and god mutually exclusive? Did you have to have both? I'd never shown a skill for anything supernatural. Nothing to suggest I could commune with the dead, so why now? How? How was Gray reaching me if he was a ghost?

Exhausted but anxious, I curled up in my bed, staring at the card balanced on the back of my desk. Held in place with a clip-lamp. Ted Williams - now dusted off - stared down at me. The same face.

If I slept, I could see Gray. I could ask him. I could see if the name Theodore sparked any memories. See if there was a reason he was reaching out to me. I didn't even believe in ghosts. Maybe the card was a fluke. Tom could see it, so it had to be real. It was the exact card. How could it be there? How could I know it was there?

"Hey?" I whispered, calling out to Tom, who rolled over and grunted back at me. "Do you believe in ghosts?"

He groaned, rubbing his eyes. A silhouette of limbs like tendrils in the dark. "Maybe. I don't know. Why?"

"I might've felt something. In the room."

He sat up. A faceless shadow staring at me without eyes in the dark. "Like what?"

But what could I say? I couldn't tell him I thought Gray's governess was there. That room three was Gray's room. That Gray might've been Theodore, but that meant I was dreaming about a dead psychic. A dead institutionalized psychic. Who burned alive. Gray burned alive. Oh my god, somebody burned Gray alive!

"James?" Tom called when I didn't answer. "What did it feel like?"

Burying my face in my pillow, I tried not to think about it. Tried to bury the thoughts. Push them down. They just kept coming. Burning hurt. He must've been so scared. Was that what I felt on the soccer field? Him burning alive? It was so hot. He didn't fight it. Everything hurt, but he gave up - like he knew no one was coming. Like he was better off letting the person kill him. Somebody killed Gray.

"Like drowning," I managed to get out. "It felt like I was drowning."

Chapter Fifteen

Closing my eyes, I sunk into blackness. The darkness swept me away. But where the shining mahogany usually greeted me when I wasn't exhausted out of my mind, there was only dusty shag. Insects - out of sight but loud. Their legs skittering behind, beneath, and all around. Invisible, hungry swarms. A breeze drifted through the side parlor. Not enough to feel on my skin, but enough that the cobwebs hanging from the ceiling waved. Tattered remains of a guidon. Or a half dozen white flags marking surrender.

"Gray?" I called, racing up the stairs. "Gray? You here?"

The door to his room stood open. Rust eroded the upper hinges, leaving the door tilted backward, readying to fall as the decay encroached. His bed wasn't there. A cot stood in its place. No sheets. Just a bare, stained mattress. Thinned from use and covered in a thick film of dust. His desk - more like a small table and chair - remained, shrouded in disuse. On the wall, where his baseball card stood regardless of time or the manor's state, only the outline - free of dust - suggested anything had ever been there at all.

A cold sweat broke out down my spine. Rivets ran along the edges, drenching my shirt as I reached out. My fingers brushed against the edges of the gap, and electricity sparked through my hand, sending it flying back to my chest. Black tipped my middle finger.

In a dream, breathing wasn't mandatory, but my chest heaved. Bursts of air coming in and out in quick succession as I tried to keep the lightness from clouding around my head and ending me back before I had searched every corner of the house for him. Gray was dead. A ghost. Somewhere here. Somehow, he had been reaching out. He had to be here.

Spinning, I raced from his room. Panicked blinded me. Stole away all sense. From the walls to the doors, I crashed, stumbling and fumbling my way as I banged and called out for him. Tearing the world apart for a sign he had been there. A sign he hadn't vanished like the Ted Williams card he cherished.

"Gray? Gray, where are you?" I screamed. My voice hoarse, itching as it caught in my throat. It hurt. Like thorns had grown there. Tearing me apart each time I called out for him. "Gray? Answer me! Where are you?"

When no more doors opened for me, my feet took me higher. The third floor had no locks on their doors. Not on the inside. Decrepit, some hung on their hinges. Others - clawed or broken into splinters - covered the carpet.

No sign of Gray. So up my feet led. Up to the Widow's Watch. Up to where Gray had died. The door and the final group of steep stairs waited for me. A small little room with windows on all sides. In the center, a rocking chair creaked. Back and forth. Nobody there to move it. Just back and forth.

Buzzing, the air thickened. Smoke churned. Swirling - invisible and thick around me, gathering with each step I took forward until I moved like resistance bands wrapped taut around my limbs, growing stronger the more I stretched them. Any moment now, they would fling me back. Throw me from the space.

In my mouth, my tongue sat heavy and dry. A useless weight meant to be calling his name, but I couldn't even lift it to lick my peeling lips.

One-two.

Slow. Deliberate as coins flipped into a wishing well. *One-two.* Coming closer and closer, louder and louder as cold rushed at me from behind. Warmth brewing - building to explode before me in the small room - emanating from the rocking chair. Back and forth. One-two. Back and forth. One-two.

The toe of my shoe fell, brushing against the entrance, and I sat up, gasping for breath. Sweat drenched me. Flatted to my face, my hair stuck. Itching and knotting as I scratched myself in the hurry to get it off of me.

Over on his side, Tom rolled over with a grumbled groan, but he remained firmly asleep. His clock flashed just past midnight, so despite the tingling across my skin at the dampness, I sunk back into my sheets - burrowing beneath the blankets as I chased the wisps of sleep which had fled so quickly from me.

"Gray!" I called out in the darkness of my mind. Lips pressed tight, so I didn't wake Tom, I screamed his name until the weight of exhaustion dragged me under once more.

Back in the side parlor, I stood in grandeur. Polished wood beneath my feet. Not a spot of dust. No skittering of insects in the walls or just out of view. Nothing to indicate the bones of that previous dream came from this place. Moreover, heat clung to the house where a drafty chill lingered once before. Food roasted - onions and garlic and spices tickled my nose, rising from the kitchen in fragrant plumes.

Though my eyes drifted to the stairs, my feet led me deeper toward the back - through the winding halls to the kitchen. Gray and I never went there together, and when I headed there alone, it hadn't been on days when I could smell the ovens working.

Turning the corner, I pushed open the swinging door, and a flash of light brown caught my eye. Racing from one end of the kitchen to the other, a short woman worked. A mostly clean apron covering her empire waist dress from the stains of her work. The tangles of her graying red hair were tied into a bun on top of her head. Neatly and efficiently done to keep it from her round face as she cooked. With rosy cheeks and a grandmotherly plumpness to her figure, seeing her instantly put me at ease. Another person's grandmother had little likelihood of killing me, and her opinions on my masculinity or preferences didn't matter. Especially not with Gray missing.

"Look at you!" the woman exclaimed, turning to face me. One hand settled on the roundness of her hips while the other stirred what seemed to be a bubbling stew. "I swear, all the young men are skin and bones. Grab a seat. Yes - yes, you!"

I stumbled back. Falling into a chair at the wooden table set back against the kitchen's windows, I watched as she bustled about the place, grabbing this and that from the cabinets as she prepared homemade biscuits and seasoned vegetables to roast while her stew simmered.

"Do you know where Gray is?"

Maybe it wasn't polite. I probably should have asked her name first or introduced myself, but my mind needed answers. I needed to see Gray. To know he was okay.Even though he was dead. And I couldn't save him. Because somebody had burned him alive.

Setting an empty tea cup before me, the woman placed a large plate of scones and pastries on the table. "Here, now. You look positively ghastly. Eat." Setting a teapot before me, she tapped its side. "Let it brew some first."

I took a scone, not sure what to do or what would happen if I ate it. "Thank you."

"You're welcome, lovey. Now, what's this about my sweet Theodore?"

Like I'd been stabbed. Her words pierced me, leaving me scrambling though I had known - had felt that I was right before I had even come here, but Theodore - just Theodore left me wrecked.

"He's dead. You're all dead." The words tumbled out, bubbling up like steam from her teapot. "Somebody killed him."

Facing me, she sighed, brushing her hands off on her apron. "I'm afraid so."

"Who are you?"

Laughing, she poured the kettle, filling my cup with steaming tea. "Oh, sweet boy, I'm the cook!"

Had she forgotten her name? My mind buzzed with questions. Would it be impolite to push? To ask?

As if sensing my distress, she patted me on the hand. Her touch was warm and gentle. "Hayward, lovey, Bonnie Hayward. You may call me Mrs. Hayward."

Another name. Another ghost. "Did - did the person who killed Gr-Theodore," I corrected quickly, but she waited with a smile, stirring the stew as I gathered my thoughts. "Did the person who killed Theodore kill you too?"

"Oh, no, dear, I died in my sleep. Six children, ten grandchildren at the time - thirteen by the end of things - I had a wonderful life. My husband went a few years later, lovely man," she told me. Her eyes sparkled. "I'm so excited to see him again. He's been so patient, waiting for me while I've been here - continuing my work, but he understood."

"What do you mean?"

Pressing a hand to her breast, she shook her head with a sad smile. "Why - I couldn't leave her.

113

Not when she'd been through so much, and everything that came out afterward - dreadful business. Truly dreadful. But when you're dead, one year blurs with the next, and they've only just scheduled to break down the foundation this year, so I couldn't convince her to move on until now, and the business with Theodore. My goodness, my afterlife has been rather busy."

All around us the manor creaked. It almost sounded like footsteps, but then the walls would follow. Thuds and groans.

"What happened to Theodore?" I pushed when the biscuits drew her attention away from our conversation.

She hummed, glancing over her shoulder at me. The heat of the oven accentuated the glow of her cheeks. "Hm? Oh, you should eat that scone, lovey. Does you no good in your hand. Same with the tea."

But I couldn't. I'd seen the movies. Heard the stories. Eating food in the underworld never ended well. I set the scone back down, pushing the teacup and saucer back.

"What happened to Gray?"

The cook sighed, brushing off her hands as she lowered the heat and placed a lid slightly off-kilter on the pot. "Oh, lovey, he died."

"But how? Why did he get locked up in here? Could he see you? Before he died? Could he talk to ghosts? Who killed him?" Question after question. They all rushed out of me.

"The smoke killed him, so we were able to pull him in between before the fire destroyed his body," Mrs. Hayward explained. Taking my cup of tea, she sipped it. Her fingers curled around the cup rather than the handle. "He was such a gifted boy. Did you know he can read minds? It's how he used to tell the difference between ghosts and humans until the medication took that away. He was so confused, the poor thing, when he lost that. Couldn't tell who was alive and who was dead."

"Telepathy?" I gasped. My mind stumbled over the new information.

She nodded - not even seeming to notice my panic. "Likely how that nasty business started."

The thudding grew closer. As I struggled to find a way to push her leisurely way of speaking to answer my questions faster, the door flew open, and a man flew into the room, sliding and falling down onto the floor. Wrapped in a straight jacket, the figure had sweatpants and bare feet. Long, dyed black hair knotted in tangles which veiled his face, trailing down past his shoulders. Scruff - not a beard but an attempt at one - covered his face, and a mad glint sparked his eyes.

Mrs. Hayward clinked the teacup as she dropped it back into the saucer to rush to the stove where her stew bubbled over. Her murmured, "Oh dear, behave yourself!" faded as the air churned, panting - quick harsh breaths from the newest phantom as he flopped, wriggling across the floor to stand without the use of his hands. His eyes focused on me. Frozen in place, I couldn't even scream as he lunged, and everything went dark.

But I didn't wake up. Instead, I slipped from one strange dream world into another. Just as dark. Just as smokey and hot, but the heat wasn't welcoming. It didn't smell like cooking meat or bread. Something slick caught in the back of my throat. An oily web dug in, finding a way to drag me under and keep me afloat at the same time.

And there he sat. A blur like an oil painting made phantom. "I believe you'll find not every phantom in Crables Manor is as welcoming as our dear Mrs. Hayward."

I blinked, trying to see through the fog clinging to my eyes. "Where's Gray?"

My heart raced, but the blurred man shifted. "I'm afraid I'm uncertain who you mean."

"Theodore," I said. "Where's Theodore?"

He sighed. "Elsewhere."

I lunged forward through the fog, stumbling and falling somehow backward into a chair. Heat flared to my right. Everything tumbled. Spinning like sitting on a whirling top. Every curse I knew flew from my lips as I growled, "Where's Gray?"

Tearing apart at the seams. These tiny pieces broke off of me. Fragments of my mind reaching out. I just wanted to hold his hand. I just wanted him back. Real or a dream. Dead or alive. I just wanted him. My whole body rejected his absence like a lost limb. Each step a reminder of what was supposed to be there - another foot to catch me. A hand to entwine in mine. Somewhere in this labyrinth of rooms and smoke - somewhere in this ghostly manor, Gray existed. In some form or another. Somewhere. And I was going to find him. Find him and never let go - never again. Because we belonged together. Two parts of the universe who had found their way back together. As insane as it sounded. As crazy as I had felt every step of the way. Gray was a piece of me, and no matter how much I tried to pretend it to be a lie - to be some consequence of repression - none of that mattered because he was mine, and I was his, and the space and time which existed between us - inconsequential as starlight.

"You're in love with him." An epiphany. Eyebrows rose, and eyes widened.

Denial wove a web around me, sputtering at the insides of my lips, but the secret wormed its way out of me. A small and quiet: "Yes."

The man sat back in his chair. His hands falling into his lap as he studied me. There was no particular color to his gaze. Everything about him blended in hues of brown and white and black and gray. No particulars. Just a blur of color from the moment he brought me in until he drummed his fingers against his thighs - growing clearer and clearer until a man in a wool suit sat across from me.

"If that is the case, I'm all the happier to have saved you..."

"James," I told him my name with no further prompting. The answer jumped from me. Others

117

hummed along the surface. Bubbling beneath my skin.

"James," he repeated. Sinking deeper into the chair, the new phantom tilted his head, considering me a moment before he offered, "I am Dr. Ose, James. It is a pleasure to meet you."

A doctor. They suspected the staff had killed him. What if this doctor killed Gray? The flames - small tongues of fire - danced in their glass lamps. Balanced on copper piping, their fogged panes occurred as much as they illuminated, but the more my eyes trailed up and down his seated form, the more at ease I became. He'd died before the 1900s. The cut of his suit - or more correctly the knee breeches and stockings marked him as from an earlier century.

"Nice to meet you too," I offered. "So…you know Gray?"

Back in elementary school, all the kids used to draw on the corner of their textbooks. Some made flip books. Little animations where stick figures walked across the pages, smiled and waved, or tipped their top hats. Dr. Ose smiled like a flip book stick man. Slow and incremental. Jarring. His off-white teeth glimmered in the gaslight. Pins and needles tingled across my skin, making my whole body shiver as his eyes narrowed.

"Of course! Though I knew him as Theodore," the doctor explained. "A bright boy. Eager to please. Shockingly well-behaved, considering his father had all but abandoned him for little to no reason. He could, after all, actually commune with the dead."

"So Gray - he's Theodore."

"Yes, in that, my good sir, I can say the Cook was honest. Beyond that, her words are rather - well, she has certain flights of fancy owed to a limited understanding of her own demise. It takes a well-trained mind to recognize when one has moved beyond the mortal coil." Just a fluttering as it had appeared, the smile waned to an almost neutral expression. Only the ends of his lips curved upward.

My stomach churned - slow and sloshing. A kind of sick. Strangely mesmerizing in the way it rose up, numbing the tips of my fingers before I even recognized what it had done. Turning my left hand over, I stared at the lines of my veins. Almost purple beneath my skin. I had never been kicked from a dream into another dream before. From one phantom to the next. Was I even still in Crables Manor?

The floors looked the same. Rich and dark. Molding squared and precise along walls, a fortress within gray walls. Bookshelves everywhere. A desk - ornate and large and already old - at the other end of this new room. A fireplace opposite - leaking heat against my right side. Across from me, the doctor sat in his straight back chair. The back towering above his head. A crown of studs - almost like used bullets - pinning the leather in place along its frame above his head.

"Do you know?" I asked.

The words slipped - tumbling out. Curling around me. Each blink lasted longer. Shadowing me in darkness as those strange narrow eyes stared. Not threatening. Not looming. Just observing. Taking in everything I did - weighing and measuring me.

Leaning forward, he reached a pale hand toward me. "Perhaps I've kept you too long."

"Do you know?" The words came out, repetition even though the details slurred together.

Dr. Ose sighed, jostling my knee gently. The world sharpened once more. A panic rising in my chest. My heart raced. On the back of my neck, cold sweat gathered.

"Do I know what, my dear boy?"

My nails dug into the upholstery. Treated cowhide curling beneath my fingers - like mummified flesh as my mind summoned the words. "Do you know who killed him?"

Pages flipped. The smile came back. "Oh, James, you already know who did that."

"The Governess."

It came without question. The plopping stones of her heels echoing - almost as if her title summoned her. A flood surged - putting out the fire, cutting the gaslights. Bubbles rushed from the piping, but the cold poured over me - *one-two, one-two*. Suffocating. All the air in my lungs pulled out until bubbles rose from my mouth and nose. Grabbing my throat, I wriggled like a fish caught on a hook.

Then I woke up. Panting. Sweating. Alone in the dark of my room. Early enough to not need to be awake but late enough to know I couldn't go back to sleep.

She had killed him. Gray trusted her. Thought she meant to keep him safe, and she had betrayed him. Tricked him. Trapped him. Burned him alive. Tumbling one thought into the next, I sunk down into my sweat-soaked sheets. She had killed him, and she knew I knew it too.

Chapter Sixteen

Can the dead be saved?

Religion and I rarely got on even before my stunning epiphany back in middle school, so drawing from theology to answer this newest riddle seemed inane. Heaven hadn't come for Gray, and Hell hadn't hunted the Governess. Both seemed like signs that neither really existed, but if the afterlife resided on Earth - a pale reflection of life hidden in a realm of dreams, what then could I do for Gray?

Nothing. Little next to it. The universe never cared for fairness. It sought stillness - balance. A rapid expansion toward a frozen return to nothingness - just spread a bit further apart than before. Entropy. Why would death be any different?

But a living object could be removed from its environment. Maybe it wouldn't survive, but if Gray had already died, what risk did I have in finding a way to keep him with me? Tie him to me so thoroughly that Crables Manor and the Governess couldn't reach him. Maybe she was powerful, but I could find the source of that power. Train hard enough. Work with Gray - the two of us, maybe with Dr. Ose's help or Mrs. Hayward's even - we could outmatch her. I just needed to work harder. Research her - find the names and dates to identify why she had such sway over the house. Why she had been able to attack Gray in the first place.

Which drove me online. Drove me to pictures I should have never clicked to see larger.

Never opened at all. Because I didn't have the Governess's name. I didn't know her timeline, but I knew Gray's.

Pacing the gap between my bed and Tom's, I counted each step, pushing the rest of my panicked thoughts aside. Every time I drew close to my computer, I steered my gaze away, but out of the corner of my eyes, his picture stared at me. Boston's famous young medium - available to those wealthy enough to pay the doctors to look away - or his father.

He sat at a plain table. Nothing to make him seem like anything more than a normal teenager sat with his father standing behind him. Two nurses - the only ones smiling in the picture - stood to his father's right between him and the doctor, who crossed his arms, looking severely put out by the whole affair, but with some rich widowed heiress sitting in one of the other seats - I doubt anyone hadn't had their pockets lined to ensure the picture ended up happening. Well, anyone except Gray. While the heiress would head off back to her mansions, he would remain locked with a ward - medicated for the very power he had been roped into displaying.

And it was him. Formal outfit - dark hair and bright eyes - tired eyes. The point of his chin and the firm set of his lips - traced, smudges overlaid on my screen as I yearned to reach through the monitor and drag him out of time - out of place. Anything to just see him. To hear his voice. Gray's gaze weighed on me. A reminder that he wasn't just a figment of my imagination. No, he was real, and I had abandoned him. Treated him as a thing for my own amusement - my own pleasure and loneliness, and the whole time, he had suffered. Murdered. Burned alive.

"A problem shared is a problem halved," his calm voice suggested from where he sat on my bed.

Without his jacket or shoes, he seemed underdressed though his clothes were fancier than anything I owned. No socks. His pale, delicate toes and narrow arches pressed against my sheets. Shifting back and forth as if he could knot his toes in my blankets. Hide his exposed skin, but it was all I could see. Collapsing to my knees before him, I wrapped a hand around his thin ankle. My thumb rubbed at the soft skin - pressing gently over the bone, and he let me, watching with half-lidded eyes. His chin resting on his forearms which laid upon his knees. The pouting curve of his lips enthralled me.

By all reasoning, I should have confronted him then. Told him what I knew - that I knew he was real, a ghost, a medium - a victim. Instead, I rose. A serpent slithering to wrap around him. As if my body could shield him from the world.

And when his long fingers curled in my shirt - his knee shifting to bracket my body, I might have wept. Maybe. With the rain, I couldn't tell.

In my arms, he shifted. Rose. Arms wrapped around my back. Lips pressed against my throat, sending a shiver down my spine. Was love always this torturous? A possessive, practically insatiable desire to protect Gray swelled in my chest, and all I could imagine was keeping him here - with me - hidden from the world. Away from the Governess and the ghosts of Crables Manor, but how? I had no idea how we managed to find each other in the first place. Was this how Simon felt? Desperate and terrified?

For the first time since Reggie screamed at him in the debate room, sympathy bloomed in my chest for Simon. I quickly stamped it down. What Simon did wasn't love, and this bordered on obsession.

"Gray?" I whispered. His name was a trembling question on my tongue.

His fingers pressed, pulling me tighter against him as he shook. Not answering. Just holding tightly to me. An anchor for him - a port in a storm I couldn't comprehend.

Huddled on my bed - afternoon sunlight filtering through the blinds before another torrent struck, we clung to one another. No reassurances. No definitive answers. Nothing but two men - only one, perhaps, alive. Holding fast. And for the first time in years, I prayed - begging whatever powers could hear me - perhaps even Gray himself: *Save him. Make him not dead. I wanted him to be real - but not like this. Never like this.*

"Stay," I pleaded. My heart sank - my body ached beneath the gentle weight of his arms around me. "You don't have to go back. Just stay here with me."

Gray nuzzled against my neck. His breath hot - like fire against my skin. We tipped. Falling together, I pulled him tightly against me, and he burrowed - closer and closer against me until every nerve of my body screamed for him. Electricity jolting me, cradling me into the black.

Waking to an empty bed shouldn't have hurt, but cold and alone, I rolled over, scouring the room for any sign of Gray - not that he seemed to remain long in my world. His visits were short. There and gone. Enough to make me question my sanity and no longer. A cruel twist of fate. A joke without a punchline.

Tom typed at his computer. His back stiff in the rigid wooden chair as he gnawed at the skin around his thumb nail. When his eyes strayed from the screen to me, he smirked.

"You helping Chad? Or did you get hit with the Crables' bug?" my roommate asked, jerking his head to nod at my computer.

The screensaver hid the image - covering it in black as the computer hummed, waiting for a jiggle of the mouse pad to bring it back to the lock screen. Which meant he'd been here pretty soon after I passed out. And that I fell asleep quicker than I had thought.

"The whole thing is pretty weird, right?" He continued, leaning back in his chair with a grin. "If you sell a guy as a ghost-psychic or whatever, you'd think you wouldn't also lock him up as a schizophrenic."

"Yeah, you'd think."

Holding his pen between his forefinger and thumb, he wiggled it up and down as he pursed his lips together, humming. "Not like his dad remarried. No other heirs. Though he didn't really have a fortune, right? So you'd think he'd take the kid back when he started making money or whatever."

Another question to add to the pile I hadn't managed to get out when I last saw Gray. I couldn't even confidently lie and tell myself I would ask. My ribs tightened. Just the thought made my heart ache. If I saw him again, I'd probably just hold on for dear life. Not that he was alive. I couldn't save him. Ghosts might be real, but necromancy? Everything had a limit. Conservation of energy might explain ghosts, but what was the physics to convert the dead back to life? Another human sacrifice? Was I that desperate? Did I love him enough to kill?

"Worst sanitarium to put him in if he did see ghosts," Tom added.

Swinging my feet over the side of the bed, I met my roommate's curious stare. "What do you mean?"

"Well, like, houses have histories, right? Maddix's looking into the background of the place. Something about the psychic dude overhearing nurses talking or something and that's why he ended up setting himself on fire in the widow's watch. Cause the first owner of the house committed suicide there like the day before some voodoo murder shit went down in the basement," he explained, waving his pen - and I could already tell his attention had jumped back to his work. His gaze drifted.

Standing, I grabbed my coat and shoved on my shoes. "Where's Maddix live?"

"Huh? Oh, uh...no idea?"

And there went my lead. Evaporated the second it was given to me. "Don't you have his number?"

"What? No. Why would I? He's kinda weird," Tom replied.

If Tom didn't, there was a chance Chad did. As much as I wanted to stay as far away from him as possible, I had no choice. Waiting out the weekend to maybe run into Maddix wasn't going to work. We only had one class together, and I'd never seen him while getting food.

When I reached Chad's room, the door was already open. Most of their hall kept their doors open - the football team bumming around from room to room, and as one of the few on that floor who wasn't on the team, Chad glared at the trio invading his room as they devoured pizza rolls on the floor between Chad's bed and Alexander's.

"James!" Alexander cheered, mouth steaming like a pizza dragon. "What's up, man?"

Standing awkwardly in their doorway, I waved as all eyes turned on me - even Chad's glower. "Hey, either of you guys have Maddix's number?"

"No," Chad retorted at the same as Alexander said, "Sure - Chad's got it."

Swallowing, Alexander cocked a brow at his roommate. "But you made that list of everybody's number after the tour."

128

Eyes narrowing further, Chad scoffed. "Fine. I have it. Why?"

"I need it. Tom said he might have a book I was looking for," I told them.

"What book?"

"Schizophrenia: Cognitive Theory - Beck and somebody," I lied. "So - can I have his number?"

"I thought you were focusing on collective post traumatic stress disorder. High school shootings or whatever," Chad said. His mind was a steel trap for information he could throw back in my face. "Why do you need something on schizophrenia?"

"Different course."

Alexander's gaze jumped between us, but he wasn't the one who spoke up. One of the other guys did, grumbling, "Sheesh, Chad, just give him the number."

Pulling out his phone, Chad clicked away. "I think I'll text Maddix first. Ask him if he has the book."

"Seriously? Your roommate is psycho," the same guy said as he took another pizza roll.

Alexander shrugged, but Chad turned his glower on the player. "So I can give out your number to the whole school. Anybody who wants it - here you go, Blake Martinez's number. What's that Jessica Gould? He's been avoiding you - here's his number."

The guy, Blake, sneered but shrunk in a bit on himself. "Fine, whatever. You're right."

"I'm always right," Chad retorted. "Save yourself the energy spent being wrong and assume that from the beginning." Glancing down at his phone, he smirked. "He's in the library. Probably your midday nap zone," Chad informed me as he grabbed his bag and walked right by me out of the room. Leaning back into the doorway, he cocked a brow. "So? Come on."

Shoving the note in my pocket, I gave Alexander a short wave. "Why are you coming?"

"Cause I know you're lying."

I grimaced. "You always think I'm lying."

"And I'm always right," Chad retorted with a self-satisfied smirk.

Chapter Seventeen

Sitting back in a chair, Maddix glanced between the two of us. His lips tugged down into a dour scowl. Books built walls around him, and he'd dragged one of the armchairs into a corner.

"I get why he's here," Maddix said, gesturing at me. "But why are you?"

Chad crossed his arms. "Curiosity. Sue me."

"Whatever."

Reaching into his backpack, he held out the book in question. "I've already grabbed the quotes I want from it for the project, so just get it back whenever."

"Cool. Mind if I get your number, so I don't have to go through this idiot to get it back to you?" I asked. Chad huffed, rolling his eyes.

"Sure," Maddix said, holding out his hands for my phone. As he typed in his number, he asked, "There a reason you guys are acting so weird? Or is that just Chad?"

"Just Chad," I said as Chad spat, "Forget it!"

Off he stormed. Stomping and glowering at everybody between him and the door. Maddix blinked. HIs eyes - wide and round - looked to me. "That was weird."

"To be honest, it's not really his fault. I lied to him 'cause he wouldn't give me your number if I told him I wanted to talk to you alone about Crables," I admitted, sitting down in one of the other chairs.

His brows furrowed. "But you're not doing your project on it."

"No. I'm not."

His gaze weighed on me heavily. I could almost hear the gears turning in his head. A smirk - small at first but growing - tugged at his lips. They twitched up on one side.

"It got in your head," he said.

I swallowed. "What?"

Dread pooled in my stomach. Roiling and acidic, it built up in the back of my throat, threatening to pour out of me. What if I wasn't the only one who saw Gray? What if he appeared to others? What if we blended to him? Maybe he didn't feel the same way about me as I did about him. A knot of jealousy tangled around me. If I let it go, it would choke me. Drag me down the same road Simon had gone. The sort of place where want destroyed having, so I stayed silent, waiting for Maddix to respond.

To my relief, he told me, "You felt something in Crables Manor. Everybody joked about it, but I sensed a presence there. Maybe multiple."

"Presences..."

"Ghosts."

"Oh - yeah, kind of. I just feel like if I know the history I could get some sleep. You know, put my mind at ease," I told him, rubbing the back of my head.

Maddix flopped over the side of his chair. He dug through his backpack, pulling out a notebook. Loose papers stuck out here and there. From the mess, he pulled a single sheet. A half-typed, half-written bibliography.

"Here," he said, handing it to me. "They're all online."

Not for the first time, I wanted to slam my head into a hard surface. A wall. A desk. Anything would do just fine. Google could've saved the day. Sure, I hadn't had a computer at home for most of my life, but it wasn't like I was Amish. I had no excuse for not thinking it through.

I believed myself better. Smarter than this. Maybe it was my weird sleep schedule. It was probably my sleep schedule. Or it could legitimately be because ghosts haunted me. Though - to be fair - I wanted to date and possibly marry one of them, so blaming ghosts seemed a bit presumptuous. It wasn't like I wanted Gray to stop haunting me. Poor guy probably didn't realize he was dead.

"Thanks."

Maddix shrugged. "No problem. Just if I get the guts to do a seance there, you'll come, right?"

"Course." Like I was going to let somebody mess around where Gray died without me. "Just text me," I offered, double-checking he'd sent himself a message to get my number. "There's definitely something off about that place."

Chuckling, Maddix gestured at the paper. "You wait. That place is nasty."

Nodding, I folded the paper, sticking it in my pocket. "Thanks again, man."

He waved me off, and I left him alone. Frustration and excitement buzzed around my body as adrenaline built up once more. At this point, I stumbled through between waking and sleep, so any progress deserved some celebration. However, in my hazy return to the dorm, I almost missed the way the world shifted around me. It was strange. Like being caught in an oil painting. A dense fog rolled in, and the color rolled out.

Shadows jumped, stretching long and tall. Looming like giants, but I assumed everything was natural. I hadn't fallen asleep. No gaps suggested that, and Gray was the only apparition which showed up outside the manor, so with none of the other markers of a dream, I believed things to be normal. Fog in the midwest in November. Weird. But Boston was right on the ocean. They had fog all the time. Sea - evaporation - all that New England mess.

Shadows - sure. Boston had sunlight, however little that meant. Fog plus sun meant weird shadows. Sure. The day started cloudy. I hadn't seen a speck of sunlight on the way to the library, but if San Francisco's fog could run, why couldn't Boston's?

I made it back to the dorm without an issue. If a shadow followed me in the fog, I hadn't noticed. It wasn't like the ghosts of Crables Manor had been particularly shy, so how was I supposed to realize I'd just led one right back to my bedroom? Gray found me straight away. Everybody else saw me in dreams, so why would it be hard for any of them to show up? Why would one of them have hooked a ride on Maddix? Sticking to him - holding tight and waiting - waiting because it knew eventually it would be led straight back to me, and haunting me wasn't as easy as Gray made it seem.

Every time I rethink it, my brain comes up with a thousand excuses. Reasons why it wasn't my fault. How I couldn't possibly have noticed. Gray occupied my thoughts. But that wouldn't change what had happened, or how the struggles of my conscious mind against the drain of sleep and stress would get so, so much worse.

Chapter Eighteen

Exhaustion weighed on me, and with the fog and rain, sleep called to me. I kicked off my shoes, and I dove face first into bed. Not even bothering to push back the covers or change. Just a diving leap -
- and I was running. Like falling through a hole, I swung in a strange flip, rotating all around to be standing again, but my legs moved - slamming against the floor before I could think. All around me - the air hung heavy and thick. Each breath left a strange, dull ache, leaving my head spinning. All the lights glowed - glass capped lanterns. Beneath my feet, carpet covered the floors, but the shag wasn't exactly the old moldy half-torn mess it usually was when it wasn't the pristine dark wood.

Slowing to a jog, I glanced around. My head pulsed with every beat of my heart, but nothing seemed out of place. Different - sure. No cobwebs. Instead, black stained the upper corners. Long strokes of charring. Gaps in the ceiling sizzled, but I couldn't smell smoke. Just the dull, thick oily air. Running a hand through my hair, I turned around, and like ripples in a puddle, the air reverberated as a blur of black and white barreled toward me.

The phantom screamed. Twisting and curling in and around itself. A beast with knotted black hair covering whatever undead face lay beneath, but its legs - long and clothed in white scrubs - gave way to blackened feet. Skin bubbled and peeling.

Stumbling, I took off. My hands hit walls which hadn't been there before as the manor stretched, growing around me. Through the newly formed labyrinth, the spirit chased me. It smashed into walls, leaving ash and blood smeared in its wake. More than once, I glanced back to see it fall, worming its way across the ground to crawl up a wall - never pausing in its screaming. No matter how fast I ran, it never fell behind.

A crack sounded. I fell forward, twisting around as my foot sunk through the carpet and the broken floorboards hidden beneath. The hole swallowed my foot and leg right up to the knee.

"Shit!"

I twisted, tugging as I shuffled backward. The creature zagged, thudding against the walls of the hall as it drew closer and closer. It seemed to realize I was caught, so the spirit slowed. Its screaming waned as it dragged the shadows - the blood and fire clinging to it - closer and closer. The phantom shuffled across the carpet. Blood oozing from its blackened toes. Cracks like sparks shot up its heels as it tilted its head, contorting the closer it loomed.

Kicking my leg, I tugged, but my caught leg wouldn't budge. The floorboards shifted. More of the carpet sunk into the gap. Stuck, I clawed. Suddenly, all those animals who had gnawed off their own legs to escape traps seemed sensible. Handfuls of brown shag broke off in my hands.

The spirit closed in - barely five feet away. It had no arms. Just a white misshapen torso.

139

Feathers and beads decorated its hair. Braids started and ended. Chunks of burned - singed ends curling, splitting apart crowned its head. From behind the curtain of dark tangled hair, two eyes stared at me. Wide whites surrounded black spots.

Each tug dragged the wood splintering into my leg. A lump swelled in my throat. The faster my heart drummed, the slower the world seemed to go. If I wrenched it up, my leg would be mangled, but if I didn't, the spirit would get me, and there was no telling what it would do, so with a scream of my own, I tugged it free. Fractured wood dug into my flesh, tearing my jeans and tearing down my leg, but none of that mattered. I was free.

Spinning, I crawled, fumbling into a run. With a roar, the spirit pursued. The faster I ran, the faster it came after me, but somehow, the manor collapsed inward. Stairs appeared where they hadn't existed moments ago, and I half-ran half-fell down them. The spirit did nothing in halves. Head over feet, it rolled down the stairs, slamming into the wall at the bottom while I continued going. Gray's room stood open. Out of the corner of my eye, I saw markings - geometric shapes and runes carved there. Somebody had upended the bed, but the spirit climbed back to its feet - taking longer this time than before - but quickly enough I couldn't delay.

Almost there. Almost there. Sliding down the rail to the first floor, the air thinned around me. A fragrance tickled my nose. Some sort of soup - a bubbling broth, and safety struck my mind. An instinctive certainty overtook my desire to try to leave the house, and as the spirit rolled down the stairs into the more open first floor front hall, I fled to the back, shoving open the kitchen door.

And the all thickness left the air as if vacuumed out. At the stove, the cook hummed, stirring before she slid to the side to cut up some carrots. The growing panic - pitched by the constant hum buzzing through my bones - vanished. My adrenaline waned, and my leg throbbed. Swearing, I fell back into a seat.

"Language," she scolded, but her eyes widened when she turned. "What have you been doing?"

"Running for my life."

The cook blinked, setting her hands on her hips. "Well, I suppose I'll have to fix you up."

"This is a dream. My leg'll be fine when I wake up," I argued, but she put down her knife and dug through her cabinets, pulling out a tin kit filled with gauze.

"I'd have you remove those trousers if they weren't tattered enough for me to see the mess you made here. Luckily, it's not too deep. No stitches needed," she assured, and from one blink to the next, my leg was bandaged, and the cook returned to her work. "Now, who were you running from?"

"I don't know. Some mad -"

"This - is very - inconvenient," a man complained as he skidded into the kitchen on his back. His black hair fanned out behind his angular face. Piercings lined his ears, and his dark brown eyes glared at the ceiling. "I'm a bloody turtle. This is - ridiculous."

"- a straitjacket."

The spirit glared at me. "Yeah - we don't all get to pick what we spend our afterlife wearing, Mr. Still-Gotta-Pulse."

Somehow, seeing his arms wriggling against the bindings made him far less intimidating. Or maybe that was the fact that he was struggling to roll over and stand up, but he kept slipping. His feet - blood and painful looking - left red marks on the floor, making matters worse as he skidded and slid every time he tried to move from knees to his feet.

"Are you going to stare? Or are you going to help?" The cook asked, not even bothering to turn from her work.

Scoffing, I grumbled, "He was chasing me. Why would I help?"

"Chasing you? Ha! Herding you from an early grave. Saving your life," the straitjacketed man hissed, finally managing to stand with a triumphant exclamation. "The doctors might've left you alone before, but now that you're not just making goo-goo eyes at Gray, they're causing trouble."

"Trouble?" Mrs. Hayward brushed off her apron, leaning against the counter as she crossed her arms. "That pair intends to isolate that poor boy until they can use him. This is their last chance after all."

"Yeah, after this go-around, this place'll be torn down. Stupid, freaking, jacket," the man growled, twisting as he tried to break free. He failed, only making himself sweat. His dark eyes sparked as they fell on me, pinning me in place. "I tried. Before you. I tried to save him. Could've done it too. Stupid limbo burns off pen. Got all these marks, but they've got to scar- "

"Or tattoos," the cook added.

"Yeah, but who's tattooing a guy in rehab?" The ghost spat. "Nobody! I didn't really have options."

Running her hands soothingly over his face, she sighed, brushing his hair back. "You did what you could. You gave your life trying, Rory. Nobody could ask more."

He leaned into her touch like an attention-starved puppy. Exhaustion ringed his eyes in purple cradles which vanished when she stepped away, and his focus returned to me.

"So. How're you gonna do it?"

I glanced at Mrs. Hayward, but she had her back to me. "Do what?"

"Save him! Mrs. Hayward and the Governess have enough on their plates keeping Dr. Ose and Dr. Carreau from Gray. Not like I'm much help like this," he informed me, struggling once more in his straitjacket. "But I know what they told me, so we can do this. Plan it out. Make your attempt work."

"Why would I trust you? The Governess killed Gray. If you're working with her -"

He slammed his head into mine, growling, "Lies! I can see him. He's already in your head.

Spinning things around. She saved him! Pulled Gray into limbo before they could use him."

I shoved him away from me. Rubbing my forehead, I gritted my teeth. "Why should I believe any of that?"

"Because it is the truth," Mrs. Hayward intoned. "While Florence might not be the kindest of people, she would never harm Gray. She sees him as her son. She's already lost one child, young man, so she isn't about to let some greedy head shrink get their hands on him now."

In the manor's kitchen, their words made as much sense as Dr. Ose's had in the study. The same frustrated indignation built up in my chest, and all I wanted to do was destroy everything. Burn the place to the ground to get Gray out. They were all dead. Who was I supposed to trust? Nothing made sense. Not that ghosts ever had, but I imagined myself a decent judge of character, and I couldn't figure any of them out. The Governess felt evil. Mrs. Hayward didn't, but she trusted the Governess. Dr. Ose left a bad taste in my mouth, and he spoke in circles, wrapping me around myself as good a manipulator as any, so I could believe he was evil, but this new ghost - whoever he was - definitely seemed off. Not evil off. Crazy off. Rehab made sense, off. I didn't have enough information.

Drowning in unknowns, I asked the simplest I could find, "Who's Dr. Carreau?"

A chill - like fingers brushing across the back of my neck - crept over me. Shadows shifted, and the light bent like everything in the room had

144

casually agreed to lean slightly, drawing out the lengths of the shadows before snapping back into shape.

Both ghosts watched, standing firm against the shifting for a moment before the ghost in a straitjacket screamed, twisting as the distortion focused on him. His hands slid through the bindings of the straitjacket. Then they curled around him, twisting back as if he were a marionette. Collapsing to his knees, he seized. Shaking and screaming silently - his mouth opened wide as terror contorted his face.

Kneeling beside him, Mrs. Hayward rolled him to his side, brushing a hand through his hair as she gently whispered, "Everything will be fine soon, Rory. It's almost over now. Just breathe."

"What's going on?" I demanded.

Her eyes narrowed, glaring up at me even as her tone remained soft. "Remember, you're already dead. He can't do anything to you now, Rory." The distortion snapped, and Rory sagged against the tiles. With a sigh, the cook looked at me. "Dr. Carreau is Dr. Ose's partner. He isolates his victims, warping their sense of self until - "

"They kill themselves or others," Rory interrupted.

Mrs. Hayward clucked her tongue. "You didn't kill yourself."

"I didn't pay attention. I knew they were onto me, but I just - just swallowed the pills like an idiot." He released a shuddering breath, adding in a whisper, "I knew there were too many. Didn't recognize them, but I just took them anyway."

My skin buzzed. A strange uncomfortable tingle like each cell in my body screamed in unison - *get out! Get out now!* But where would I have gone? Somewhere in this house, Gray existed. Stuck in limbo - not entirely dead if Rory was to be believed - somewhere, capable of one day being free and real and alive with me - Gray existed, so how could I turn my back on this? Even if everything in me suggested I'd more than likely end up dead?

Nodding, I said, "Okay. How do I do it? How do I save him?"

A sharp smile spread across Rory's face. His teeth swirled - a mix of creamy whites and pale yellows. From there, the swirling spread, and though I knew by the movement of his mouth that he was talking, I couldn't hear a word he said until the screaming started again. The whole kitchen dissolved into a Van Gogh painting. Then popped -

- and I sat up, slamming my forehead into Tom's.

"Shit!" he cried. "Ow!" Rubbing his brow, he glared at me. "You okay?"

"What?"

His hands dropped to his side. "You were screaming in your sleep."

I blinked. "Oh - nightmare, I guess."

"You really should go see a counselor of something, man. It's free," he reminded me, but he didn't press further, climbing into his bed.

146

Staring down at my hands, I counted my fingers. Not a dream. As if that helped. As if I didn't have the same number of fingers here as I did in the manor. As if the manor was really a normal nightmare. It didn't matter. I could feel it in my bones. I wouldn't get back there tonight. Nothing could ever be that simple.

Rolling over, I almost swallowed my tongue. A tall shadow loomed. It almost looked like a man in a long coat. Whipping around, I forgot to breathe until my eyes landed on Tom tugging up his blankets. It must've just been him. The shadow disappeared the moment he clicked off the lamp which curled around his bedpost. None of the other ghosts left the manor besides Gray. Most likely the rest couldn't. I had nothing to fear in my dorm room except annoying my roommate into hating me, and I had Tom. That would never happen.

Chapter Nineteen

Reading through Maddix's list, I found a web of connected articles and urban legends - horrible histories which expanded back and back into the history of Crables Manor. Back to its building during the decade prior to the Civil War. Florence Wilson married a man from a wealthy family, who gifted them a large mansion with a widow's watch. The land owned by the manor had once extended to the coast, though I couldn't imagine any ship could be caught coming in when hard coastlines rather than beaches formed its property line.

The family - the Sullivans - had two sons. After the marriage of the eldest, the war broke out, and he marched south, leaving his pregnant wife behind. When the man - Henry Sullivan - died shortly after, his brother took over the family business for a short time before a mass tragedy, which led to a servant finding Florence Sullivan dead in the widow's watch. She had committed suicide. Stranger still, her brother-in-law and her husband's entire family were discovered slaughtered in the basement. Carved into bedrock.

All of that, I could confirm. It was the tales which arose around it which left me with an aching head and increasing discomfort.

According to urban legend, the Sullivans had practiced human sacrifices dating back to the twelfth century. At least two sons were born, but the eldest always died. Most went off to war, but others died of sickness. All very bland deaths. The sort people expected and wouldn't question, but each generation, the family gained more and more power wherever they were. However, some had noted this only occurred if the first son was married with an heir conceived. Sometimes, the second sons married the widows. Others, they simply cared for them, but every single time, the first son's child would also die - except at a very young age without stated reason.

Which led to speculation - as the Governess hadn't had a child. In fact, they clearly stated she had miscarried after hearing word of her husband's death.

That's what they said, and with an incomplete ritual, the second son would have to be sacrificed in his brother's stead to continue the line. Obviously, having knowledge of his brother's death being less than above board, the second son wasn't about to let that happen to him. Notes commenting that Henry Sullivan's mother was pregnant - despite her advanced age - seemed to confirm this theory for some, and they suggested the second son, Charles, had discovered that fact, leading to him massacring his family to avoid his brother's fate; however, while the family wasn't extensive, he couldn't have cleanly killed them - and there weren't specifics. Nobody knew exactly what happened, but some hypothesized backlash due to the incomplete ritual. Others suggested the wife's suicide was actually a self-sacrifice as she demanded revenge, resulting in whatever occult being the family worshiped turning on them.

All of this seemed ludicrous, but I spent several weeks - months really - with a dead psychic from the mid-twentieth century, so who was I to judge?

One thing none of the history suggested? That she was a bad person. That the Governess would have any reason to hurt Gray. But - then I came across the pair of doctors who bought the manor, transforming it into a sanitarium. Dr. Ose and Dr. Carreau - who later set the entire place on fire after nurses presented evidence that the two doctors were experimenting on their patients, encouraging them to give into their darker impulses. Homicide, suicide - every creepy story I'd stumbled across online seemed to be repeated either by them to their patients or their patients to each other. It was something out of a Edgar Allan Poe short.

It made the decision simple. Back in the kitchen, I leaned against the counter, studying Rory. He struggled, tugging at his bindings. His gums bled, but he kept gnawing as if that would free him.

"I could try," I offered again.

He shook his head. "Won't work."

"It is all in his mind, darling," Mrs. Hayward reassured me.

"Well, do you need to take it off to show me the marks I need to save Gray?" I asked, and his eyes sparked. The madness slipped away just a bit as he shook his hair out of his face.

Smirking, he nodded. "Yeah. I've got a picture. They took pictures."

"They?"

"Autopsy photos," he clarified, and my stomach lurched.

"Where would I even get those?"

He tilted his head. Eyes narrowing, Rory hummed, considering my question carefully. "They probably sent my brother some copies. I think."

"That's not helpful. If it isn't publicly available, I can't get to them." Running my hands over my face, I sighed. "There's got to be some other way."

"Possession would work," Mrs. Hayward offered, never looking away from her stew.

She always cooked the same things. Stew or soup or something in that big pot of hers. Part of me always wondered if one day I'd lean over and see a human eyeball bumbling up like in a witch's cauldron. I never got too close. Mrs. Hayward and Rory hadn't exactly popped up in my searches yet.

"I'm not letting anybody possess me," I informed them.

Rory shrugged. "Don't need to possess you. Just let me follow you back out of the dreamscape. Outside the manor, I shouldn't be in this getup."

"So I'll be able to see the markings?"

"Or I'll have a free hand to draw them," the straitjacketed spirit affirmed.

Shaking my head, I couldn't find a reason to object when I still needed his help. "Sure. Follow me back to the dorm."

"Great!" Rory leapt to his feet. Sauntering over to me, he grinned up as he stood on his tiptoes to look me dead in the eye. "Now…wake up!"

He slammed our heads together, and I groaned as I rolled away from the wall.

"You okay?" Tom called groggily.

Rubbing my forehead, I huffed, "Just getting acquainted with the wall."

"Then be quiet," he complained, rolling over to go back to sleep.

However, I wasn't alone. Standing beside the bed in leather pants, a white shirt, and a leather jacket, Rory stood with his hair pulled into a ponytail at the base of his neck. Tattoos covered his body, and as he turned, surveying his new surroundings, I got the distinct feeling I would regret letting him come out. This worsened when he spun around to look toward Tom's bed.

All calm dissipated from his face. Shrieking, he flashed between his cool leather-clad ensemble and the straitjacket horror movie maniac look. Back and forth, he went as his cry rang through the dorm, rattling the windows before he exploded. Just poof. A bright flash of light, and he disappeared. All the while, Tom remained asleep.

"Shit," I grumbled, jumping out of bed to look around, but he was well and truly gone.

Gray hadn't done that before, but something told me that getting out of the room would help - or maybe I just didn't want to be there when somebody came knocking to complain about the noise, so I grabbed my stuff and changed before

152

running out. Out on the busy streets, I walked alone. The chill swept right through my sweater, but I wasn't about to go back in without an explanation as to what had made Rory panic. And explode.

"God, I miss sunlight," Rory complained, condensing right beside me.

He fell easily into step with me. Sunglasses hiding his eyes as he tilted his head back as if to preen in the sunshine. It was freaking cold, so I'm not sure how great it was when it did shit all to warm anything.

Pausing to wait for a light, I glanced around before hissing under my breath, "What was that about?"

"What? I like sunlight," he reiterated.

"I meant the screaming. In my dorm room."

Looking at me over his sunglasses, he asked, "What screaming?"

And he actually meant it. I could see the confusion in his eyes. For a moment, I debated wasting time to ask him, but he seemed fine, and I didn't have time. Gray didn't have time. In a few weeks, Gray would burn alive for the last time, and if I couldn't reach into limbo and pull him out, he would be dead for real.

"Are all your tattoos for the ceremony? I'm never gonna be able to hide the neck ones," I told him, nodding at the black spiking up like a sharp collar.

"These?" Tugging down his collar, he revealed the twining barb wire. "Nah. Half of these are just mine."

Without being able to take a picture, my options were limited, but it wasn't like I could get all the tattoos at once anyway. I had only so much money, and going too big too quick would probably catch attention. Thank goodness I was eighteen.

"We'll start with the body tattoos and work out. Hopefully line art won't be too expensive," I grumbled, crossing the road with the ghost in tow.

"I bet my old buddy Zeke still has his shop. It's only been like twenty years, right?" Rory announced, taking the lead. "He's superstitious, so if he knows you got me around, he'll probably do it for free. Good cause and all."

"If he reports me as being crazy, I'm gonna be locked up," I grumbled.

With a shrug, he wove his way through the city. Despite having been in Boston for the last few months, I hadn't explored too far beyond the area between my dorm and campus. The couple times I had, Tom had been there too, knowing exactly which way to go - or having someone else around who did, so I wasn't exactly confident following a ghost from the eighties. Uncertainty still dogged me. Popping up when I least expected to find myself doubting. Perhaps I ought to have recognized it. That sinking feeling in the base of my stomach. As we moved further into the city - on new roads of which I barely caught the names, doubt churned inside me.

"You sure you know where you're going?" I demanded.

He scoffed, glancing over his shoulder at me. His bright eyes narrowed. Curling up on one side, his lips smirked at me. "Relax, kid, this city isn't exactly everchanging."

When I opened my mouth to remind him just how long it had been since he had been alive - let alone free, he glared, stunning me to silence. What was I supposed to do? Keep arguing with the guy only I could see?

Besides, it was pointless. Forty minutes later, we were there. Zeke's shop remained. A black sign marked it out: **Zeke's Tattoos.** The neon sign insisted it was open, but nobody seemed to be around. I'd never been to a parlor. Good Christian boys didn't get tattoos - or so my parents said. Not that I asked them. Dad just scoffed, making snide remarks when he saw somebody with a tattoo. Especially women. Not that his critique of anything remotely outside his own experience turned out positive, so there I stood, my first time in front of a tattoo parlor - with a ghost.

"Not the most creative shop name, sure - but this guy's brilliant," Rory assured me. I nodded, and he shoved his hands in his jacket pockets. "You gonna go in?"

"Yeah - just give me a minute."

Cocking an eyebrow, Rory leaned back against the window. "How are you gonna get runes all over your body if you can't even walk into the store?"

Ghost had a point, so in, I went. Everything smelled clean with a burnt edge. Like someone had tried to wipe down lit bulbs with industrial cleaner. As I stepped inside, a sensor on the door rang, and a burly man stepped out of the back. The picture of a Hell's Angel - the guy looked almost seven foot and at least three hundred pounds. Completely bald with a Bruce Willis sort of shape to his head, he had multiple brightly colored tattoos down both arms and around his neck. His dark brows furrowed, and he lumbered over.

"I'm guessing you're not Shannon," he murmured, glancing into a book behind the receptionist's desk.

"Ah, no."

He sat down at the stool behind the stand, studying me. "If you'd like to make an appointment, I have some time open tomorrow morning. I'm afraid I'm doing inventory at the moment."

"Zeke!" Rory cried, surging forward as if to hug the man. "You got old, you fat bastard!"

His arms went right through the guy, who kept watching me with an increasingly concerned expression. As Rory reeled, Zeke asked, "You okay, kid?"

"You Zeke?"

"Yeah. I'm the owner."

I nodded, fighting the urge to turn tail and run. "I'm looking to do some full body tattoo work, and I'd like it done as quickly as possible."

"Sure. I'll write you in," Zeke assured, pulling out a pen. "What's your name?"

"James."

Rory growled and leaned over his friend's shoulder. "Shannon's not in for another couple hours. Get this guy to schedule you." Unable to answer him without looking crazy, I sent Rory a pointed stare, and the ghost rolled his eyes. "Tell him I sent you. Tell him the idiot Crow sent you."

What did I have to lose? "The - the idiot Crow sent me."

Zeke fumbled the pen. His head snapped up, and he stared at me, gaping. "Excuse me?"

Rounding me, Rory whispered in my ear, demanding I say word for word what he said, and despite feeling like a freak, I did. "The idiot Crow said if I needed a tattoo, I should get it from - from your bald self. Considering you still have the shop after the watertower fiasco, Rory suggested I should be equally impressed and concerned, especially since he's seen your aim when you were drunk - and he highly doubts you've gotten significantly better."

"Stop," Zeke held up a hand, cutting off Rory's weird rant. "What the hell is going on?"

"I'm not lying," I told him. "Rory said you were my best bet."

"Rory Haggard died before you would've even been born," the gruff looking man returned, but he spoke softly - as if just saying the words brought him unspeakable pain.

"Ask me something," I offered. "Ask me something only Rory would know."

Running his hands over his face, Zeke inhaled slowly, but the air didn't seem to inflate him, and when he breathed out - staring almost blankly at me - he seemed to collapse just a bit more. "Why'd he do it? Ask him that."

I glanced at Rory, who sighed, "Shit."

When he offered nothing else, I said, "He's just saying 'shit.' Do you mean why did he kill himself? Cause, he didn't."

Zeke shook his head. His lips wobbled, and his eyes filled with tears. "I fucking knew it," he sobbed. "I knew that dumb bastard wouldn't off himself."

"Course not. I promised," Rory insisted.

"He says he promised you that he wouldn't," I told Zeke, who nodded solemnly, slamming his hand down on the desk. "That's actually kind of why I'm here. He was trying to save a kid named - "

"Gray," Zeke cut in, nodding. "Ari told me. Said Rory was going on and on about ghosts and this kid named Gray. He asked me - asked me to sneak my equipment in. I still have the drawings!"

Jumping to his feet, Zeke pulled out his wallet. Inside, there was a neatly folded piece of worn paper. When he unfolded it, he revealed a drawing of a man - back and front - covered in runes and lines. Common sense told me I was in for a full body of symbols, but the full breadth of it didn't strike me until I saw the sketch.

"Looks about right," Rory affirmed, and my stomach sank further.

Swallowing, I nodded slowly. "You still have that."

Zeke nodded, running a finger over the edges, smoothing them down. "It helped remind me - before - about how bad things can get. After he died, I got myself sober. Proposed to Angelica."

"Fucking finally," Rory cheered. "She was too good for your sorry self."

Shaking his head, Zeke laughed almost as if he could hear him. "Love of my life. Too good for me, but she said yes." His eyes - big and sad as a basset hound - lifted to me. "You can see him, right? Is he here? Can you thank him for me?"

"He's right there," I said, pointing at Rory who shifted. "He can hear you."

Zeke focused on the spot where I'd gestured. "I got two kids now. Morgan's in high school - thinks she knows everything. Fucking genius. And - ah - my older one - he's...he just got into college out in L.A." Tears gathered in his eyes. "We named him Rory."

Rory swallowed. His brows furrowed, and he glared up at the nearest light, stubbornly refusing to look at Zeke. Growling, he stomped his foot. "Damn it," he growled. "It's not - it's not fucking fair. I was supposed to be there. I got clean, so I could be his best man when he finally got the balls to ask. Goddamnit!"

Above us, the lights flickered, and Zeke sat forward. "Was that him?"

"It means a lot to him that you named your son after him," I offered as the ghost raged, shifting between leather and a straitjacket as his frustration and torment twisted him.

Zeke probably meant the best. He honestly seemed like a good guy. A bit gullible but that worked in my favor this time, so I couldn't be too mean about that. But as he pulled his collar done, showing off a black bird in flight, he just made the situation all the more difficult as he said, "Got this for him too."

It was stupid. I knew the ghosts were real. If Gray was real, it made sense. These were people once. Living, breathing, walking, talking people with lives of their own and people who loved them, so it shouldn't have struck me so hard in that moment, but I couldn't seem to get a hold of myself. Rory raged. Zeke sniffled and looked ready to sob. I just wanted to sink right into the floor and disappear. This was too big. Worse still, I couldn't save them all. Even if I got Gray out of there, Rory would still be dead, and unlike probably every other dead person in the world, he now intimately knew the world had moved right on without him - but for better or worse, without exactly forgetting him.

"I've got to get those," I nearly shouted, pushing my emotions down. Gray needed me. The guy I loved could be saved. Nothing else could matter. "There's only one more chance to save Gray."

"In the next six weeks!" Rory snapped.

Frowning at him, I added, "And I've only got six weeks to get all of it."

Zeke frowned. "Okay," he said, nodding. "For Rory, I'll do it."

"Really?"

160

"Pro-bono and all, but I can't - I can't in good conscience let you get this all at once. Six week, right? Okay...yeah, we can..." he pulled out his appointment book, righting in my name on all the subsequent Saturdays for several hour blocks in the early morning. "Chest, back, left leg, right leg, upper arms, lower arms - six weeks."

"It's gotta be done before January 1st," Rory told me.

All the Saturdays aligned, so it was only the last one. "Can we move the last to the 30th?" I asked him, pointing at an open slot. "I have to be ready and in position on the 1st?"

"Course."

Biting my lip, I tried to put a finger on the unease settling in my stomach. Everything seemed to be going just fine, yet I'd never felt more nervous. Probably just from going into getting my first tattoo. The chest designs were intense with geometric blocks of black and runes carved up here and there.

"Thank you," I said. "For believing me."

Gesturing for me to follow him, he washed his hands before sorting his tools. "Just bring him in when it's done. I'd like to meet the kid Rory died trying to save. He's got to be something special."

"He is."

Chapter Twenty

Everything swirled around. Soft and
yellow-lit, the gaslighting warned me as quickly as
the way my lungs tightened in the thicker air.
Despite the heat, the room sent chills up my spine.
Goosebumps rose on my arms, and I could see blue
taking over beneath my nails. Still, I sunk deeper
into the chair. Exhaustion pinned me, and as the fire
crackled to my right, I forced my eyes to focus.
Back in the study, I sat across from Dr. Ose.

"Welcome back, James," he said. Legs
crossed, he reclined with his hands folded in his lap
- a pen settled between two of his fingers. "How
have you been sleeping?"

My nose scrunched as I shook my head.
"What?"

"Narcolepsy can be a difficult condition, but
it is treatable," he assured me. "Schizophrenia as
well."

A slow dawning realization overcame me.
"You're - you're acting like I'm one of your
patients."

"Aren't you?"

Fighting against the weariness in my bones,
I pushed myself up. "Mrs. Hayward and Rory told
me all about you. There's plenty of articles about
you and Carreau."

He smiled. His face blurred, so I couldn't
say exactly what he looked like. White and
brown-haired - dressed in a suit. "I'm sure there are
numerous articles. Likely more than a few about

Florence Sullivan and the massacre which happened here as well." He didn't give me a moment to respond. "Regardless, you'll find our dear Mrs. Hayward is an eternal optimist. While well-meaning, she's too kind. The Governess trapped your young gentleman in limbo - a terrible fate if he had any of his memories. Luckily, Dr Carreau and I were able to minimize damage - "

"You're gaslighting me."

The black sphere where his eyes should have been blinked. The swirling movement of a Van Gogh swirled in the streaks of brown and peach across his face. If I could focus enough, I might have smeared him. Rubbed my hand across the wet paint of his face. Might even make my eyes focus a bit better.

"James, I need you to concentrate. I believe you're having another episode," Dr. Ose said.

His tone rocked, low and rolling as he spoke, but it wasn't nearly as calming as he likely intended. It itched. Overly prepared. A highly practiced lure - as deadly as a siren. The same voice we were told to use - objective but not too distant. Trustworthy. An absolute lie.

Something lunged at me. Ose didn't seem to move, but a flash - like lightning - danced across the thick air. Silver. Sudden. Pain - sharp and sudden - pierced me. Dragging my mind back from wandering, pain silenced the distraction of my over-energetic mind. Carved deep into my chest, the lines of my tattoo ached. They cracked. Bleeding and peeling -

"You were saying…" he urged, but the words slurred, drawing out and slowing as the warmth in the room drained.

A flood of cold swept through. The thick air rippled, exploding and thinning and chilling as stones plopped - *one-two one-two* -

And I woke up - panting and cold and drenched in sweat. Tom hadn't gotten back, so Rory remained on his bed, lounging as he swayed - rocking as if he were in a hammock. When I rolled out of bed, jumping up and ripping off my shirt - he sat up.

"What's going on?"

I didn't answer. Couldn't. All I could do was stare at the lines. They remained pristine. Perfectly the same as they had been when I fell into bed - exhausted from the adrenaline drop after the spike of the needle repeatedly piercing my skin.

Rory swung his legs over the side of Tom's bed. "He got in your head, didn't he?" He hovered, inching closer toward me along the edge of the bed. "You should eat something. Sugar helps."

Sugar helps - the dead man suggested sugar. Part of me wanted to ask him what drugs would go best with my descent into madness. I'd never even had a beer or smoked a cigarette. Alcohol and tobacco didn't seem enough to balance the panic thrumming through me as my adrenaline soared and crashed back down. The ache of the tattoos clawing at my psyche, leaving me half-convinced I had been attacked.

Tugging back on my shirt, I dug through my desk for something before giving up and raiding Tom's snack stash. "There's got to be a way to keep him out of my head."

"Not without risking your connection to the house and the rest of us."

"Shit."

Shrugging, Rory floated back, careening through the air. "It's six weeks. Count it down."

Six weeks. Six weeks - and I would be with Gray again, one way or another. The twinge in my chest remained.

Chapter Twenty-One

Sitting in a test, head down and trying to keep my eyes focused on the words, but they blurred. Turning topsy twisty upside down. Syrupy thick saliva. Barely able to swallow it down before the thickness choked me. Nothing made sense. Rory whispered in my ear the answers, claiming he saw them on Cheyenne's paper - trying to help me. Only making things worse.

Who cheats by ghost? Me, apparently. No hope of passing otherwise. My back hurt. My chest still itched. Nothing infected. Zeke assured me. Checked me over and cleaned me up like a boxer's coach, sending me out to get smacked down again. Nights filled with clicking heels - stones plopping in puddles. Thick air and thicker lies - molasses smooth and dark in the swirling eyes that might have been embers or just the actually empty abyss of his soul. An underline in my coursework on how hypocritical doctors could be. How they said they were helping as they stitched you up the wrong way. A frustrating few who screamed while the good kept their heads down - kept working, grew restless and tired and yelled back only to be buried more thoroughly than the dead.

I've had good doctors. I came here to be a good doctor. Wanted to sort my brain and find people interested in reaching out, finding ways to combat the ignorance that pervaded my hometown. The desperate clinging to history because the present was too abysmal. Too depressing as all the smart kids left - the rich kids - any kid who could. I wanted to be a good doctor. Meet good doctors. Ones who I could open up to - talk about the lies and fears and repression and years of terror - knowing my father will abandon me, pretend I never existed - call me hellspawn and spit at the sight of me.

Good doctors - they existed. I met them. They taught me. Even my old pediatrician cared more than my dad - listened though I never told him the truth. When everyone talked about how it was better Reggie was gone, the doctor spoke out. Tried to reach out - and despite his wife and once lauded family life, people left his practice. Side-eyed him though they'd loved him before that. His wife - fierce and ruthless - might've burned us all if he hadn't gotten a job in the city - taking them away while her eyes cursed us all for being so arrogant, ignorant, set in ways I couldn't escape.

There were good doctors. And good people. The debate team never abandoned Reggie. I could've told them - Marie with her bright red lips and fierce glower, surrounded by friends like-minded and those who had sneered when in high school she had ruled with a mind made of steel. Looks left the boys melted. But she didn't change. Swore like a sailor, refused to back down and turned the words thrown against her - the traps baited to capture her confidence and turn it into a sin - and though some drifted away, the bulk wanted to be her - wanted her to keep them safe and bully away those who stalked and bullied them that no amount of undermining lost her ground.

We didn't speak by then. My parents would've disowned me just as quick if I went out with a girl like Marie - someone able to speak her own mind and control her own body. Only thing worse than that was if I were gay. So I pretended I wasn't, and I kept my eye on the prize, citing Harvard. That mattered to them. Good son. Something to brag about - point to and cheer. If I graduated without a girl from college - then they'd be upset, but I wasn't going home. They weren't paying for my schooling. I just had to find the courage. Tell them. Then they wouldn't want me to come home anyway.

"Hey," Rory hissed, tapping the paper in front of me. "Get your head in the game. Half the students left already."

All the multiple choice done. Essays to write. Can't cheat on those. I could do this. I studied. These had been on the guide I made. Midterms hardly mattered. I had this.

Rory stalked me to the front table when I was done. He glared all around like it was their fault I had sat flustered. They didn't know I was in pain. Inside and out. Covered in brown lines. Had thought they were black - not that color mattered, but brown, Zeke said, would be easier to hide. Easier to cover in the end. Weren't they black? They looked so dark. Bloody even where there wasn't any blood. Dark against my pale skin - hadn't I been tan?

Handing the packet to my TA, I turned, heading up the stairs and out. Rory - my phantom shadow - followed. Mumbling along the way, "Finally got the courage, and the brat's not even here."

"What?" I grumbled.

Before he could answer, Cheynne bounced over to me. Her blond hair bouncing in pigtails. "Heard you weren't heading back home for Thanksgiving break."

"Yeah…"

Her lips twisted into a condescending smile. "Maddix told me about your research. Thought you'd like to know - I'm going back to the house on Thanksgiving."

"Going to bring the ghosts a turkey?"

Rolling her eyes, she tugged me along toward the coffee cart. "They don't do tours of it on Thanksgiving, so we can do a seance without worrying somebody will show up."

"We?"

"She means you," Rory informed me.

Cheyenne side-eyed me. "Everyone in our group who's staying behind. You, me, and Maddix. Probably Chad too."

Of course. I couldn't get lucky. Chad had hung about, glaring at me with a level of suspicion. Somehow, I had become the Moby Dick to his Ishmael. Who wanted to be some weirdo's white whale? Didn't matter. Truth was stranger than fiction, and there was no way he would be able to figure out what was going on with me. Not like he believed in ghosts. I hadn't. If I didn't have the itch of healing tattoos, maybe I'd still have days denying it. Well, the tattoos and Rory.

Fuck, I wish Gray had haunted me like this. Spent nights curled around him. That was all I wanted. Him back in my arms. Rory - off wherever he planned to go when his mission to save Gray was done. All of this was for him. Tattoos, dealing with Rory, faking I wasn't going absolutely out of my mind between lack of sleep and nightmares and hauntings by Victorian shrinks and a Civil War governess - and her cook? God, the whole thing was a mess. There were older houses. The manor wasn't even two hundred years old. Heck, it wasn't even a hundred and fifty. How could that sound so young when Gray being dead for over fifty years seemed so long?

"So you're coming, right?" Cheyenne asked though I could see in her eyes that refusal would be met with nightmarish determination. I didn't have the energy to deal with her. And - to my surprise - I didn't want to either.

Sighing, I shrugged. "Sure. Whatever."

"Good." Turning to the barista, she ordered then glanced at me. "You want anything?"

"Nah, I'm good."

"You look like you're going to pass out."

Rory shoved forward. He grabbed for a scone, but his hand slipped right through as I answered, "That was my last exam. I'm going to go crash back at the dorm. Tom headed out last night, so I've got it all to myself."

Rolling her eyes, she told the barista, "Add a small hot chocolate and that scone to my order."

Her pink-painted nail pointed right at the one which Rory had been struggling to pick up. My heart stuttered. Both Rory and I froze. "I really don't need anything."

"Heard you loud and clear. The scone's for me and I owe Angela a hot chocolate," Cheyenne informed me, and with a flip of her one pigtail, I was as good as dismissed.

Chapter Twenty-Two

Rory paced the length of my room. He seemed more at ease now that Tom was gone for Thanksgiving, but he eyed the door with a nearing hysterical madness. The same insanity I had seen in him when he first chased me down the halls. Maybe he had been gone too long. Spent years waiting for somebody else to be dragged into the madness. Someone else who would see Gray and understand that he needed to be saved. Or perhaps he had simply been out of the manor for too long.

"I don't like this," he whispered.

My chest tugged, the skin a bit tight, but the pain had finally left. Even the ache off my back lessened. I had only a few more weeks left. Then I would be marked - tattooed all over as my arms reached into the void of limbo and drew Gray out. It would be good. It would be the best. My connection with the manor would fade, but my life would never be the same. Never return to what I had known. I would, in that moment, recognize who I was at my very core. The person who my parents couldn't accept. Who I still struggled to acknowledge without self-loathing taking over. All for Gray.

But as I sat in the chair - Zeke's needle painting my skin with the latest markings, I almost vomited. Panic swirled in my stomach, demanding to know whether Gray would love me - could love me - when he was free. Did he even want me? Had he wanted Rory? I never asked. Not really. Hadn't been able to bear questioning whether Gray had the

172

same relationship with Rory that he had with me. I had no right to be jealous. They seemed not to be together now, and Rory had died. Horribly. If I wasted time being jealous, I was no better than Simon, and I had seen how well such ridiculous jealousy went. Isolating Gray once he was finally free would be cruel.

No matter how I rationalized, the thoughts haunted me. Another ghost for my collection. What-ifs threatening to tear me apart as my mind turned them over and over again like playing cards. Each one promised something more. Something fouler. Crueler than I could bear after everything.

A chill passed through me. Up to the elbow, Rory buried his arm inside me, pulling it free when I looked down at it. "Stop panicking. It doesn't help."

"I'm a guy - haunted by actual ghosts - going back to a haunted manor to see if I can get in contact with...ghosts." Rubbing the bridge of my nose, I sighed. "Can you even interact with physical objects?"

Gritting his teeth, Rory swiped his hand across my desk. Nothing moved. Not even a single paper fluttered. "Maybe your friend is actually psychic."

"You were standing right beside me, and she didn't seem to be able to see you," I pointed out.

It would be easy enough - wouldn't it? To see Rory if she could have. Cheyenne hadn't said a thing though. Nobody had noticed Gray either. Only me. Otherwise, they would have said something.

"Or she thought you'd think she was insane?" Rory suggested. "If you couldn't see me, what would you think if she had mentioned a strange guy following you around? I mean, obviously, I look pretty fly, but you already think she's annoying. Crazy is just a step away."

"You're making this more than it is."

He cocked a brow, crossing his arms over his chest. "And you're crazy if you think some board game is the way to talk to Gray."

"Then what would you suggest?" I demanded. My fingers curled into fists as I glared at the phantom. Paler than when he first came, Rory stared back. His nails clawed at his forearms through the leather of his jacket. "Not like I can just call him up."

"Maybe if you slept -"

"When I sleep, I either don't see anything, or I'm jacked by that gaslighting lunatic."

Madness circled in his eyes. Like sharks, the insanity loomed closer, smelling the blood in the water - released, leaking from him until he would return to the man I had first met. The monster who writhed, tethered and bound in stained white canvas.

My stomach rolled. Churning in my guts, it urged me back. The same nerves alit beneath my skin. A flare of panic. Run-run-run, my mind screamed, but I held my ground, staring him in the eyes. Holding onto the man behind the madness. The man who had died trying to save Gray. Just like I would.

"Do you honestly think she could see you?" Spoken aloud, the words hung between us like frost painted on a glass. Somehow emphasizing the gap between us - living and dead.

Bowing his head, Rory retreated. He stumbled back into himself until the back of his legs nearly touched Tom's bed, but the opposing sides of a magnet, he bounced away, repelled until he collapsed upon my own. Electricity coursed, pulsating in the air. Leather jacket - straitjacket - hands clawing at his forearms - hands hidden by thick white fabric, stained from inside out with rusted red. Black lines gathered up around his neck. Ink stains climbing, animated serpents made of half-formed runes - too strong to be born of temporary measures.

"Maybe."

I didn't believe him. He didn't believe him. His eyes shifted back and forth. A strange waking sleep, but the longer I watched, the less he seemed to see me.

"Rory?"

No response.

A monstrous shadow loomed. Where no glass stood, a divider formed between us, and though my mind knew it couldn't be real, I had no way to fight against the way it bloomed, taking every inch it could to push me back and silence the yawning fear clawing its way to the surface of my mind.

Then he seized.

His body tensed. Teeth slamming together as the muscles in his jaw jumped. Left and right, he rolled, shaking and sinking. Vanishing into the mattress below as if vanishing through a portal to another world.

"Rory!" I screamed, throwing myself forward - through the barrier that didn't exist to reach out - to grab at his body. No other thought than to roll him onto his side. As if he might choke. As if he could die again. "Rory! What's going on?"

His pupils constricted to pinpricks. The smooth curls of his hair matted, knotting around each other as he clawed. Tears poured down his face. Rivers formed through dirt which hadn't been on his face before, and when my hand touched him, cold burned at the tips of my fingers.

How could someone like you save anyone? You can't even save yourself. Look at you - the world was better without you. Your brother - you've seen him - look how much happier he is without you? Better without you. Stronger. Happier. You just brought him down.

Soft and deep and endless, the voice spoke - words shifting in the shadowy cold which gathered like a blanket around Rory's form. Sending a fog of cold dread - tension to pain. Out of the dark, a man formed. Leaning forward. Looming. Hands steepled - pressed against his lips. The long coat of his gathered about his knees, shifting even as he stood still. Silhouetted, he pulled away. The sharp ridge of his nose - gentler than I might have expected. A slope which seemed almost spritely in its upward turn, but the way those lips pressed, quirking toward one side as he shifted, the darkness stared right into me. His tongue traveled the course of his bottom lip. Smirking. Meeting my gaze and dragging me inside the darkness of his empty soul. A black hole. Empty and hungry and feasting.

Hello, James.

Turning to face me, he tilted his head back, showing off the scars across his throat. Lumps and curving bumps - like someone had cut and cut, but unable to stop him, they finally held him down, pressing and squeezing until his throat collapsed, vocal cords and trachea smashed, and now he stood here. Haunting me. Haunting Rory. Tormenting a ghost.

Such a pleasure, I'm sure. We haven't yet met, but I'm quite the fan. Rather impressive - all this mess. Few handle such stress well. How have you been feeling? You look...tired.

And I felt it. The weight of exhaustion fell upon my shoulders, heavier than it had already been until my knees buckled, but my fingers held fast. Knuckles white as I curled them into Rory's jacket as he stilled, panting and paler than the phantom had ever been.

"Get out!" I commanded. "You aren't welcome here."

Tilting his head, the new spirit smiled softly. As if he cared. Gently. Kindly. Why did he look like Gray in that moment? Not everywhere. His hair - pale blonde - grew long on top and kept short upon the sides. Slicked back, his hair fit better on a model than on a doctor - even one as monstrous as this. He looked too young - too modern to be a ghost from the manor, but when he moved, the air rippled, showing something darker underneath. A shadow of a man. Darkness curling like smoke. For all the youth of his face, Dr. Carreau's age showed in his eyes. Bits of chipped ice. Muddled and too pale a hue.

Unwelcome? But you invited me?

When I lunged toward him, my hand outstretched, the shadow of his existence shimmered, and an implosion stole away his face, leaving over the shadow.

If you insist...

And fingers wrapped around my wrist. Rory rolled, curling around my hand and groaning. "He's not gone. Not really."

"Well, maybe Cheyenne can banish ghosts," I grumbled.

He weighed nothing, shifting between standing and sinking through the arm where he leaned on me. Grabbing my coat, we left the room behind, but the chill remained. The weather taunting me.

"As long as I'm around, we can't - you can't..." Rory panted, his breath unnecessary and invisible even as white mist curled from my lips. "He'll be back. Carreau always knows where I am."

"How about some holy water? Salt?"

His bright eyes jumped to meet mine. "None of it worked. There was a priest who came around on Sunday afternoons. Offered service. I asked - but he couldn't do anything. None of the prayers helped." His lips quirked into a rueful smile. "Maybe I didn't believe enough."

"Guess I'm screwed," I joked, but the words fell flat.

Rory pulled away, stumbling a few feet away. His body drained but already growing stronger once more. "I can't go back to that room. That's got to be where he's set up camp. If I stick around, he'll have a straight line to your head. You've got Zeke. Three more weeks, and you'll be ready."

"You said there's a ritual I have to start six days ahead of time. The one with honeyed water…" even the idea of it left my stomach churning.

"It's straightforward," he assured. "No food for six days beforehand. Just water and honey."

It seemed counterintuitive. Right when I had to be strongest, I had to fast. Empty my body out to avoid getting sick. I could risk it. Eat up. Argue it was for my strength, but the idea that my inability to keep my feet under me and my stomach from emptying itself onto my feet might prevent me from saving Gray, I can't. Anything that could help. Anything that might give me that extra inch - that edge I need.

"Tattoos and fasting. Check."

With a cut nod, Rory fell into step with me. "Next sleep, I'm gone."

"Who knows? Maybe you'll be able to slip back when we go the manor," I said, but he didn't acknowledge.

Shoulders slumped and dark circles cradling his eyes, Rory watched the people walk around us. His fingers twitched. Dancing across his thighs, they lurched forward, falling back as the desolation within his eyes grew greater. When a crowd pushed me further aside, he vanished - invisible and insubstantial. A coloration of light they could neither perceive nor touch. In that moment, the ghost seemed smaller. A young man closer to my own age than either of us likely cared to admit, yet for the years which would never touch his face. Aged only by death and addiction.

But when the crowd cleared, he shook his head. The dimming light of a November day passing easily through him as he straightened his spine and swallowed. Whatever he might have said died in his throat as he looked up - Professor Haggard of Psych 101 headed toward me. His usual double espresso in his hand and a small smile on his face as he marched straight ahead. His eyes on some journal article held in his hand; the front cover folded back.

Rory's eyes widened. His lips parted as he listed to the left, aligning their paths. Though he didn't need to breathe, the phantom's chest swelled, rising as if he might float off the ground with hope.

Head popping up, Professor Haggard stared straight at Rory. Their heights were similar enough that their gazes seemed to meet. A spark of recognition. Small but potent.

Then his head turned, and with a small wave of his journal, Professor Haggard said, "Hope you're making the most of your break, James. We're having unusually nice weather for this time of year," and walked right through Rory.

And like an idiot - that was when it finally clicked. How many lectures had Rory spent following me around the last three weeks while avoiding one particular class? Not once had I made the connection. I'd only heard Rory's surname the one time when I first met Zeke, but that didn't seem good enough.

"I'm so sorry."

Rory shook his head, rubbing his hands over his face. "Don't say anything." Tears poured down his face, and in the afternoon sunlight, he shimmered - less and less there as he whispered, "Please don't say anything."

Chapter Twenty-Three

Side by side, we sat, letting the roar of traffic talk over us. Engines churned. Exhaust curled and rose before spreading clear, leaving only the taste of it in the air. Once or twice, a bus rumbled up to us. Brakes squeaked. I waved each one on until I lost count. All my senses honing in on the phantom sitting beside - curling further and further into himself as he shut himself off from the world.

With his elbows on his knees, Rory ducked his head. His fingers knotted in his long dark hair, but he kept silent, and I didn't have the courage to push him to speak. Up and down, his back rose. Breathing though he had no need. Perhaps the motion ingrained itself. Burned into his memory. A reflex not even death could steal away from him.

What could I possibly say? I hadn't even realized my professor was his brother. Once I knew, I didn't have the courage to add anything else. To tell Rory he was my advisor too. Tell him we could schedule something. Find a way for him to communicate. Because there had to be a way. Zeke believed me. Maybe Professor Haggard would too.

But I could see it. The way he slumped, caving in upon himself. Knew it before - respected it once. Professor Haggard was a skeptic. He believed in the power of the mind, including its ability to trick us, so how could I explain Rory without suspicion? Surely someone better than me -smarter, more talented could have found any information Rory might tell me to identify himself to Professor Haggard, and with every risk I already took, how could I add another? I needed Harvard. I couldn't go back. Not with Gray coming. If I saved him - I couldn't go back to pretending I was someone else. I wanted to be me. Wanted to be me with him. Finally free.

With a shaky exhale, Rory sat up, leaning back against the back of the bench. "He's happy, right?" It wasn't actually a question, but I nodded quickly, recognizing the sort of affirmation he wanted when his eyes slid to me. "Good. That's...that's good. He deserved - I'm - I wasn't the best brother. Six years difference."

He rubbed his palms across his thighs, pressing the heel of his hands into his jeans as if he might resist the urge to claw himself apart. Closing his eyes, he inhaled slowly. Gradually, the transparency of his body darkened, fading until he seemed as real as he had the first time we had met. His breath even curled - white vapor - from his cracked lips.

"It's good. I'm glad he's happy now," Rory murmured, and a weight shifted around him.

I swallowed my questions. Nothing gave me the right to ask them. We were allies of sorts. Thrown together to save Gray because he had failed, and I was his last hope of success before they knocked the house down, forcing the die cast all that time ago to finally fall - and not in Gray's favor.

So I reached out. My hand took his, and as our fingers entwined, tears gathered, rolling down his cheeks as he stared up at the sky as if he could see some sort of answer there.

He held tight. His grip almost broke my hand, but I bit my tongue, refusing to flinch away from him when he needed such a simple thing from me. An anchor from the storm in his mind. The nightmares which likely haunted him even when Dr. Carreau wasn't there to speak the words. A monster made of half-truths. Fears he knew. Potents of a future which he hadn't intended but unfolded regardless of his best intentions.

"If you want - after it's all done, I could introduce him to Gray...if you think that might..."

"No." Rory shook his head. "If he's happy, I don't want to bring up the past."

"Okay, but if you change your mind..." I murmured, letting the promise lay unsaid between us.

I meant it. Even though standing before anybody with Gray seemed impossible - a dream. An impossibility that I tried so hard to believe could happen when everything about my life had become surreal. But Gray had to be real. His face hung heavy in my heart. The soft curve of his smile. Eyes - bright and clever and soft - gentle with me in a way I never expected. His long fingers - hand in hand with me. Every detail hung around me - another link in the chain which bound us two together, and the feel of him in my arms - my cheek against his smooth dark hair, and the stuttering anxiety of his shaky breathes against my skin - an anchor which would keep me safe or drag me down.

Either way - I didn't care. I wanted to live with him or drown with him. A madness, perhaps, but I existed in the dramatics of a romance I hadn't thought I would ever have a right to claim as my own. Maybe someday someone would label me insane. Call me asocial, dissociative, or simply delusional, but whatever sort of romance this ghost story became, as long as Gray was free, nothing else mattered. If we could be together, all the better.

"Hey, eager beaver, what's got you glum?" Cheyenne demanded, bouncing over to slide right through Rory and sit beside me.

At the intrusion, the phantom sputtered and shattered like a cloud of smoke dispersing. He wasn't gone. I could feel him - a shifting presence stretching out from me like a shadow.
Fighting the urge to grimace, I told her, "Just got some cabin fever."

"Man, you could've come with us and Leilani to breakfast this morning before she had to head off," Maddix suggested, adjusting the backpack over his shoulder. Tracking my eyes, he smirked. "Thought the ghosts might be a bit friendlier if we brought some snacks."

Cheyenne scoffed and rolled her eyes. "While Maddix stuffs his face, we can respectfully make contact."

Glancing around, I frowned. "I thought you said Chad was coming."

"As if I'd want that jerk to come," Cheyenne grumbled. Jumping up, she held her head up high. "Let's do this!"

We trailed after her, letting Cheyenne forge the path. I had spent the last few days memorizing the best routes. Studying every street between my room and Crables manor. In case something happened, I could find my way there in my sleep.

From the outside, the manor rose like a tombstone. The architecture was so unlike everything surrounding it. Cast iron wrapped around. A fence of black spikes covered in vines and overgrown bushes. Even the trees curled, gnarled by association though it seemed tall and the same as every other tree in the area. Nothing special in the fogged glass. Dusty and dirty and dilapidated - warnings strewn to scare those like us away. Caution tape. Bright yellow. Posters hung, warnings of construction to come, but we ducked them easily enough.

"Can you feel it?" Cheyenne asked. Her lips stretched in a manic smile.

Reaching out, Maddix set his hand on the wooden frame of the collapsing porch. "It's like the house is vibrating with energy."

"Should be," Rory scoffed, an invisible whisper in my ear, "with how many people died here."

Suicide, sacrifice, massacre, flames, pills, and pain - a stench of desperation and agony seeped into the pores of the wood. Leaked through the gaps in stone. Burrowed into the earth, thick and cloying as blood. Dark storm clouds hid the sunset. Not a single star lit the path, but it was better this way. No

186

lightning either. Nothing to frame the already horrifying history of the house.

"Do you think we'll get Theodore? Or maybe even Florence?" Cheyenne chattered excitedly as she jimmied the door open. Catching it before it could slam, she stepped over the threshold, ducking under the tape meant to block our way.

I shrugged, following her inside. I took the bag from Maddix, so he could get in without falling over, I sighed. "Why don't we start small? Maybe Rory Haggard."

"Who?" Both blinked owlishly at me.

"Rory Haggard. The patient from the 1980s..."

Cheyenne rolled her eyes, tossing her hair over her shoulder. "He overdosed on pills. Why would he be around?"

Shutting the door behind us, I glanced to a shimmering on the stairs. Rory sat. His eyes like daggers, but there was a determined set to his lip. Back in his straitjacket, he bowed his head, ducking my gaze though the rest of his posture remained the same.

Facing my classmates, I shrugged. "Just a feeling..."

Maddix's brows furrowed. He seemed to look right into my soul before pulling the board from his bag. "Not like we're gonna refuse whoever comes around."

"Yeah, but it's always nicer if we can invite them around," Cheyenne argued, but with a huff, she grabbed a blanket out from the bag, setting it on the dust and dirt covered shag rug. "Let's see who answers." Kneeling down, we gathered around the board, and feeling like a fool, I set my fingers down, praying that this would work. Six fingers - a pointer from each of our hands - settled on the indicator. "Remember," she declared, "keep your fingers on it until we say goodbye. We don't want to have anybody following us out of here." Cheyenne tilted her chin up, staring into space as she declared, "Is there anyone here?"

"That's it? Should we say hello or something first," Maddix asked, but Rory stood in the gap between the guy and Cheyenne.

Stretching his bare foot, he settled it on top of the indicator and with a determined scowl upon his face, he gave a sharp tug. Cheyenne and Maddix cried out in surprise, and even Rory's jaw dropped as the indicator moved, falling firmly on YES.

"Oh my god," Maddix moved to rear back, but Cheyenne hissed, "Keep your fingers on it until we say goodbye!"

"You're not screwing with me, right?" he asked.

Cheyenne snorted. "Shut up, Maddix. Sorry about that...could you tell us your name?"

Cautiously, Rory settled his foot down once more, slowly drawing out the letters of his name as Maddix and Cheyenne called them out in unison: "R....O....R...Y....Rory?"

They both looked up toward me. Cheyenne huffed, "You better not be messing with us, James."

"I'm not," I grumbled.

Already, Rory moved the indicator, spelling out as rapidly as he could. The words forming with a growing fury - "This is working. How is this working? The manor must be getting ready for the cycle to repeat. Like the veil is thin."

"What are you talking about?" Cheyenne demanded. "What cycle?"

Rory's mouth opened. His eyes met mine, but right as he moved to speak, arms reached out of the emptiness behind him, and he flew back, vanishing once more into nothing. In his place, a tired looking middle-aged man came.

Dark brown eyes watched us, half-lidded. A similarly dark beard covered his face with only the first few curls of gray scattered there and in his slicked back hair. After seeing him swirling - lit in yellow fire and whirling like a Van Gogh - this was the first time I had seen Dr. Ose in his full form. From the gauntness of his cheeks to the ever present smile which bordered on menacing as he shifted his attention from Maddix to Cheyenne before landing squarely on me, he embodied a cinematic villainy.

"Why'd it stop?" Cheyenne muttered.

Her eyes leapt about as if she might be able to see the ghost to whom we spoke, but when Dr. Ose knelt, reaching out with his pale fingers to move the indicator, every instinct in me screamed like a cornered animal. I wanted to run. But Cheyenne had said to hold fast until we said our goodbye, so I forced myself to free, fighting against the panic rising inside my mind.

Slowly, Ose moved us. "The Solstice," the bastard lied. "The closer it gets, the thinner the line between life and death."

"He's lying," I growled.

Maddix frowned. "Why would Rory lie?"

"Don't talk like he's not in the room," Cheyenne scolded. Searching above the board, she called out softly, "Sorry these guys are being idiots, Rory."

"It's not Rory," I informed them, but they looked at me in disbelief as Ose's lips quirked into a smirk.

"No apologies needed," the murderous ghost spelled out. "What are your names?"

Names had powered, didn't they? But Ose wasn't a fairy or something. He didn't have power outside the house, did he? But he had Dr. Carreau - who apparently had decided to haunt my dorm room, and I couldn't be sure the other doctor hadn't followed us to the manor, so what was I supposed to do? They didn't see what I saw. Both of them believed it was Rory talking. What was I supposed to do?

"I'm Cheyenne, and this is Maddix," she announced to the room before glaring at me. "And that one is James."

"He knows. We've met," I spat.

Maddix blinked. "What?"

"Met him?" Cheyenne repeated, and Ose laughed - slimy and slick as oil - as I realized my mistake.

190

"I can see ghosts. That's why I got interested in Theodore Thompson." The lie came out so easily. God, I never wanted to get good at this, but what choice did I have. Silence only ever went so far, and eventually people ask questions, so I knew how to lie. Knew how to bend the truth, and I wasn't about to do anything less than everything to fight against Ose. "I can see him. He's not Rory. He overpowered Rory and is lying to you."

"Rather perfect, don't you think? Making a claim no one else can disprove," Ose spelled, forcing our hands this way and that - making us puppets.

"James, that's not funny..." Maddix murmured. His eyes jumped from the indicator to me to Ose, following the line of my glower. "I think we should stop."

Glaring between us, Cheyenne hissed, "If he's not Rory, who is he?"

"Yes, James," a voice whispered in my ear. Hands slid over my shoulders, and Dr. Carreau leaned against my back, whispering in my ear, "Who is he?"

Surrounded - all eyes on me. The words slithered back down my throat. When had the lights grown so dim? I couldn't do it. Couldn't sit there, pretending nothing was wrong when we were getting exactly the two ghosts I didn't want. I just wanted to talk to Gray. Wanted to see him. Ached to be with him again, but Carreau pressed firm against me, and Ose stood, looming as Cheyenne and Maddix waited for me to answer.

A light flashed over us, and Maddix screamed, rearing back from the board. "We're going to die!"

"You idiot! You broke contact!" Cheyenne yelled, but the ghosts both dissipated in that moment. Vanishing just like Rory, and I could breathe again.

"Wow. So this is how you three decided to waste your evening," Chad scoffed, dragging his flashlight across the three of us. "Don't tell me you seriously believe in ghosts, James. I get those two idiots, but I bet Alexander good money your issues were repression."

"What. The. Hell!" Cheyenne leapt to her feet, whirling on Chad with such murderous rage that both Maddix and I flinched back. "What is your problem? Did you honestly stalk us here to - to make fun of us? You're such a pathetic grade school bully, Chad. Grow up!"

Rolling his eyes, Chad held up a cylinder of paper. "The office here has a more thorough picture of the original floor plan than I could find online."

Cheyenne gaped. "You're kidding."

"This one has markings that match up with some photographs I found online of the criminal investigation into the massacre." Which apparently should have been more impressive than it sounded when he added, "Do you know how weird it must have been for them to waste time photographing it back then?"

"Late 1800s - yeah, weird photos, so...we done here?" I asked, standing up and backing away from that stupid board. My whole body itched, and a chill settled inside me which I couldn't fight off.

Chapter Twenty-Four

Waking up in Mrs. Hayward's kitchen was like being rocked to sleep. Soft and gentle - slow in a way where the slicing of vegetables, which could have been a horrifying chop, became a methodical whisper. Soothing and made all the better for the salty, savory aroma of some kind of broth. Always the same meal. Same vegetables cut over and over again. The afterlife had to be a boring place to eat, or maybe - as far as Mrs. Hayward perceived - I just popped in and out in the same few seconds of the same day.

If she had been as unaware of her death as Gray, perhaps she would have thought of me as the strange narcoleptic boarder who randomly collapsed and awoke in her kitchen.

Pushing myself up, I ran my hands through my hair. The symbols. I needed an answer for the symbols on Chad's map. They congregated in the basement. While Chad could check out all the books, hoarding them in his room, the old plates for the investigation photographs couldn't leave the library, so while finding them had been labor-intensive, I had prints now.

And they weren't particularly pretty. An old couple, their second son, and a half dozen random relatives massacred, and while the investigators attributed it to a mass suicide, there were symbols carved into the second son's body - the brother-in-law of the Governess. The one who needed to be sacrificed after his brother's death failed. And the only one I could talk to was Mrs. Hayward. The Governess continued to kick me out of the manor whenever she came around, so I couldn't interrogate her. Not on this.

"Mrs. Hayward..."

She hummed softly. "Yes?"

"The Governess - her husband's family, were you still alive when they died in the basement?" I asked.

Glancing over her shoulder, she smiled. "Of course, lovey. Nasty business. Served them right, though. Dying so far from God. If you're curious, you could go see them - they should still be down there. They can't move around, but you might get some answers out of them. My George always said - never die low. There's some sound advice if I ever had any."

That static white noise of a broken television echoed through my brain after she spoke, and no matter how I turned the dial, I couldn't say anything more productive than: "What?"

"Oh yes, all of that nasty business - it's their doing that poor Teddy is trapped like he is. Bless Florence for bringing him to the widow's watch. If he died on another floor, who knows if we could have kept him safe this long," Mrs. Hayward explained. "The doctors died on the second floor - but Dr. Ose seems to be able to anchor Dr. Carreau - allowing him to wander further than he should. I swear - they could talk the Devil into a knot."

"How is that..."

"Further from the altar - or something like that." She waved a hand, dismissing my question to continue her tirade. "I died on the first, so I can move about, but I'm rather tied to this room. Not that I mind. Spent most of my days here anyway, lovey, and when the time comes, I suspect there's a kitchen in Heaven with my name on it."

"What about Rory?"

"Hmm? Oh, poor doll, died on the third floor."

As if he could hear us speaking about him, a scream echoed, rattling the boards above our head. The happy cheery kitchen flashed like lightning struck, and Mrs. Hayward vanished. Torn curtains hung on the windows. Shattered glass in rotting frames left the whole floor a sprawl of tiny crystal points. Smoke rose from the oven. Wind ripped through the room, and the screams continued. The door to the kitchen hung off its hinges. Dust drifted down with each rattling of thunderous steps, rumbling and rolling. I could almost see Rory struggling, stumbling and smashing into walls before he fell, whirling on the floor until he could find his way back to his feet.

Something pulled - my stomach ached, itching as something anchored its way inside of me, throwing me this way and that as the world swirled around me. Until - with a gasp - I awoke with arms around me, and a weight against my chest. Dark hair - beautiful and familiar with a small nose and familiar long lashes.

"It's just a nightmare," Gray whispered, shifting to stare up at me with his large beautiful eyes. "Go back to sleep."

My heart skipped a beat. I could feel it. The lurch as I studied his face - how long had it been? Beautiful. Shit, I missed him. Cupping his jaw, I caressed his soft skin with my thumb. With a smile, he leaned, pressing into my touch, and I couldn't bear it.

"I love you."

His lips parted into the most gentle smile I had ever seen. Pushing up, he pressed a delicate kiss to my lips. "Love you too."

Nothing in my life had ever been as soft as this. We curled around each other. Entwined as sleep rocked me down - until my mind caught up with my body.

"Gray!" Sitting up, I grabbed his shoulders, forcing him to wake and meet my gaze. "If I'm not here, you need to know - I'm coming for you."

His brows furrowed. "Where would you be?" A glimmer of black at my ankle pushed me to move faster. Tugging up the fabric, I showed off the new tattoos on my leg. Eyes widening, he gasped. "James - what? How?" Tentatively, he reached forward, brushing the tips of his fingers against my skin. "Rory had these - he...in pen...he drew them on his skin, but they-they burned off.."

One-two - no, no - no. She couldn't come yet. I need more time.

"Because he was trying to save you, and I'm going to do it," I exclaimed, reaching for him. Part

197

of me expected him to pull away, but he threw himself forward, nuzzling into my neck as he curled against me. "I'm going to get you out of here. I promise."

One-two - not yet. I hadn't had him in my arms long enough. I need him. Gray and I - we deserved time.

But the world rippled, my lungs squeezed - too large in my too small chest as I woke, cold sweat gathered on my brow as I stared at the dark shadows playing over Tom's bed. At first, I wanted it to be my mind. Too many late nights and days spent with ghosts had me seeing them everywhere, and even with Tom back, the room felt too wide - too big without Rory around.

However, a dark form stretched above him. Crowding closer and closer. The form screamed its name to me - Dr. Carreau. He loomed. His dark form curling over my roommate as he slept. My mouth went dry.

"Tom..."

He snuffled into his pillow.

The shadow coalesced. Carreau grinning at me like the Cheshire Cat.

"Hey...Tom?" I called, sitting up, but he only murmured in his sleep.

Lunging across the room, I reached out to smack the phantom away, but Tom's eyes opened, leaving me to almost slap him instead.

"Shit!" He rolled back to the far side of his bed. "Crap, man!"

"Sorry, you were - " Excuse. I needed an excuse. "You look like you were having a nightmare."

Snorting, he cuddled back up in bed. "Sure. Man - you sure you weren't having another nightmare yourself?"

"Maybe - sorry about that," I murmured, shuffling back to bed.

And like the amazing roommate he was, Tom just laughed. "Seriously, you must've been going stir crazy all alone in this room."

Curled up, I could only agree. For now, though, the shadow of Carreau had dissipated, but the doctor hung over the room - not thick and noxious like Ose, but with an oily slick presence which coated my skin, leaving me hyper-aware - sweating and calm-panicked. Purposeful adrenaline.

Just three more weeks. I could do it. Just three more weeks.

Chapter Twenty-Five

Wake up. Go to class. Counting down the moments until I could sleep - and not see Gray again - only to start over. Because why would I want to see the man I fell in love with? The one who inspired me to cover my body in tattoos that I couldn't appropriately explain to my parents - not that I ever intended to go back home after I finally had the man of my dreams - *literal dreams* - in my arms, but the closer the day came, the darker the circles became under my eyes. The less food seemed appetizing. All I wanted was Gray.

His dark hair and bright eyes - the slight upturn of his lips to the left whenever I remembered something he had told me before - no matter how small it seemed. The blush - pale pink that flushed dark across his pale skin - whenever we touched accidentally. Brushing our fingers together. Our shoulders. The contented sigh when I curled around him or when he settled, nuzzling into my shoulder. Soft and so vulnerable. Or the smirk - honestly, any of his expressions, or the stubborn and cocky way he stood his ground, never letting me take the lazy way out. Keeping me honest. Keeping me grounded when he should have been the least grounding presence in my life. A ghost, and yet my best essays came from spitballing ideas with him. My calmest nights had him in my arms, or his fingers combing through my hair. I ached to do nothing else.

Instead, I wake up, shower and dress to deal with the social niceties. Because Gray cared about those too. If he ever popped up, I wanted to leave a good impression. The gaps hurt. Long and difficult and horrifying in a way that no distance had any right to be.

"Hey," Tom greeted, sliding into a seat beside me. "Dude, you missed breakfast."

I shrugged. "I'll grab brunch or whatever after this."

His eyes narrowed, but it was Tom. Tom didn't ask hard questions. Not really. He poked, but then he backed off. Because he was an awesome roommate, and he understood I was - weird. Or something like that.

"Here." Sliding a bagel and orange over to me, Tom proved he was a better friend than I deserved.

"Thanks, man. I owe you."

Tom rolled his eyes. "You owe me so freaking much." His lips twisted into a sly grin. "But, I think I know how you can finally start catching up."

He wanted something from me. Probably nothing big. This was Tom. Last time, I ended up finding myself in Crables Manor on a murder tour. Odds weren't bad that this time would end better. Or at least less emotional. Not like I could realize my dream boyfriend was a real ghost a second time.

Ripping off a chunk of bagel, I told him: "Sure, what do you need?"

"This Saturday - I need a second guy for a double date. You in?"

A double date? Why would I ever want to be

involved on a double date? *In what world would he actually think that's something I would want to do?* I hadn't had to fake being straight in so long. I let myself - let myself feel for so long. Let myself believe I was free of all the expectations weighing me down, but I hadn't actually told anyone, had I? Well - nobody but Zeke, but I needed the free tattoos, and I hadn't exactly told him everything. I never said the words to him even, did I? *I'm still trapped.*

"Uhhh - a double date?"

Reading my tone, I wanted to scream. Wanted him to feel the unspeakable, but he just shrugged. "Danielle said yes to a date, but apparently, Maggie got dumped, so...I said I'd put in a word with you." He smacked my shoulder. "Apparently, you're considered to be one of the hottest freshman psych majors."

The less I wanted their attention, the more people paid to me. Just like high school. All their eyes on me. I couldn't refuse the dates. Not all of them. My dad would've started asking questions. Made jokes about my standards. Too high. Nose in the air. *Too good for my own or a pansy.* Both would've become daggers - turned against me, sharp and deep and I couldn't do this here. Boston - east coast - freedom, right? I had to be. This meant I needed - I wasn't - *but that would mean telling him.*

Maybe I could trust him. Tom would understand. *He joked about Chad and Alexander.* But he also commented that Alexander was hot.

Speculated on the sexuality of others while safely dating a woman. But he described himself as demisexual. He joked about crushes. Like the uncontrolled rush of infatuation was *hilarious*. *Ridiculous*. Something to be reveled in and joked about. Something beautiful. Light and gentle and welcome in all forms - amusing in all forms. So he would understand. Hell, knowing Tom, he'd probably be elated to be the first to officially know. Accepting and loving and a better roommate than a messed up guy like me deserved.

>*He'd probably be better for Gray than I am.*

Cold and twitching and dark thoughts. Shoving more bagel into my mouth, I shrugged as best I could in what I hoped was an apologetic way. Tattoos - I couldn't go because I had to get the next set of tattoos. Just my arms left. "Sorry, I've got a standing date for Saturdays."

His eyes narrowed. "Shit, you got a girl? How did I not notice?"

"Nah, man, I'm getting a tattoo." *And now he's going to ask questions.*

"Tattoos?"

Tugging down my collar, I showed off the beginning of my chest tattoos. "It's a couple sessions, but I'll lose the deposit if I don't show up." *Liar.*

Why yes, doctor, I lied. I grew up lying. These thoughts weren't unusual. Growing up hating myself, I struggled with more darkness than light, and every single day, I swallowed back, cutting off

203

the pieces of me that threatened to kill me - to drag the weight of a world that would hate me for who I was inside, and all of it with this goal in mind. Get away. Go to a big fancy college - go to Harvard. Because Boston had to be progressive. Not NYU progressive, but they offered me more money than NYU, and if I headed out west - I wasn't west coast material. Not brave enough or loud enough, and if you aren't west coast material, you aren't NYC material, but Boston - I could do Boston. Pull myself back together. Stitch the pieces back on me which hadn't decayed. Ease myself into being who I told myself I couldn't be.

"What the hell - man, when did you - "

And that wasn't Tom, but he'd reset - hopefully - by the end of the class, so I just gestured at the professor and the lecture, mouthing my thanks for the bagel and pretending, with everything I had - pretending I could explain away what drove me. *Because I was a coward.* Shut up. *Who used tattoos because I failed to say that I was -* that was my secret to tell - *Chad already knew. Alexander and he bet that my insanity came from repression.* I wasn't crazy. Which meant these thoughts invading my head weren't me.

Shoving them, I focused on my professor. *Rory's little brother.* Well hello, Dr. Carreau. I'm not getting near him. *Poor Rory - he seemed devastated when he saw how happy his brother was on his own. Without his drug addict, waste of space -* now he wasn't even trying.

204

Maybe I was cocky. Maybe I thought I was just too good. If I could recognize which thoughts were mine and which were Carreau's, how could he possibly get to me? Rory told me. Talked about the way Carreau twisted him around himself until up and down no longer made any sense, and he fumbled - swallowing the pills he was given without consideration to the other forces at work. The doctors worked as a unit. They supported each other. A terrible, warped pair of geniuses - fiddling inside the heads of the living until they could find a way to get a body of their own, and I believed I knew better. Dreamed I could recognize the voices. Separate them from myself.

But they just kept coming. Clawing their way inside me until my brain screamed the names over and over - questions I couldn't answer. What if Gray no longer loved me? What if I saved him only to have everything torn apart? All these tattoos, scarring my body without meaning - it had meaning. Saving Gray - it wasn't just because I loved him. *Not just because I loved him. That was only part. I wanted to be useful. Give my life meaning because the moment I admitted what I was out loud - it would find its way back to my family like a flood. A trail of blood which would never wash clean. Cut me off at the root. If I could save Gray - save him and keep him, I had to be worth more than the nothing I would be to my father - my mother - who would call me ungrateful. List out all they had done for me. The weight of their expectations - their doctor-to-be*

205

son dismissed and forgotten. Not that they'd tell their friends. Better everyone think I was a big city doctor. Too smart to come home. Better ungrateful than -

"Shut up," I hissed.

Tom frowned, brows furrowing. "You okay?" he whispered.

"I'm fine." *I lied.*

Scratching his head, he sighed. "You sure, you okay? Seriously, James, you've been kind of normal lately, so I tried to forget about that insomnia or narcolepsy whatever you had, but you're kind of freaking me out again."

"Sorry - just...arguing with myself. You know - intrusive thoughts." Not the right move. Not the right answer - who would think it was normal. He actually understood what that meant. *Better to brush it off as stress. How many white farm boys get into Harvard these days?* "Just ignore me."

Though he nodded, his face did some interesting acrobatics. Skeptical - disbelieving that I could be anything other than his concern. That he could ignore me. If I could swing it on my scholarship, I needed to get a single next year. Or a single in a suite - something so nobody would know my sleep habits. *All the bad habits that would chase Gray away.*

For once, Carreau was right. I wouldn't have to worry. Next semester, I'd have Gray. *Who didn't have IDs or a place to stay.* I could work. Dropping out would be a pretty shut door, and Gray would always feel guilty. *I'd always hold it against him if*

I did. Gray and I would work on that together. The two of us - we could do it. Could figure it out. Those weren't decisions I had to make on my own, and it would be easier then - easier to admit to what I wanted, who I was - *because Gray could handle it. After being locked up the majority of his life - because he could commune with the dead, Gray deserved the responsibility of being my emotional crutch.* That - that wasn't true. When I didn't deal with ghosts who wanted to kill me, that was when I'd make life-changing decisions. *Like getting tattoos. Or taking in an eighteen-year-old from before the turn of the century.*

And the worst part - I couldn't even argue with him, so I held my tongue. Pushing it down. Swallowing my outrage and the excuses, concentrating on surviving. Two more weeks. I could do this. Just two more weeks.

Chapter Twenty-Six

"All right, that's all I have time for unfortunately," Professor Haggard said, dismissing us.

Shutting my notebook, I groaned, stretching. "Brunch?"

But Tom just frowned. Between the short dark fuzz of his buzzcut and the glow of the half-dead lights above our heads, the lines of his jaw seemed sharp enough to cut, and when - after a weird offbeat - he finally smiled and put his own stuff away, I could almost smell the thick miasma of Dr. Ose's study. *Warm*, choking, like breathing in smoke. The scent wound itself around my nose. Thick and cloying even when the pair of us stepped into the hallway, but in the clouded light of mid-morning, it faded once we exited the building.

"So what's really going on?" Tom demanded on the old pathway to the nearest cafeteria.

I shrugged. "What do you mean?"

"You're acting weird again."

One of these days, I'd tell Tom everything. He deserved to know. Not because I owed him anything. Though I probably did. Owed him the honesty of a friend - which was unfamiliar because the last 'friend' I had ran away to California because his boyfriend - *and my crush* - made his life a living Hell. If that could be called friendship considering. I never told Reggie the truth either. *Simon would've made the whole result miserable if I had.* Bad enough for him to suspect.

Now wasn't the time. Not until Gray was safely in my arms. "Just stressed. Finals this week - not going home for Christmas..." But Tom was. He planned to leave Friday morning. "Wait - aren't you heading home Friday?"

Grabbing my arm, he pulled me out of the middle of the path. "Dude, you don't do well when stressed. You need to calm down. You're hyper-focusing, which might be great for whatever you're actually concentrating on, but I doubt it's all your classes at once."

"I appreciate your concern, but seriously, man, I'm fine."

"Fine?" His brows leapt up before furrowing low over his dark eyes. "You're not planning ahead. You aren't going home..."

Of course. Tom and his perfect home life - which was why he was such a great person, *better than me*, had him stumped. Why would I not go home? I could tell him the right lie. Again.

Running a hand through my hair, I took a deep breath. "My folks can't afford that. Anyway, not like I'll be alone. A lot of the international students stay behind."

"That you know?" he asked, and when I didn't immediately answer - because he knew I couldn't, Tom continued to roll right over me. "Maybe you've forgotten, but I room with you. I call my dad weekly - sometimes even streaming for the game. My mom and I text almost daily. You haven't talked to either of your parents the whole time you were here."

"One, you aren't around me every hour of every day, and two, you and I aren't the same. Our families aren't comparable," I argued, catching my voice raising quickly enough to keep it low, but not quickly enough for Tom not to notice the uptick.

Crossing his arms, he tapped his foot. "Why?"

"Hell if I know. Some guys get lucky," I retorted.

He snorted, but his eyes blazed with a focus which terrified me. For all his talk about hyper-focus, I wasn't the one with an Adderall prescription. As nice as Tom could be, every ounce of his concentration on me *threatened everything.* If he realized what was happening, no way he'd understand. *Or believe.* My actions added up to a one-way ticket to a psychiatric hold. I couldn't afford to lose even one day. Risk losing Gray - *or my scholarships.*

I had to tell him the truth.

No. I could do this on my own. I didn't need Tom to figure things out. Sure, I had help, but I had this. Two more tattoo sessions with Zeke, and then I'd camp out in the manor to ensure I was there when the time came. Reach into limbo in the attic, drag Gray out, and figure out the rest once we were safely back in the dorm.

When Gray sat beside me, then I could tell Tom. Tell him everything, and *if he thought I was crazy*, fine. Because Gray's life wouldn't be in the balance. We had another semester together - *and if*

I expected him to help hide Gray, I needed to stop waiting and tell him now.

Stop it. No matter how much Carreau whispered in my ear, I wouldn't do what he wanted. I saw him - felt him - recognized his evil. I wouldn't let him bend me around myself like he did with Rory.

"My parents have certain opinions, and I'm not somebody who they'd want around at Christmas." Not somebody they'd want anyway. They would hate me. Make me hate myself - *more than I already did*. "It's complicated, and I'm not ready to talk about this yet. Maybe after finals - or hell if you could give me next year, I -"

Tom threw an arm around my shoulders. Pulling me into a one-armed embrace, he guided me onward toward the dining hall. "You don't have to tell me right now. I know I'm putting you on the spot, but you're freaking me out." We got a few paces in awkward silence before he added, "Come back home with me. My parents always wanted another kid - "

"Thanks for the invite, but I'm good. Finishing up my tattoo, spending some time figuring out how to deal better." Maybe even figuring out how to be honest. Find a way to reassure myself lies weren't necessary.

Prepare for when my parents called. When they asked why I didn't come back on the bus. My mom would ask if I hadn't been able to afford the ticket after all and offer to buy one. Ask if I was eating enough - sleeping enough. Until I told them the truth, they would keep caring. She'd care. My dad would tell her I was a young man - spreading my wings. Probably tell me to make sure I hit a service, but at eighteen, he considered his responsibilities completed. I got into college, didn't I? I survived and looked like I'd end up a productive member of society.

That would take time. But it was important. Better I get everything out of them - the hatred and the attempts to save me. Odds were my mom might try to reason with me. Tell me I was mistaken. Confused by the city. By the City. Like all cities were exactly alike and held the same temptations. For her, I'd have to stick my ground. Tell her again and again - find a way not to get angry - not to yell or cry or tear myself apart when she blamed herself. She always did that. Verbally punished herself to push me to fold. I couldn't live like that. Live in the unknown - Schrödinger's gay. Wasn't that the trick? Everybody else balanced between the two - was or wasn't - but the cat knew. I knew.

My dad wouldn't give a second chance. He'd dismiss me. Disown me. Tell me to forget about them. Act like I was suddenly more on my own. As if he paid a cent toward my education or anything else. I had bought the ticket to Boston. I paid for my school supplies. Everything was me.

"Hey, come on," Tom called, waving his hand in front of my face. "You're zoning again."

Better pay attention. Would hate for a positive coming out experience before I threw myself on the proverbial fire.

Shut up, Carreau. That sick reverse psychological experiment wouldn't work on me.

"Sorry."

Though he nodded, any ease I had earned myself stood on shakier and shakier ground. Just two weeks, and after this Friday, I wouldn't have to hide my actions from anyone. I'd have the dorm room - and pretty much the whole dorm - to myself for the next four weeks. Two weeks of that would be with Gray.

Or dead.

Either way, I'd be with Gray.

Chapter Twenty-Seven

Tom rushed around our dorm room, throwing this and that into his duffle bag as if he would be gone for months instead of the few weeks for the holidays. If I were a better friend, I wouldn't be nearly as excited to see him go, but all I could think was how much easier saving Gray would become without him around. Plus, Carreau hung around the room, lurking in my thoughts - and probably Tom's too - which meant I had no idea when he would strike next. The less people around to mess with, the better off I'd be. At least I could recognize his influence.

"So - Cheyenne and Chad are coming back up on New Year's for some memorial for Theodore Thompson. Apparently, he died on the 1st or something, and the place is getting torn down at the end of the month," Tom informed me, and I nodded along, pretending this was new information. "I mean, kind of weird. Spending New Year's Day hanging around an abandoned rehab center - kinda weird, but that's Cheyenne for you."

Sitting back on my bed, I set aside the book I had faked reading. "What about Maddix?"

"What about him?"

"Generally, when Cheyenne does anything related to Crables Manor, he's along for the ride," I retorted.

Tom shrugged, shoving the messy pile of clothes into his duffle as he tried to zip it. "Normally, you're involved too, but it seems they didn't invite you. Anyway - Maddix'll be in Texas. Cheyenne's in NYC; Chad - is Chad, so ya know, you'll be around. I told them you were interested."

Of course, he did. I couldn't be trusted to be left on my own, so he was going to have the crazy crew check in on me. I bet it was Carreau who gave Cheyenne the idea of a vigil. Having them around would make the whole thing more difficult than it had to be. Zeke scheduled me for the 30th, so I'd just camp out from the morning of New Year's Eve until it was done. Unfortunately, I had no idea the exact time. None of Maddix's or Cheyenne's research pointed to a time of death, and Rory hadn't given me any specifics. We had been arrogant to think we had time to discuss more details later.

With a sigh, I rolled my eyes. "Thanks for the playdate, mom, but I've got plans."

"Plans?" He reared back and turned on me. "What plans?"

"A friend of mine is coming around to Boston," I told him. Better to build up Gray's arrival sooner than later.

Brows furrowed, Tom crossed his arms over his chest. "Who?"

"Gray. He's sticking around a while after, so you'll probably meet him."

Even though he nodded, I could see uncertainty in his eyes. "Friend from back home?"

"He's actually from around here," I offered before jumping to another topic. "When are you planning to come back?"

"The Friday before classes start back up."
Glancing at his cell, he ran his hands over his short hair. He stuffed it back into his pocket and grabbed his coat. "Shit! I should've already hit the road."

"Need help bringing your stuff down?"

Tom shook his head. "I've got it. See you next year!" The door had almost shut behind him when he kicked it open again. "And keep your phone on you!"

"Sure thing, mom. I'll keep my phone charged and ready for your motherhen calls." I waved, and with a pointed look, he headed out.

After a few minutes, I rolled over, studying the ceiling. Come tomorrow - my right arm would be covered. Just the left after that, and I'd be done. Prepared to pull Gray through to this side - to the land of living permanently. Out of limbo.

And then what? What comes after? How would I be able to face him? To tell him everything that had happened - the decades which separated him from the world he knew? Would he be happier having survived? Or would this strange new world seem darker to him? I hoped not. I hoped he'd see everything and want to stay with me. Then again - what choice did he have.

Maybe that was the appeal. Someone who couldn't leave me. If that were true, I would be just as bad as Simon. Inevitably, I'd chase him away. How could he want to stay with someone who caged him? While his world would center around me for a while, I had to create an environment where Gray could thrive. *Impossible.* Difficult - but

I could do it. God only knows how - but I had to be able to do it. Saving Gray meant nothing if he woke in a world which haunted him more than the limbo where they trapped him.

With the lights on, I fell asleep - the manor dragging me under quicker perhaps for Carreau's presence in the back of my mind. But the place I awoke wasn't anywhere within the old house that I remembered ever being. Stone pressed into my back. An entire stairway pushing up against my skin while my feet - bare - pushed into crackled stone. Spots of dirt gathered there. Not dust but actual earth. A single light bulb hung from the ceiling on a long cord. Back and forth, it moved like a pendulum. Electricity flickered around its coil.

In Ose's office, the hair hung thick and heavy. A blanket which weighed over everything, spreading across the limbs and pressing down until I couldn't tell where I began and ended. Inside this new room - the basement? It was almost like there was no air at all. Each breath returned with empty lungs. Cold crawled across my skin. Not enough to draw me to shiver, but a resonating frost which dragged every speck of heat out of me until only the emptiness remained.

But I wasn't alone. Something slithered in the dark out of the corner of my eye where the light couldn't reach no matter how far it swung. Whispers hissed low. Something unfamiliar in its familiarity which lingered long after it should have died, and though my head spun in the thin air, I recognized the symbols carved into the rough faces of the wall. No amount of paint could cover them. Not enough bleach in the world to clean off the blood on this floor. Even a whole foot of dirt over the top couldn't hide the red.

The world hummed. Low and resonating through the stone. Too low. Deep in the belly of the beast - the monster built into this house rested here. In this basement, and none of the spirits moved. They hung - women and men sprawled where they had breathed their last breaths. Fallen and tormented - because they believed it would give them power. A massacre.

"Soon." A man's voice echoed in the dark.

He curled at the foot of the stairs. His body almost leaned against my leg. Everything in me screamed to run back up those stairs, but I hadn't come down them. My legs wouldn't work. They resisted every urging as the man hummed. When he spoke, his lips didn't move. His entire body vibrated like it was made of sound.

"Soon."

Soon what? Soon it would all be over. Soon the spirits in the house would be free once the construction crew wrecked the place and broke the runes - broke whatever spell bled into the floors and walls? Something so powerful not even fire could burn it out? Or would the dead face something worse after it was done? Had they planned to summon something? Would all the souls - even those like Rory and Mrs. Hayward - get drawn into something hideous and evil? Drawn down into the belly of the beast?

If I got Gray out, would we both live with
that guilt for the rest of our lives? Or would the
markings on my arms tie me to the same fate? I
didn't intend to sacrifice anybody. I had believed
my soul to be my own in those moments when I
found myself believing I had a soul at all - that
anything more than my eyes could see existed. That
there was something bigger than all this, but with
this magic - with ghosts - it made it a bit easier to
hope.

"Soon."

Swallowing, I found my voice. "What is
soon?"

In the far arc of one of its swings, the bulb
froze. Electricity hummed, crackling as it flickered.
All across the room where they lay, the spirits
vibrated - calling out the word again and again:
"Soon - soon - soon…"

A shadow swirled - tall and humanoid, and
when a new voice joined the echoing mess, the
racing of my heart sunk at Carreau's thrumming
tone. *They always say that. Soon - soon -
soon…pathetic. They cannot tell time. No idea
what is happening above. It isn't a warning. They
are begging. Caught and stuck and driven mad.
How much do they despise each other? Caught in
this Devil's Trap with those they murdered and
who murdered them. Poor little souls.*

Above me - where stone met wood - the
stairs creaked. Dressed like a nineteenth century
dandy, Carreau sauntered down the steps. His blond

hair perfectly combed. As his half-lidded eyes scanned the room, only disdain colored his features.

"Did you bring me down here on purpose?" he asked. His voice sounded far gentler but just as deep as when he threw his thoughts directly inside my head. "No - you don't have the skill for that, do you? This must be that ridiculous woman."

My palms pressed, pushing against the stairs, but I couldn't move. Every muscle in my body strained, but I was just as paralyzed as the spirits surrounding me. Despite that, I asked, "The Governess?"

He blinked at me - his long eyelashes fluttering. "Hayward."

The cook? The surprise seemed enough to override whatever part of my mind told me I had to keep still. Standing, I shifted to face him. "How about you go off and see your boyfriend, and I go off and see mine, and we pretend we didn't see each other?"

His nose wrinkled. "If I release my hold on you, there's a chance you'll wake up, and I won't be able to follow you out. It takes a considerable amount of energy."

"Why don't you just follow Tom home for Christmas instead?" I offered like the self-centered jerk I was. "Get some of that positive energy or whatever?"

In a swirl of darkness, he flickered. Around and around the bulb swang, casting his shadow larger and shorter on the walls until the man vanished, and only his shadow remained. Then

220

darkness stretched out once more. At the top of the stairs, the door clicked, swinging open, but the moment my hand rested on the doorknob, I woke up in my bed alone.

Chapter Twenty-Eight

Christmas music blared through Zeke's shop. His needle buzzed, humming through the air as he bowed over my arm. Already, the symbols and lines curved over my shoulder. Stark black against my ever paling skin. After so many weeks, I ought to have been used to the pain. Piercing my skin again and again, the ink painted me, joining me to the house and turning my body into a weapon. A knife to pierce the gap. The last piece of a horrible puzzle so many had tried to finish before me.

Pulling back, Zeke sighed. "Almost done. I swear, kid, you're pretty tough." My skin burned. "And lucky. If any of these had gotten infected..."

He didn't have to say it. I begged him not to in my mind, and as my luck would have it, he fell silent. His eyes shimmered as he stared down at the black lines twining down my forearms to where he had left off at my wrists. Hands were delicate. Complicated. As if the rest of the markings which netted my body were anything else. A single wrong line, and nothing mattered.

To come so close and to fail because of a line on my back I couldn't see. It haunted me. Back when Rory still stuck to me outside the manor, I begged him to look at the lines again and again. Each time, he proclaimed them right. No matter how many times he said so, I found panic building up inside me nonetheless.

Wiping the sweat from his forehead, Zeke settled forward to start again. "Just a bit more. Then the next arm next week..."

"The 30th," I corrected.

Sitting back, he nodded. "Can't believe it's almost here. You're staying over at that place from the 31st on, right? I looked into it - into the kid, like you said, and they didn't have an accurate time of death, but it was early, wasn't it? Just a bit past midnight on the 1st?"

"Yeah."

Bowing over my arm once more, the needle shook, but I held still. I breathed through the pain, ignoring the way my hand wanted to twitch. Fighting against the urges building inside me to move. To pull away. I could do this. I would do this. For Gray. I could throw myself on the fire - risk it all for him. When the end finally came, we would be together, curled around each other in the emptiness of that crypt. The corpse of this nightmare might gather around us, but I would break him free of the selfishness which bound him - the thirst for power built into the foundations by a family who massacred themselves, the greed of two doctors twisting the world around them to fight for a chance at a life they only served to abuse, and the rest could fall aside.

Even Rory. Mrs. Hayward. Were their lives worth risking the balance? Hadn't Rory died chasing this exact goal. He understood it. For addiction - whatever madness burned in his veins thanks to Carreau and Ose, he had to have recognized what this might mean for him. Even the Governess - if she truly cared for Gray like the other two said - her spirit, where would it go in the end? And why did it strike me now to care? Why so close to the end?

Like a fool, I begged myself to be selfish. If I could focus on Gray - on the weight of him in my arms and the way his existence would utterly change my world (for the better, I had to believe this, always for the better), then I could not distract myself with the horrors and the sacrifices of those who had drowned themselves to give him life once more. They knew the cost. God help us all - we knew the cost.

When Zeke pulled back, the pain remained. An itch and burning spreading up and down my arm. My nerves - still unaccustomed to the process - screamed, sending signals to my mind which refused to follow, but they would dim. The ones on my back barely itched anymore. When all this ended, Gray might trace them. I imagined it sometimes. The way his long fingers might slide across the dark marks over my body. Even when I wished for our love to be something pure - untainted as it already seemed too dark, I couldn't stop my mind from going elsewhere. To the breathless way we kissed. He flushed every single time. His cheeks pinked. Flushed and pretty as he nuzzled into my shoulder, horrified and excited, and the excitement won every single time.

And he kissed me just as breathless. What started as his hand in mine turned to his lips upon my cheek, drawing closer and closer time after time until the soft brush of his lips against my own sent my heart racing. I would never forget that kiss. Curled on the bed he claimed was mine back before I realized how real he was. Back when I threw away life for the dream of him. Before the world rewarded me for my suffering - my anguish with the sweetness of his affection.

"You know the deal," Zeke announced as he set his equipment aside. "If there's any peeling, let me know. We can do any last minute fixes on the 30th. I haven't taken any other appointments."

"Thank you."

The big man smiled, but it didn't reach his eyes. Tears gathered on his lower lid. "Rory was my best friend. He - shit, kid - he's the reason my life turned out this good. I've got my own store - the most beautiful wife, best kids...god, I wish he had lived to see all this." The tears spilled over, and he rubbed them away with the back of his hand.

Suffering seemed a measurement of love. Rory said he didn't want Professor Haggard to care about him or to be trapped by him, and thinking that kept me from bringing up the unknown of what might happen to Rory when this was all said and done. If he and the other spirits went down in a not great way, Zeke deserved to believe otherwise. Rory would've wanted it that way.

"Still, thank you."

He nodded, waving me off. A week without food started easily enough, but after fighting in that chair for hours, I could feel the hunger brewing in my belly. It slunk around like a snake, slithering here and there until it could push and curl within the core of me, leaving little for me to do but keep moving forward. Luckily, Tom wasn't around to notice this. If he realized I hadn't eaten - and had no plan to eat for the next week - he would wreck me.

Or report me to health services. Talk about a group I didn't need to deal with - not now or ever. It would be hard enough finding a lie to cover Gray once I got him out. If they caught me - what would I even tell them? I couldn't even find the right lie to completely get Tom - my stupidly awesome roommate - off my back. What would a bunch of psychologists think? Kid goes through insomnia and depressive periods - tattoos himself in six weeks - full body. Well, full from the neck down. I could never wear shorts or short sleeves again without someone seeing what I had done, but that wouldn't matter once I had Gray.

And wasn't that dangerous? Putting all of my happiness onto one person. Someone I couldn't talk about - not until he was here with me. Someone who inspired me closer and closer to the edge - almost had me hospitalized - though it wasn't his fault. Never was his fault. But how would somebody else see it? What excuse could I use? Was I doing a religious fast for Christmas? Self-punishment for breaking away from my family? Which they'd probably think was a bad sign too. Maybe they'd even call them. Tell my parents that their son was having suicidal ideations.

Which wasn't true. I didn't want to die. I just wouldn't mind it if it meant being with Gray. Death wasn't the end. Recognizing the unhealthiness of that thought should have gotten me some credit, but I knew how those people think. Every thought I had slipped closer and closer to reason enough to institutionalize me, so I had to keep them to myself. Just one more week. If I could bully my way through, it would be fine.

One arm left. My chest swelled with something. Not hope. Nothing so positive. Maybe anxiety? That weird stomach churning uncertainty where everything headed in the right direction, but it couldn't last. I couldn't recognize why. Wouldn't know until I had stubbled right into the trap, but after a rough night, Carreau hadn't shown himself. Small wins, right?

Of course, Tom sensed my mood from miles away. Or he just had shit timing. My phone rang, and with a huff, I answered, "Hey, Tom, guess you made it home safely."

"I texted you when I got in last night. Didn't you see my text?"

Rubbing the bridge of my nose, I held back my sigh. "Yep. Didn't you see my response?"

"So...weren't you getting another part of your tattoo today?" he asked.

"Yep. I actually just finished the appointment and confirmed the last one," I told him as I headed back toward campus.

A wheezy inhale came down the line, but whatever caused it must've not lasted long as Tom quickly pushed, "When's that gonna be?"

"The 30th! Just in time for the New Year."

Humming along the line, Tom said something to somebody on the other end of the line before coming back and asking, "So - you got any plans for New Year's Eve?"

"Nah, I'm not really planning that far in advance."

More mumbling and then distracted - "What about the vigil with Chad and Cheyenne?"

I would have Gray by then. No way would I spend time with those two considering. "I won't be around for that."

"Won't be - where're you planning on going?"

This was ridiculous. "Tom - you're home. Be with your family. Enjoy it. Bye," I said, and I hung up on him.

Seriously, that guy took motherhenning to a new level. Sheesh, maybe he'd be better once he had a chance to calm down and realize I could take care of myself.

Ha - like that would happen.

Chapter Twenty-Nine

There came a time when hunger shadowed me. Even in the blank abyss where dreams took me when the manor wouldn't have me, I couldn't escape the bile churning - eating at the emptiness. All I wanted was to spend another night in Gray's arms. To know he understood. We never discussed his death. Never spoke of what it might mean for me to bring him back, so the uncertainty weighed on my shoulders - leaving me unbalanced.

"Hush now," a soft voice whispered. A delicate finger pressed into the furrow between my brows. "You'll give yourself a headache worrying."

Warmth radiated. Around me, the cold which haunted me in the last day or so when my stomach begged to be fed, I forgot how another person felt. The warmth of touch. Alone - without Gray or any of the clusters of my classmates, the frigid air crept into my bones. But in his arms, I learned the lesson a thousand times over.

Slowly - no energy to sit up - I opened my eyes, and Gray smiled down at me. His lips curled. My heart skipped a beat, and the cold urged me to bury my face into his stomach. Hadn't he seemed the cold one? Trapped in the strange world between life and death - hadn't he chased the feverish apathy away from my mind in the beginning? Back when this was only a dream, hadn't his touch eased the fire inside me? Now, just the sight of him set my skin ablaze - rushing red through me as his gentle touch warmed and grounded me in equal measure.

"We should talk," I murmured into his shirt.

Softly, he shushed me. "I haven't seen you in days, James. We can take our time."

One day, after I saved him - days when I could support us - ensure his safety and my own - in those days I would be patient. Take time to simply enjoy the ease of his presence. Of my body against his. For now, I needed to plan, to be certain Gray understood and would come through this whole. Despite every bit of me wanting to curl around him, I pushed myself up, brushing a strand of hair behind the soft curl of one of his ears.

"Have you noticed my tattoos?"

His eyes rolled. "I wasn't about to comment. It is your body."

"I'm not getting them for me. Do you remember Rory?"

Gray blinked. Pulling away, he studied me. I had seen the expression before but never on his face. Simon looked at Reggie like that. Like he belonged to him - like I belonged to Gray.

My heart pounded, and my dick stirred - because I had no sense of propriety. All I could think to do was pull him close, kissing him. Our tongues entwined, and the gentle closed-mouth pecks of our early romance became something else entirely. Pushing him down onto the bed, I pressed between his long legs. Trailing his hands down my back, he tugged at my shirt, stroking up the skin of my back beneath. With a gasping breath, I pulled back - throwing off my shirt before diving down to press against him, aligning our bodies from lips to crotch.

We rocked together, refusing to part. Each of his soft moans, I swallowed. The arcadian gentility of our love broke. Everywhere he touched seemed to burn. Heat spread through me. All I needed - the smoothness of his skin when I pushed up his shirt, shoving the fabric to gather in his armpits - exposing the lithe slimness of his stomach and chest. The delicate trail of hair which disappeared beneath the waist of his pants. Chasing his breath with my fingers. Buttons flying. Hands on my shoulders. Nails dug into my skin.

"James," he whispered, gasping for breath between my kisses.

"I got them for you," I confessed. "To free you from limbo. Get you out of Crables - bring you home with me."

"Limbo?"

Nuzzling into his neck - down from his jaw to his shoulder when he shifted away from my desperate mouth, I groaned. "They're tearing down the manor in the spring. If we miss this year, there won't be another."

All heat left me though my body protested the sudden shift in mood. Pressed so tightly to him, how could I not be torn between want and terror? This could be the last time I touched him - kissed him - how could I not be horrified yet desperate to touch him all the more?

"What are you talking about?" Gray asked, taking my face in his hands. His eyes scanned me, and when he frowned, I wondered what he saw. "Rory told you - he told you that you needed these tattoos to save me?"

When I nodded, a soft choked sound slipped from between his lips. I couldn't bear the pity brewing in his eyes. "I'd do whatever it takes to save you."

"Oh, James…"

His lips brushed against my cheek as he pulled me down, holding me close as if to rock a fretful child. I allowed the touch for a moment, but the longer the silence remained between us, the more awake I grew, feeling a tug in my gut to fall asleep in his arms and wake back up in my bed. This could be the last time I ever saw him. He needed to know I had tried. That I would try until the life left my body.

When I shifted back, he let me go. "Gray - you died - do you remember?" Shaking his head, he squirmed, moving up the bed and away from me. "In the widow's watch...they tried to kill you. Lit the room on fire, but the Governess saved you. She pulled you into some kind of limbo. Every year, you relive it, but with these -" I showed off the tattoos across my body then my bare arm. "Once I get the other arm done tomorrow, I can pull you through. Bring you back to life...with me."

"James -you have to hear yourself. You sound…" he closed his eyes, shaking his head.

"You know this place isn't right. Time skips and jumps. The ghosts! You have to remember the ghosts," I cried.

All the while, he shook his head and whispered, "No."

"Gray isn't even your real name!"

His eyes - wide and bloodshot - focused on me once more. "No. Stop it, James. This isn't funny."

"I'm not trying to be funny. I need you to know! If I fail...I need you to know that -"

Covering my mouth with his hands, Gray swallowed. His pale throat almost glistened in the room's dim light. "James, I know Rory is persuasive, but he's an addict. No - no don't argue, James. He's a bad influence. He lied to you. I'm fine. I don't need to be saved. I wanted to come here. I asked to be admitted to Crables. My father wanted to pretend nothing was wrong, but I wanted to get better - and I am getting better," he insisted. Calm and sure, he spoke, "You've helped me so much, and I don't care what Rory told you - but you didn't need to do this."

"What year is it?" I demanded, tearing his hands from my lips.

"What does that matter?"

Holding onto his delicate wrists, I tried to summon some sort of courage. Only desperation showed up. "The Curse of the Great Bambino broke - you think that might be important."

"And it will be when it happens," he retorted.

Pressing a kiss to his palm, I tried once more. "You used to call me a boarder -"

"Denial. I'm still recovering."

234

"It's -" but his fingers pressed to my lips once more.

Softly, he shushed me. "You were doing so well lately."

This was impossible. I hadn't been doing well. If the whole mess of my Harvard life - of the future for him and the present for me - if that existed only as a mad hallucination, I had been spending far longer there than in Crables. Tattooing as a patient also wouldn't have been possible. He couldn't see that. Like he said - this was all denial. Denial he had died. Denial - but he had to fight - had to be just as ready for the shock of another time when I pulled him out.

"Your real name is Theodore Thompson. You were a renowned medium - people came from all around the world to have you connect them with their dead loved ones. Your father died in 1948 - six years after you supposedly burned in the -"

"Shut up!" he screamed, pulling his wrists from my hold. His hands covered his ears as he cried. How cruel. Even as horrified as I made him - I still wanted to kiss him. To silence his terror with my mouth like some beast. He deserved more from me. "My father's alive. It's not - it's only 1942. I'm alive. Oh god, not again."

"Again…"

All of my confidence vanished with that one word. He seemed smaller. More delicate for the horror on his face. I wanted to scoop him into my arms. Wrap him up and promise to make all his fears go away, but I had scared him. I couldn't lie to him. Couldn't pretend I was being less than truthful - and maybe he should have been scared.

The door flew open. Ose stood with a white coat on his shoulders. "Nurse - escort Mr. Thompson back to his room."

An invisible force entered the room. *One-two. One-two.* The clicking of heels as Gray listed to the side, half-carried and half-dragged toward the door.

"Calm down, James," Dr. Ose urged, grabbing my upper arm and stepping between Gray and me. "Nurse Florence is only taking Theodore back to his room to calm down. You want him to feel safe, don't you?"

"Stop lying!" I raged, struggling, but my muscles protested. Hunger burned in my veins. Knuckles against wood. My dorm room door swung open - hadn't I locked it? Voices like I was under water. Someone - who was that? Fingers against my pulse - that wasn't Gray. That wasn't Ose.

The dead doctor held me. "Just focus on breathing, James. You'll get through this. We've done this before. Deep breaths - can you do that for me?"

Rolled onto a stretcher - screaming, crying - I had to wake up. Something went wrong. Caught between two worlds. Useless in both. They were taking Gray away from me. They were taking me away - I couldn't. I had to -

"Stop!" I demanded, an echo of Gray's earlier pleas. "I'm fine. Leave me -"

An ambulance. Sirens. Oh god - oh god - this had to be a nightmare. They couldn't keep me. Wouldn't I? Why did they come? What if they made me eat? I had to wake up. Had to stop before they put in an IV or feeding tube - would they know I hadn't eaten? They couldn't - couldn't they? Just an IV - but would that count?

"No," I groaned as the last vestiges of energy abandoned me.

Dr. Ose smiled - his eyes - pools of oil - swirled as he leaned over me, chasing me as I fell awake - caught between the two. "Shush now, James. It's almost over. Just breath. In. Out."

Chapter Thirty

Waking up screaming, I scared the E.M.T. beside me and myself. He pressed a hand to my chest, calming himself down as he checked my vitals over as if I were some kind of junky awaking from a bad trip.

"No I.V.!" I demanded.

"Do - " he tried to talk, but I wasn't about to let him roll right over me.

"My name is James Madison - freshman Harvard psych. I stayed here for the break because I hate my family, but I got a little too excited with all the free time, so I crashed hard. I'm not on drugs," I informed him, struggling to sit up, but they had me strapped down. "I might've had some alcohol at a party, but I'm fine. I don't know who called you, but - "

"Some nice tattoos you've got, James."

All the blood drained from my face, and a burgeoning sickness brewed in my stomach. Zeke wouldn't have called, and the only one that knew besides him was Tom. Tom couldn't have done this to me. "Shit, did Zeke call? I have an appointment today! Did I sleep through it? He's such a worrier."

Shaking his head, the EMT shrugged. "We got a call from your roommate. Said you were having some dark thoughts..."

No way. Tom wouldn't have done this to me. If I missed a few of his calls or sent them to the reject abyss, it shouldn't have made him call 9-1-1 on me. I didn't have to answer to him. All my talk about him being a great roommate - completely proven wrong. He had wrecked me. I couldn't eat, but I couldn't say that until asked, or they might think I had an eating disorder. Was there a holiday which I could use? Ramadan? Shit, I didn't know enough about that to work. Did Jehovah's Witnesses also refuse anything intravenous? Or was that just blood? Come on, James - think!

"No dark thoughts here. I'm fine - great even. Have an appointment for the future - today, I guess, but tattoo appointment works as prior planning, and I'm going to this vigil with classmates," I lied, grasping the bits I could to try to find a way to escape this mess. They couldn't keep me under surveillance. Basics - prove I had future plans, no signs of depression but not too much overenthusiasm. Answer the questions. Keep it concise. I could do this. "I've pulled a couple too many all-nighters on a couple online games."

"Oh, what game?"

Crap - what was the online game Maddix talked about? "Halo."

"Halo, huh? I thought they shut down the online release…" the EMT studied me, waiting for my reaction on being called out.

"Fan-mod."

Nodding, he leaned forward. "I know Zeke. He's a nice dude. He won't give you trouble about rescheduling your appointment if you end up missing it."

239

"I have to be there. He was coming in just for me. It would be a dick move to miss it," I told him.

I just needed to stay calm. The more I panicked, the harder it would be to get out of this. And if the room stopped spinning, that would have been nice too. I could handle it. Sure, Gray didn't believe me, and he might go catatonic when he realized he wasn't dead, but I would have brought him back, so that was fine. I could handle this. They couldn't keep me here.

It didn't help my case that I blacked out again, waking up in a room that sure as heck wasn't an Emergency Room. No curtains. Who did they think I was? I couldn't afford a private room. Unless my scholarship included some pretty amazing healthcare. Did it?

The door opened, and an older man in a white coat and glasses walked in. He had that little string which went around his neck in case his glasses fell off his nose, they would just hang about his chest. He glanced up at me over his lenses.

"Good afternoon, Mr. Madison. I'm Dr. Ben Kedves. Do you know where you are?"

Inhaling, I glanced up at the bags hanging and the line connecting them into my arm. Maybe an I.V. wouldn't count. I wasn't about to panic in front of a psychiatrist. I could still get out of this. Just needed to stay calm. Talk clearly.

"Last guy I talked to was an E.M.T., so I'm guessing Boston General."

The man nodded. "Your friend, Tom, was very worried about you."

Did they always give up the ghost? It felt off. Weren't we supposed to keep some confidence? Or maybe I hadn't gotten to the lesson yet where humanization through familiar name-dropping happened.

With a sigh, I shrugged. "Tom's kind of a worrier. Normally, I'd appreciate it a bit more, but if it's afternoon, odds are he made me miss a tattoo appointment that was being done as a favor."

"Yes, they mentioned you were concerned the artist - a man named Zeke? - would be upset," the doctor informed me, slowly drawing closer to the bed as if feeling out how close he could get without startling me.

"His kid just started college, and he was willing to help me get my tats done before the New Year. Zeke understood how important this was to me. See - I come from a small town, and there are parts of me that I couldn't really address while I was there, so coming here allowed me a safe environment to become the person I wanted to be." There. That had to be close enough to the truth to work. He had to understand. I didn't have to say it yet, right? I could. I could do it. If pushed, I could come out to this guy. He was a psychiatrist. Probably saw weirder coming out stories, right? If I looked like a guy getting a handle on his sexuality rather than someone killing themselves for discovering it...shit, such a thin wire. I could do this. I had to do this. "Tom has - he's not exactly

241

someone I can confide in, so this wasn't something I wanted to discuss with him until I was ready."

More nodding. "Sure. It can be tough to talk about things to our closest friends before we're ready." He gestured to the chair beside my bed. "Do you mind if I sit down?"

"Whatever will get me out of here fastest. Even if I can't get the tattoo finished today, I'd like to at least apologize for wasting Zeke's time," I replied.

He hummed but sat down. "It's your first semester at college. That's a big change for a lot of people."

"Took some getting used to - same with Boston. Had a bit of trouble sleeping earlier in the semester," better to admit it now than to deal with Tom having said something and me looking like I was keeping information from him, "I got myself in order for the end of the semester. A's across the board." Somehow. Knowing that would probably piss Chad off. Maybe I should go to the vigil to tell him.

Crossing one leg over the other, Dr. Kedves furrowed his brow. "James, when was the last time you ate anything?"

"Breakfast yesterday?" I lied, dropping my head in feigned guilt. "I got really into this game online..."

"Yes, Pete - one of the gentlemen who brought you in - mentioned it. Halo? My nephews are into it. I wasn't aware there was an online version available..."

Crap. Either I folded and opened myself up to the possibility of another failed lie, or I hedged my bets and presented as the sheltered midwestern Christian freshman who just discovered porn and refused to own up to it. Gray was kinda like porn. I mean, he got me hot and bothered, and I wanted to push him down and - there we go.

Blushing - thank you, Gray, I shifted. "Yeah - some fans made it."

Another over the glasses look - pensive. Good, look at me. See a horny college student newly awakening to his sexuality - let me go. I could handle this. Zeke understood. We'd reschedule, I'd be there still twenty-four hours ahead of the window when Gray might relive his burning. Sure, the tattoos on my left arm would be pretty fresh, but I could do this. We could get through this, and then Gray would be here, and I could talk about things, because I'd have to because Gray would be here, and maybe Gray would have 1940s biases. Maybe he wouldn't want anyone to know, and I'd be an absolute mess because I'd question whether he really wanted to be with me or had some sort of savior complex -

No. Those thoughts were making my vitals wonky. Think horny thoughts. Kissing Gray before things went south. The way he felt in my arms. Pressing against him and feeling the hard line of his interest, rocking against my own erection. I just wanted to feel his legs wrapped around my waist - pump into that round ass of his. For a guy that delicate, he filled my hands just right, and his lips made me drunk. That was the furthest we had gone, and it had been amazing. We would be amazing together.

"I know you've got a lot going on, but with everyone gone for the holidays, this might be the best time. No disruptions to your academic schedule." No - no - no. "It's only a seventy-two hour hold, so we'll have you for a bit of a long weekend. Get some good food in you. I know what they say about hospital food, but I think you'll be pleasantly surprised - "

"I'm really fine." My heart spiked, and there was nothing I could do to stop the way it raced or how his eyes shifted to the monitor. I had to find a way to get out of this. Had to get the runes completed - get to Gray -

"Tell him to get my brother," Rory whispered, hovering at my side. "He's got hospital privileges, doesn't he? Tell them he knows you, and he'll see that you're fine."

I wanted to ask how he got back, but talking to myself wouldn't exactly give me the best chance of getting out. "Please, call in Professor Haggard. He's one of my professors. He knows me."

Dr. Kedves frowned, but then - by some miracle, he nodded. "I can see if Dr. Haggard is free to come in early. He's in tomorrow evening, so you might have to wait until then. Can you do that?"

Morning. I could do morning. Get cleared in the morning - tattoo in the afternoon - straight to Crables. "I prefer sleeping in my own bed, but if tomorrow's the best I can do..."

A small smile rose to his calm features. "I'll reach out and see what I can do. Why don't you get some sleep?"

And with that, he left me alone with only a ghost as company. Shifting to sit in the newly vacated seat, Rory chewed at the skin about his thumb nail, twitching his feet as he crossed first one leg over the other and back and forth, switching which leg balanced on the other. His whole itchy demeanor screamed withdrawal, but I couldn't ask him about that. Not know. I had to concentrate. Keep my focus - keep Rory here and Carreau out. This was a love story, wasn't it? They always had a race to the end. I just had to stay focused.

"Fucking go to sleep, kid," Rory commanded. "I'll wake you when something important happens."

And the dark abyss of dreamlessness stole me away.

Chapter Thirty-One

Polished, gleaming dark woods spread through Crables Manor. High ceilings and a roaring fireplace greeted me, but the flames shifted, more like shadows, consuming the light around them, black holes with tongues.

Heels clicked. No longer in their slow drumming pattern. They rushed around above me. Feet thundered. Bodies rolled; blood spilt. Rory's screams echoed in the unfurnished hallows of Crables Manor as I stood at its threshold - for the first time in my months neither inside the beast nor awake.

The ghosts I had seen in the basement - silvery specters, paralyzed in death by their murderous deeds in life, burrowed and buried in the tomb they had constructed - the temple to some unknown monstrosity - rose up through the floor. A fine mist of their overstretched consciousnesses spreading, leaking and trailing over the smooth wood.

"James!"

My eyes leapt to him. Though his hair remained perfectly in place - loose as it cascaded over his pale forehead, his clothing matched those I had left behind in the waking world. Soft pants and shirt - the gentle bindings of those not fighting their confinement. He said he wanted to get better, hadn't he? Said he decided to go into Crables Manor despite his father wanting him to stay at home.

Did he wish to cure himself of his sixth sense? Or his homosexuality?

I hadn't asked. Hadn't had the chance to, and an always anxious part of me needed to know - but not know. Not yet. Not when he was in front of me, trying to get to me with terror lighting his eyes.

"Gray," I called in return, and maybe I should have been more cautious. Maybe I shouldn't have run through those spirits, but how could I have resisted his panicked call? He stood upon the stairway, glancing back and forward as if he couldn't tell which way led to a worse fate. "I'm coming, Gray. Just stay there!"

His long fingers curled about the railing as he pressed himself to them as if to shield himself. Tears gathered along his dark lashes. "No!" he cried. "You've got to wake up, James. Get out before they get you too!"

"Not without you!"

I jumped without thinking. The mist buzzed about my feet, but it was thin. I could see the floor. I could get to him. They were paralyzed. Even if they spread about my feet, they couldn't stop me.

But they did. They wrapped around my legs, clinging as they wove their way up my calves. Becoming as thick as molasses, they solidified. Hands grabbing, arms wrapping, faces pressing as they condensed.

"James, you have to leave!" Gray pleaded. Tears poured down his face.

God, I just wanted to hold him. To wrap my arms around him and carry him out of this hell.

Everything hurt. I just wanted to lift him, carry him, hold him, steal him away from the nightmare, and in his beautiful eyes, I saw my own reflection - torn and bloody and frozen in time. Unable to protect him.

However, this was just a dream. Another stretch of horror built between death and my imagination. I couldn't get to him. They bound me up, stole away the strength in my body and pressed into the joints until my knees buckled. Eventually, if I remained, they would drag me under.

Static electricity buzzed along the lines of my tattoos. The black lines glowed, burning brighter and brighter beneath my clothes. The ends on my left shoulder where they curled around buzzed. Sparks flying, snapping out into the thick air.

I reached out, trying to press my weight forward, but my feet remained firmly stuck. "Gray - I'm coming! I promise! I'll get you out of here!"

"Don't," he sobbed. "It could kill you!"

"Gray - "

"I'm sorry." My world spun as he backed away. "You were right. It's easier if I forget, but I can't - not when it's - not when it's this close. I'm going to burn again, and I know this will be the last time. I don't want you to see that. To live with that! Please, just forget about me! I'm already as good as dead."

"I can't," I whispered. "I love you."

He shook his head. "This is my mess, James, and I don't regret it. Not a single moment if it meant meeting you. You're brilliant, and there's some fantastic man out there who'll sweep you off your feet."

"I don't want anyone else," I roared, fighting against the burning in my arm and the lead weights of the dead wrapped around my feet. "Gray, I love you. I'm not leaving you here!"

Shadows curled down the stairs. Ose and Carreau descended with their white coats and slick smiles. At first, Gray flinched away, but as his eyes landed on me once more, he lurched to the side, almost flinging himself at them.

"Take me," he pleaded. "Let him go! Please!"

Carreau wrapped his arms around Gray, pulling him into his chest as I screamed, unable to find words as I fought futilely. "Oh, little bird, you know we can't do that."

"We need two bodies, Theodore," Ose said - his swirling image clear for the first time as he set his dark eyes on me. Licking his lips, he pulled Carreau into a heated kiss, pressing Gray between them. "I can't wait to truly touch you again," he moaned.

His fingers slipped through the ephemeral shades of Carreau's shadowy form as the hall stretched, taking Gray further and further from me. The two mad doctors nuzzled each other. The softness of their expressions contrasted with their hands, positioned like claws on Gray, holding him in place between them.

"Don't! Gray! I'm coming for you!" The electricity buzzed along my body, and my blood rushed, pulsating beneath my skin as I managed to lift my foot. The mist crawled up my body, their hands grabbing at me. "Governess? Florence!? Help me?" I begged. She always came when I mentioned her - even the allusion to her had sent me back to waking as she stole Gray away. Maybe this time - maybe she could save him.

Somewhere above us, Rory shrieked. Like a banshee, the cry curdled my blood, drawing darkness in from the edges of my vision. Two arms stretched from the wall. Delicate hands wrapped around Gray, pulling him free as a somber face stared at me. Pale gray eyes in a dour countenance.

The room rippled. Blackness consumed, but all I could hear was his final cry as Gray proclaimed, "James, I love you!"

Chapter Thirty-Two

Why don't you eat something?

"I'm not hungry."

The hollow pit in my stomach disagreed, but it had the decency to not protest out loud. Back and forth, less than twelve but not quite so small as to be eleven steps took me from one end of the room to the other. All along, the stand followed, cold metal in my hand as the IV continued to drip, hooked into me. Pumping me full of nutrients, right? They had to be sterile. Sterile meant pure. I could still save Gray. Ose and Carreau couldn't - wouldn't win. I just needed to have some way to verify the time. Needed to be sure what day it was.

"Maybe you should sit down," the doctor suggested, but he made no move to force me.

Shaking my head, I began the loop once more. "I'm good."

"Pacing won't bring Dr. Haggard here any faster," he intoned.

Not that it mattered. He said Professor Haggard agreed to come early. He said it was afternoon on December 31st, but there were no windows, and he could be lying. Just because we were taught to minimize anything that might break the patient's trust didn't mean he wouldn't believe his lies were in good faith. If he thought lying would help me...no. This wasn't Crables. He wasn't Carreau - or Ose. He had no reason to lie. I'd been reasonable. Extremely accommodating and thoughtful. Avoided overly emotional reactions.

Refused the burning desire to tear the room apart. I
just needed to talk to Haggard. Rory would help me.
I could get through to him. I could still do this.

"While we're waiting, let's talk. Why do
you think Tom believed you were struggling?" He
waited, but I could only shrug and deny. "Your
grades are good. You've obviously formed some
strong friendships - especially with your psych
classmates..."

"Cheyenne - a girl in my psych group
project - had us do this lucid dreaming experiment.
That messed up my sleep cycle. Things got rough
for a while, and I'm pretty sure that freaked Tom
out, but I got myself back together before
Thanksgiving. I don't think one all-nighter should
get me seventy-two hours in here," I retorted,
pausing to meet his eyes. Eye contact mattered. I
had to look impatient - not anxious.

On the bed, Rory stretched. His arms
remained trapped in long sleeves, but the bindings
seemed looser than before. Almost as if he could
unloop them with just a bit of contorting, but I
couldn't ask. Couldn't talk to him at all. Not
without looking absolutely insane. We couldn't
coordinate. All I could do was wait. Hope.

"So you believe Tom..."

"Overreacted. He's got a great family," I
told the doctor. "He doesn't exactly understand that
might not be the case for everyone."

"And it isn't true for you?"

Here it was. Drop the bomb. Get the pity
and hope it would be my jail free card. I just had to

253

say it, but - what if he thought it was a reason to believe I would hurt myself? What if they called my parents? What if they tried to use this to send me back home? Put me in one of those conversion camps - like Ted Hennisy's cousin went to - the ones my dad said weren't tough enough.

"No." I leaned against the end of the bed, staring down at the psychiatrist. "I got into Harvard on my own. Paid my own way here. Applied to all the scholarships I could, wrote essays, worked three jobs. If my parents knew about my savings, my dad would've expected me to give it to the family - to his beer fund and the church." Dr. Kedves nodded solemnly, but while his eyes remained on me, I could see his pen moving. "I'm breaking away from them, and - yeah, sure, the process hasn't been smooth, but this is the best I've been in a long time."

He nodded more, darting his gaze to his notebook. "How long have you been planning to get away from your family?"

"Parents," I corrected - not that I had any other family. "Since middle school."

Another nod. "Any particular reason?"

"Tell him," Rory commanded. Sitting up, he stared at me. His tan face pale and eyes wide. "Don't make Gray the first person. He's gonna keep so many of your secrets. Don't make you loving him one of them." His hand reached out, resting on my shoulder. The bindings of the jacket eroded away.

Maybe it was the weight of his hand. Maybe the small bit of reassurance was all I needed. Just a bit of encouragement. So easy to give, yet no one had known before, and I didn't dare to tell them. Not after -

Closing my eyes, I sighed. I could do this. They weren't here. I could tell the truth. He didn't seem like he'd be the same...but not everyone disgusted by someone like me looked a certain way. Made it all the harder to say it. To hope that Dr. Kedves didn't intend to use it against me. As if the people I love could be turned into a weapon - the way I loved and who I loved being daggers all too easy to turn against me.

But Rory was right. Gray deserved to never be my secret - not once I'd brought him though. If I didn't start saying it now, it'd be all too easy to pretend I had good reasons not to own to it later.

"I'm gay."

Dr. Kedves studied me for a moment. His eyes softened like melting chocolate. "Have you told them?"

"Not yet."

"What about Tom?" I shook my head, and his brow rose. "Am I the first person you've told?"

"First living soul," I confessed with a shrug that I could tell wasn't nearly as blasé as I had hoped. "But Zeke - I wandered into his shop, and I think - I think he kind of realized. I couldn't say it, but…"

My heart thundered in my chest. I tried to focus on the frustration and desire to leave - the voice demanding him to connect the dots and let me go. To see that I was dealing with things the best way I could. Most of me - most of me was just relieved.

"And you stayed here over Christmas break to avoid your parents..."

"I've worked so hard to accept who I am and admit to myself that I'm gay - I don't want to have to go back to hating myself - to find myself having to play along or get the shit beat out of me or worse. But..." I trailed off, glaring at the door, but Professor Haggard seemed like he'd never come. "I'm not brave enough to tell them. I know what they'll say, and I know they've never been exactly great with me anyway, but I'm not ready to - I'm just not ready. Not yet."

"I imagine that's a very difficult place to be." An understatement but I could appreciate his sentiment.

Still, he seemed to expect a response. "Honestly, I just feel rushed. Tom would've understood to just let me take my time and figure things out if I had told him, but I'm not ready to tell him. He's my roommate, what if he freaks? And even if he doesn't - he's not exactly the best secret keeper."

As he nodded, scratching words into his book, a knock echoed before Professor Haggard opened the door. Immediately, Dr. Kedves jumped to his feet. "Dr. Haggard! Thank you for coming so early!"

"Of course," his eyes slid to me. "James, glad to see you up and around!"

"Rearing to clear up whatever mess Tom made," I informed him.

"Yes, why don't you eat while I confer with Dr. Haggard," the psychiatrist encouraged, and with a sigh, I made a show of getting into the bed and starting to open the sandwich until he nodded, head bobbing before Dr. Kedves guided Haggard aside.

While I pushed the tray away, Rory scoffed - leaning halfway through the door. "The doc thinks you aren't a suicide risk." I resisted responding, but hope swelled inside my chest regardless. "My brother doesn't believe Tom's prone to exaggeration, but he does believe it's a misunderstanding." He came back, flying to my side. "Cover the sandwich! Don't take it! It doesn't matter - they think - "

The door opened, and both doctors stared at me as I blinked. "So am I getting to go back to my dorm room?"

"We agree that it would be best -"

"They're going to keep you as a precaution. Tell them about - crap - there has to be a way - if they'd let you talk to my brother alone, I could - "

"Dr. Haggard personally knows the tattoo artist - "

"I've known Zeke for years. He used to run with my brother. I can assure you - he'd understand the situation, and I can pass on a message to him if you'd liked - "

"I told him about Gray! He saw the tattoos! Show him!"

All their voices blended. A cacophony beating me down like the ocean's tide beating, rushing, eroding the ever weakening shore. Setting down the uneaten sandwich, I rolled up the sleeve of my right arm, and one by one, they fell silent. Dr. Kedves frowned, brows furrowing, but Professor Haggard paled, and Rory gasped - his hands reaching out in wonder at his brother immediately recognizing the marks on my body.

"That's - that's an interesting design," Professor Haggard whispered, and the older doctor frowned all the more for his contemporary's tone. "Where did you find it?"

"Zeke," I said.

Gliding around his brother, Rory studied the lines of his face. "Tell him - tell him you met Gray. I told him. He'll be curious. He's always so curious. He'll want to know."

"I'd like to get it finished, and if we could go to Zeke's, I'm open to explaining more. I'm sure you have questions for him. Win-win. If you still think I need another forty-eight hours in here after that - fine." All the lies in the world couldn't darken my soul enough to stop me from trying to get to Gray.

After a moment, Dr. Kedves reached out, but Professor Haggard flinched, pulling away as a shade shifted across his face. "Why don't you explain it now?" Haggard's shoulders squared off -

tension straightening his spine to military perfection.

"You plan on keeping me here against my will. I've calmly answered all of Dr. Kedves's questions, but obviously, that isn't working. If I failed to recognize that..." I gestured for him to finish the thought himself. "Plus, the food in here is horrible. I'm craving some Chinese from The Great Wall. It's right down the street from Zeke's."

"Dr. Haggard..." the older psychiatrist warned, but my psych professor held up his hand.

"Okay, James. Why don't we see if Zeke's up for that deal?" Pulling out his cell phone, he dialed the number and set it on speaker phone. All the while I prayed Zeke could be subtle. Could play along.

"Zeke's Tattoos. Zeke speaking."

Staring me down, Professor Haggard lifted the phone slightly closer to his face. "Hi, Zeke. This is Ari Haggard, Rory's brother? I'm here with James. He says he had an appointment with you yesterday."

"Yeah! Should've known you two would know each other! I'm glad the kid's alright. He's never missed an appointment before," Zeke informed the room.

Leaning forward, I forced a smile. "Sorry, Zeke! Pulled an all nighter and scared my roommate. Any chance you can do the left arm today?"

Zeke chuckled. "For you, kid? Of course!"

Frowning, Professor Haggard asked, "Why

did you say you should've known we'd know each other, Zeke?"

"He knows I'm a psych student at Harvard," I said before Zeke could reply.

"And you can't shut the kid up about your class," Zeke added. "Talks my ear off whenever I'm working on him. Professor Haggard this and that - not that I understand any of it."

"Of course." His lips peeled back into a snarling smile. "Well, I'll make sure James makes his appointment. Four o'clock?"

"Four o'clock! I'll be there."

And with a curt goodbye, Professor Haggard shut his phone. "Let's get your clothes."

Dr. Kedves sputted. "Dr. Haggard - I would highly recommend against - "

Haggard turned the poisonous grin to his peer. "I'll take over Mr. Madison's care from here, Dr. Kedves."

Rory flew back. His hands tearing at the growing sleeves of his jacket. "Hold off," he cried, "Just a little longer. I've got to stay here - he needs my help!"

But whoever heard his pleas failed to listen. A shadow loomed, and with an ear-piercing scream, Rory dove over it, vanishing along with the towering shade of what I could only guess was Dr. Carreau. However, even freed from the phantom's influence, a mad glint remained in Professor Haggard's eyes.

A run to Crables Manor. I could do it. Whatever it took. Just one night more. I could save him.

Chapter Thirty-Three

Putting back on clothes after wearing the
loose hospital gown felt like what I'd imagine a
snake would feel trying to crawl back into a
shedded coil of skin. I tugged at the hems. They
weren't mine. The doctors cut them off - ridiculous,
cause they didn't need to assess me, but there I was
- with sweatpants and a T-shirt and hoodie that
weren't mine. Clean but not right.

Luckily, my shoes and socks were my own.
Underwear too - thank goodness. They offered me
the tattered remains, and while I grabbed my wallet
and room key, I let them chuck the rest. Not worth
the effort to bring them back to the dorm just to
throw them out.

As I struggled not to squirm, Professor
Haggard stared me down. His usually jovial eyes
narrowed. Lips curled. He fought the distrust
blooming. I saw it in the twitch of his mouth - the
unsettled shifting of his weight from one foot to the
other, but although his dark mood differed well
enough from his natural state to draw Dr. Kedves's
concern, it was not enough to stop whatever messy
path we had made between each other.

"I can lend you a coat," Dr. Kedves offered,
reaching over to give me his own, but I held up my
hands, shaking my head.

"Boston's got nothing on my hometown. I'll
be fine. Professor Haggard's giving me a ride, so
it's not like we're walking, right?"

A curt nod from Rory's younger brother. "I'm parked right outside, so let's head out before we're blocked in."

Walking with us, Dr. Kedves glanced at the security guards and nurses along the way. Everyone seemed tense. Their shoulders low and hands calm, but something in their eyes gave them away. A feverish herd panic at seeing one of their own acting so out of character.

Brushing his hands down his white coat, Dr. Kedves frowned. "Maybe I should come with you -"

"He isn't the only patient tonight, Ben," Professor Haggard reminded his colleague. "Come on, James, we don't want to keep Zeke waiting!"

With a nod, I followed him. Despite the hum of the engine indicating he left it idling, he hadn't bothered to put on the heat, so my breath curled - white puffs of vapor escaping my lips with each exhale. For a moment, I couldn't be sure if he would turn it on, and when he sat down in the driver's seat, his brow furrowed as he stared down at the wheel, seeming to fight with himself over how much of a jerk he intended to be.

Reaching over, he turned up the heat. "Are you sure you want to do this, James?" His eyes focused on the road ahead as he shifted into gear. "You're too smart to not have realized how personal this is for me."

Goddamnit, why couldn't Rory be here for this? I sucked at comforting people. Not that he wanted that. He wanted something - maybe for me to be contrite. To apologize for something - maybe he thought I desecrated his brother's memory, or maybe he personally hated anything to do with Rory nowadays. I knew what it was like to have a toxic family, and as useful as Rory had been - as much as he obviously loved his brother, that wouldn't change if he was a bad presence in his brother's life. Cut out by death or otherwise.

"I wouldn't be doing this if it wasn't personal for me too," I informed him, having nothing else kinder to say.

His frown returned, but my resignation seemed to give him pause as he pulled out onto the road toward Zeke's place. "How did you find the design?"

"It'll be easier to explain at Zeke's."

His mouth twisted this way and that as if he fought off the words which threatened to escape him. As we slowed at a stoplight, he sighed. "Is this about Theodore Thompson?" He asked then shook his head, moving on before I could answer. "You didn't write on him. I would have kept a closer eye on you if you had."

Blinking, I toyed with the vents, shifting the direction they blew the heat around me. "Why?"

"Because there's one every year."

And they all failed apparently. "I didn't realize these tattoos were so popular."

"They aren't. As far as I know, you're the first who's gone that far. The rest just schedule vigils or make shrines - Theodore Thompson, the patron phantom of Harvard psych students." With a forced laugh - dark and deep in his chest, he pressed

265

a bit too hard on the accelerator, jarring us forward, but he glared out at the road ahead, acting as if I hadn't just slammed forward, auto-locking my seatbelt as it snapped to hold me back. "I'll be happy to see Crables Manor ground to rubble."

"Well, no shrines here. Theodore Thompson had a weird and short and more than slightly screwed up life, but he was just a guy. Medium or psychic or whatever - 'more things in heaven and earth' et cetera et cetera," I returned.

His eyes glimmered in the dark. "Then why did you get those tattoos?"

Rather than repeat my earlier answer, I remained silent. Shadows stretched - ephemeral yet ancient beneath the city's lights. Though I hadn't eaten, the intravenous fluid helped settle my head. Hopefully, the clarity would last. Odds lended me to making a run from Zeke's. Crables Manor may have been a good distance away from the shop, but I had about twenty-four hours to get there. No supplies. No time to twiddle my thumbs and gain the confidence (or the nervousness) of extra time. A mad dash to the end - if Professor Haggard sincerely intended to bring me Zeke's at all. Having never been to the hospital - or its psych ward before, I had no idea how to tell where we were. Lost in the shifting neons and LEDs, he might've brought me anywhere.

Within a few streets of Zeke's place, I recognized my first road name. My roiling stomach calmed. Not relief exactly. More so a certainty that I had made it to the next level. Acknowledgement of

what lay ahead. Too much room to fail. No chance
of being left alone with Zeke to plot out my escape.
When this ended, I owed that man more than I
could possibly repay. If I died doing this, he'd
probably never forgive himself.

I couldn't think that. I needed to push aside
all else - nothing else mattered but Gray. Otherwise,
I would stumble before the finish line. Choked.
Zeke had a wife and children. His life would go on
with or without me, and any guilt he might have if I
screwed this all up would be fleeting. Not like I
knew him. Not like Rory. We weren't best friends.
Doubt probably haunted our interactions.

Liar. Lying to myself again. Breaking the
promises I swore in the silence of my mind. Pushing
aside the grief and panic - I had to embrace what I
was. To absorb the strength innate to my struggle -
as unfair as the years of hiding were, I survived
them. Survived the rumors, escaped them more like.
Watched how they tore two people apart in such
different ways, but I wouldn't make the same
mistakes - wouldn't guard jealously a treasure
freely given. The world didn't have to know if Gray
didn't want them to, but I refused to hide myself
away. Disguise my love as anything else. If we
lived, we'd be together. If I died, how noble would
that be? To die for love.

Sickness brewed once more in my stomach.
Thinking dangerous thoughts. Not tonight. Not
tomorrow. Neither Gray nor I would die - for love
or anything else. I'd win. I spent my life fighting the
odds - to not get caught, to keep secrets (my own

and those forced upon me), to escape - I could face this impossible peak - surmount it.

Parking in front of the store, Professor Haggard turned off the car, shifting to face me. "Are you sure you want to do this?"

Flicking the lock, I opened my door. "I'm not Rory, professor. I'm not a risk-taker."

"Which makes your recent behavior all the more concerning," he pointed out, but he made no further protests.

Zeke waited at the door. His smile large and bright as he saw me, but the brows furrowed - peaking upward in concern when he glanced at Professor Haggard. They kept in touch, hadn't they? It would be beyond awkward if this was their first meeting since Rory's death.

"Hey, Zeke, sorry I - "

Shaking his head, Zeke reached out, setting the heavy weight of his hand upon my shoulder. "Don't worry about it, kid. It's all good." His eyes shifted to Professor Haggard. "Ari."

"Zeke, I hear your son started college this year."

With a wave of his hand, Zeke beckoned us into the warmth of his shop. "Yeah, he's doing great." He guided me to the chair as he pointed over toward a new painting hanging beside the reception desk. "That's one of his. Managed to sell some through a couple local places in L.A."

"Los Angeles? Well, I suppose it's better than if he had ended up in New York." Professor

Haggard slipped his hands into his pockets, sauntering over to the painting.

While he focused on the blurred evening cityscape, I settled into the chair with Zeke at my side. I tugged off the hoodie, pulling up the sleeve to leave my left arm exposed as he carefully aligned the transfer paper to match up with the lines coming down from my shoulder. As he pulled the paper away, leaving the light stencil behind, he pulled up a hand mirror.

"Lines match up, what do ya think?"

No shimmer came at my side. Rory remained wherever he had gone and Carreau with him. All the lines matched. I had studied the drawings, redid them with Rory's guidance again and again. Every bit of the guide fit the mental image I had created with each redraw. With this, my body would end the cycle. Bring Gray back from the dead. Victor Frankenstein had nothing on me. I would drag a body - fully formed - from nothingness.

No matter how I talked it up - panic brewed inside me. I wasn't anything special. Gray saw the dead. He dealt with the afterlife for most of his life - although neither of us had actually talked about that. And maybe we should have. Maybe then he would have understood his situation. Helped me not panic about mine. What if I failed? What if after this I lived - to listen to him burn alive again - for the last time - knowing that I failed him?

"Yeah, yeah - it looks good."

269

At my side, Professor Haggard frowned. "You look a bit pale, James. Are you sure - "

"I'm sure," I said, cutting him off.

As Zeke's needle hummed to life, Professor Haggard stood before me. His eyes studied my face. "We're here. Zeke's working on your tattoo. I think it's time you explained yourself."

"Rory mentioned Gray to you, didn't he?"

The same dark phantom fell across his features. "You said this wasn't about Theodore Thompson."

I shook my head, careful to keep my arm still. "It's not. This is about Gray."

"My brother described Gray to me in detail. If you're discussing the same person, you'd be talking about Theodore Thompson," he proclaimed. "A man who is dead."

Explaining this would be a waste of time. Rory had faith in his brother - thought the guy could help, but skepticism failed to cover his adversarial hatred - unadulterated loathing frankly - for anything to do with Crables Manor and its ghosts. I could not give him faith in what I could not show him. Without Rory, I had no way to confront him. No history to throw his way to argue my case. Worse still - if Zeke doubted while he had a needle to my arm, what would happen? Would he finish the markings?

"What if that weren't true?" I asked instead.

Haggard crossed his arms over his chest. "Then your argument against the hold would be rather lackluster."

See - waste of time. I couldn't convince him. In spite of everything, I recognized a lost cause. The more fervently I argued, the worse this would be for me. My best efforts would be useless. However, if I tried to lie, I risked making Zeke uneasy - and perhaps pushing him to believe I tricked him. Still, if I stumbled too long, there was a chance the man would want to argue for me - offer up evidence from when I had Rory with me when we first met.

No matter what - I'd be running out of here. My best bet - I couldn't even begin to calculate. I needed Rory, but my odds of him showing up were worse than pathetic. "Did you ever tell anyone else about Gray?"

"Only the man tattooing you." His lips squirmed. Fighting against what expression, I couldn't tell. "Before I realized he was just another drug-induced hallucination."

"But Rory wasn't on drugs at Crables Manor," I pointed out.

Glancing away, the professor leaned against the back counter. "With as long as my brother spent on drugs, having hallucinations and dissociative symptoms even after being clean for a period of time - long enough to go through withdrawal but not significantly beyond a handful of weeks - isn't uncommon. Additionally, with his relapses..." Haggard shook his head. "I was naive to believe him at the time. Honestly, the fact that our mother allowed me to see him in that state..."

"She didn't have much choice," Zeke noted, lifting his needle from my arm as he spoke. We had talked during my other sessions, but somehow, his words made me far more nervous now.

Sneering, Haggard glowered. "They were divorcing - not dying. If anything, they ought to have feared his influence."

"Whatever - not to sound like a dick, but I really don't care about your brother issues or family issues," I announced, cutting their argument off before it could continue. "If you only told Zeke - who was clean at the time - about Gray, how do you think I found out. From him? And what? He convinced me to get the same tattoos your dead brother tried to draw on himself? The same ones which he pulled from the very foundation of Crables Manor?" And a handful of ghosts - but again, ardent cynic.

With a sigh, he sighed as Zeke continued his work. "No. I don't believe Zeke would bring that up unprompted, but I also don't believe I was the only one Rory mentioned Gray to."

"I don't know anyone living outside this room who knows about Gray. Theodore Thompson - sure. But Gray? There's the three of us, and I only know about Gray because I met him." Before Professor Haggard could argue, I pressed on. "During the lucid dreaming project - I thought I was screwing up. Some freaky old manor and the most frustrating person I had ever met. But then Halloween came around, and Cheyenne took a group of us on a Boston fright tour - that included a walk through Crables Manor."

"As she mentioned when she argued that her, Maddix, and Chad could all cover Thompson from different angles. Funny how almost half of those attending knew about Thompson, but you believe that you never had any exposure to the building prior to that night," he retorted sarcastically.

Struggling not to roll my eyes, I sighed. "I considered that."

"And what disproved you being subconsciously influenced?"

"Zeke? You mind?"

He nodded, lifting and backing off enough for me to tug my wallet free and pull out the Ted Williams baseball card. Both men gaped. Leaning forward, they stared at it like I held up a pure gold. "I found this exactly where it was in my dream. In Gray's room."

"You could've bought that," Professor Haggard argued - his voice choked and disbelieving - though I couldn't tell if that came from what I showed him or his retort.

"If you think I could afford that card, you haven't been paying attention. I bought the plastic to hold it in. I thought Gray would be pissed if he found out I had his prized possession stuffed in my wallet, but I couldn't bear to leave it in my room." My lips curled into a smile as I set it down, shifting back into position for Zeke to continue. "Careful with it. Gray's dad gave that to him."

"Cards like these can be faked," he floundered, running a hand through his hair.

"He knew things," Zeke added. "Things he shouldn't have known when I first met him. Came to me, and it was like talking to Rory again."

A harsh forced laugh escaped the psychiatrist. "And what? I'm supposed to believe you can see ghosts? That some attempts at lucid dreaming awoke some psychic ability in you?"

"I'm not special. Crables Manor is special. There's a reason it's considered to be one of the most haunted places in Boston. People died there by the dozen. A family killing each other in the basement. The widow dead in the watch. Cook in the kitchen - two doctors died there, your brother." I tried to contain the wince as the needle crossed down to my wrist. "You've spent how long getting papers about the place, and you didn't once consider that there might be a reason so many people were attracted to it? That they became almost possessed by it?"

Another disbelieving scoff. "I've read your work, James. You never struck me as a believer in the fantastical."

Staring him in the eye, I tried to call out - tried to get across why that shouldn't have been the defense he believed it was. That my own skepticism should've underlined the truth of my words. "When a life is on the line, should my cynicism be the reason that life is lost?"

"Thompson died decades ago."

"Then you don't mind giving me twenty-four hours to prove you wrong."

He blinked. "What?"

"If you are so certain that you are right, it shouldn't matter. I have no intention of killing myself. I plan on being alive January 1st, so your conscience can be clear. I'm not suicidal. I'm not manic or insane." Shoulders falling, Professor Haggard frowned, his brows curving upward as his expression turned pitying. "I know how ridiculous this sounds, but every time I believed myself to be wrong - every single time I started to not believe, I've been proven wrong. What sort of scientific mind would I be if I failed to reconcile my results to the data when the data has clearly opposed all prior suppositions?"

"When your results run counter to logic, you first should reanalyze your sources and their mechanics. A card in a room isn't enough to rationalize the existence of ghosts," he argued.

"What do you have to lose if you give me time and find yourself right?"

"Your life!" Haggard exclaimed, leaping forward as if to interfere, but Zeke's hands remained steady as did I. Standing before us, the professor clenched his hands into fists. "You can tell me that you aren't suicidal, but that isn't the sort of reassurance I need. We're doctors, James. You were found unconscious - severely dehydrated and malnourished, yet you refused to eat. When questioned, you claimed to be playing a game that doesn't exist, and if you were almost any other male student, I might believe you were hiding the embarrassment of a masturbation bender, but your room was pristine when they found you."

This time, I didn't bother to hold back the grimace as Zeke resolutely pushed on toward the end. The lines were almost complete. Just a bit longer. Haggard might've been in decent shape, but with adrenaline coursing through my veins, I could lose him in the streets. "What if you're right? What if this is all some breakdown from me having to face that I'm basically an orphan the moment I come out? That my folks'll disown me, and I'm freaking out because I promised to own who I was when I got here, but it's a hell of a lot harder than I imagined. Maybe that's happening. Maybe you're spot on, but if you stop me from doing this, I'll spend the rest of my life wondering. I'm asking you to let me go - not even twenty-four. Hell, give me until ten o'clock tomorrow. That's all I need. Give me time, and if you're right - and nothing changes, then I won't fight against you." His gaze wavered, and I pressed, "We both know how much easier that would be."

"You're asking me to bet my career - "

"I'm not. We both know where I'll be spending that time."

Adjusting his jacket, he stepped back. "And what? I'm supposed to chaperone you to Crables? Wait until Cheyenne and Chad show up for that ridiculous vigil."

"Probably not the worst overnight spent with a patient."

Haggard fell silent, leaving only the buzz of Zeke's needle as he finished the design to carry throughout the room. Back and forth, the professor paced. Questions haunted him as much as they did me, but I couldn't bet on them answering him. I had mapped out the route in my head. I could get there. The busses would take a while to be informed, and I had my pass on me. Race across town. Wait until the flames and screams started. Reach in and pull Gray out. With him at my side, the professor couldn't deny the truth, but I had to make it until then.

When Zeke finally finished, pulling away to set his equipment to be cleaned, Haggard sighed, shaking his head. "I've already taken a risk bringing you here for that idiotic tattoo."

"Then what else do you have to lose?"

"Ari, he knew things - things only your brother would know," Zeke argued on my behalf.

Holding up a hand, Haggard shook his head. "Don't. Zeke, just don't."

"Rory didn't kill himself."

Something broke inside him at that. Like a puppet whose strings were suddenly cut, he sagged almost crashing down upon himself. "Nobody can know that. He overdosed. Accident or suicide, none of that matters. He's dead, and indulging my student's mental break isn't going to bring him back."

"But it could bring back somebody else! He wanted to save Gray. If James can do it -"

As their argument enveloped them, I shifted, backing away slowly. Zeke had to know. Had to have planned this, but I had no time to appreciate the way he angled Haggard to lose track of me.

Rory and he probably had years of practice, but the moment he did, I ran. Out in the cold air with only the hoodie in my hand. My body burned - raging with heat. Adrenaline - from what was to come. From the pain of the tattoo which itched and buzzed up and down my arm. Whatever it was, it inoculated my body against the cold, leaving only the long shadows and sudden lights of Boston between me and Crables. A scream - my name, and thunderous footsteps behind me. I could do this. Down the backroads, dodging between streets and climbing a wall blocking off one section from the next to drop down and climb onto a bus which rumbled off as I tugged on the hooded sweatshirt. Steel rumbled beneath me. Brakes squeaked as they released. I could do this. I had to do this.

Chapter Thirty-Four

My nerves buzzed, charged with a near indescribable panic. A few other riders huddled here and there, spread throughout the bus as it rumbled down the road, getting closer and closer to the manor. They had a map of the bus route. Sitting before it, I studied the roads, trying to memorize the smaller routes from the various stops to Gray. With his car and phone, Professor Haggard could easily send the cops to collect me, so I jumped off two stops early.

Underneath my feet, the world spun. Tilting and listing as restless as a boat, but I held my balance as I raced through the back roads. The map hummed, fading faster and faster from my mind as hunger grew once more in my belly. Adrenaline could do nothing to stop its coming.

Just a bit further.

Lights flashed; yellow tape blockaded the front, and cops mulled about the front entrance. A small crowd gathered, watching from the street. Apparently, Cheyenne hadn't been the only one who considered this night a good one for a vigil, or maybe these people came here like a New Year's Eve tradition.

Every now and then - somebody would set off fireworks. They whistled and broke overhead, and it would get worse at midnight. Louder and louder until midnight. Their booming roars deafening, hiding the screams as Gray burned again.

"You better not have been responsible for this," a familiar voice hissed.

Snorting, the guy standing next to Cheyenne crossed his arms over his chest. "If I planned on doing this, I wouldn't have shown up. This is a waste of my time. I'm heading home."

Chad and Cheyenne. They were here.

When Chad shifted, heading toward the train station to take him back out of the city, Cheyenne reached out, grabbing his sleeve. "Come on! Let's find a way inside!"

"Around the cops?"

She laughed with a shrug. "They won't even say why they're here. If we buy some of those kids some firecrackers or something, they'll get distracted and we can sneak around the back."

Pulling up my sweatshirt's hood, I crossed toward them, keeping to the shadows, trying my best to look casual. None of the cops glanced my way, but that didn't stop my pulse from soaring. "I'm with Cheyenne."

Whirling around, Cheyenne almost shrieked, but quickly, she covered her own mouth. Her eyes widened and then narrowed as they studied me before she whispered, "They're here for you, aren't they?"

Chad snorted. "Why would they be here for him? Looking like shit isn't a crime."

"Tom decided my not going home for Christmas deserved a psych hold." My mind screamed at them, begging for them to believe me. Trust me. Ignore the way exhaustion cradled my eyes. Ignore that I had run away from what amounted to a 72-hour nap and chat session. Cheyenne's gaze dropped to my wrapped arm. "James..."

"Oh - no," I said, lifting the sleeve. "Just a new tattoo."

Running a hand through his hair, Chad knocked off his hat. "Man, you've got to be freezing."

"I'm fine."

With a frown, Cheyenne huddled around, pulling Chad closer to angle them between me and the cops. "You're not acting like you. What's really going on?"

"He's having a breakdown, obviously," Chad grumbled. "Question remains - were you headed this way before the hold? Or did Tom's concern push you over the edge?"

I shrugged - helpless to argue against either. Not because he was right or wrong, but my eyes remained on the watch, waiting to see the first sign of light behind the dirty glass.

Rubbing my eyes, I shook my head. "Chad - come on. You know the floor plan, right? There's got to be a better way in - maybe an addition? After the fire?"

They shared a pitying look, and I couldn't - I couldn't just stand there and hope they would listen to me. I could see it. They had no intention of helping me as I stood now. Suspicion - concern - would stop them.

Grinding my teeth, I clenched my hands into fists. Pins and needles stuck me between the cold of the winter's air and the heat of my rapidly beating heart. "Cheyenne, you know there's a legend that on this night every year - "

"Theodore's screams can be heard from the widow's watch," she finished. With a tilt of her head, she considered me. "Apparently, the guy - Rory Haggard - thought Theodore could be pulled back out. Like he was in limbo."

"Wait, Haggard? Like Professor Haggard?" Chad asked.

Both Cheyenne and I nodded. "Yeah, his brother was the guy who supposedly set fire to the place and then overdosed."

"But he didn't. I wasn't lying, Cheyenne. Ever since that lucid dreaming project, I keep dreaming about this place and everybody who died here - especially Theodore," I admitted, and while Cheyenne leaned in closer with curiosity, Chad rubbed his hand over his face. "I get it sounds crazy, but if I don't try, I'll always wonder. Isn't college supposed to be about going after crazy ideas?"

Chad snorted, laughing as he cocked an eyebrow. "Don't try what?"

"He wants to save him," Cheyenne murmured.

"What?" Chad scrunched up his face.
"Who?"

"Theodore," she and I spoke in unison.

His brows jumped, pushing up toward his hairline as he glanced between the two of us as if we'd just come out and told him we were bitten by zombies. "Okay, now you guys have put me in a weird position. I don't want to agree with Tom. Don't make me be the guy who agrees with Tom."

"What are you even talking about? You've been messing with me all semester," I retorted as Cheyenne nodded along. "Goddamnit, Chad, I'm not asking you to believe me. I'm asking you to help me, and if you can't do that, just stay out of the way!"

I didn't have time for this. I couldn't. I had to get inside the manor. Had to get to Gray. Out on the street, I couldn't hear. People talked too loudly. The fireworks came faster and faster, closer and closer together until I could barely hear my own thoughts - which made it all the more startling when Chad unzipped his jacket, grabbing me.

Stripping off his jacket, Chad manhandled me closer to the building tugging the hoodie from me. "If we switch clothes, it'll be easier. We're about the same height."

"Crap, Chad. Give me a second - I can - seriously?"

He tugged on the hoodie then forcefully pushed me into his jacket, slamming his hat down on my head. "After this - you're going to go back with Professor Haggard. You're a freaking mess, man."

"Fine, whatever," I grumbled, adjusting the hat.

"Now...we just need someone to distract the cops, so we can jump the side fence and sneak through the kitchen..." His eyes slid over to Cheyenne.

Shoving us back, Cheyenne huffed. "I get to be lead author on the paper for this."

Which was ridiculous. Even if everything worked, nobody would believe it enough to accept a paper - especially not in a peer-reviewed journal, so I nodded, and Chad scoffed. "Be my guest."

With a toss of her hair over her shoulders, she crossed the street. When she reached the other side, she stepped up onto the sidewalk - a particular chunk with the fewest people, but she fumbled, collapsing with a sudden shriek. The cops glanced up, and one moved immediately to help her.

"Move it," Chad huffed, guiding me quickly around the back. None of the lights were on, and the black iron fence blocked all access, but climbing up on the wall, he dragged me to his side. "You first."

My arms ached. Exhaustion and hunger warring in my body, but I hurled by body over, rolling into a crouch in the bushes. A moment passed and Chad fumbled down beside me. With one hand on the back of my neck, he shoved me around, keeping me low to the ground as we snuck along the side, dashing across the yard toward the door.

The door opened easily enough - the lock broken by someone who must have come before us. Dust and mold clung to every surface. The same as it had been when Maddix, Cheyenne, and I had come for the seance. Nothing seemed out of place as we crossed from the kitchen to the back stairs.

"So...you're going pretty far out of your way based on a dream." Glancing at me out of the corner of his eye, he waited for a response. I hated how he dug.

"Yes. I'm gay. You were right. Congratulations," I spat.

His eyes narrowed. "That's not what I meant."

"I don't care what you meant, Chad. If all goes well, Gray's alive - and I've got to figure out how to deal with a guy who died in 1942," and there was too much to think about. So much that threatened to suffocate me just considering how much.

But Gray would be alive. I dreamed of it. Yearned for it. The weight of him in my arms. Holding him close, kissing those soft lips, pressing him against my body, my hands sliding against his smooth pale skin. Just the thought of him had me heated. I wanted him. More than I had ever wanted anything in my life, I ached to be with him. To wrap him in everything soft and warm and wonderful. Hide and burrow into the blankets with my arms wrapped around him. Tuck him into my chest. Kiss his forehead and sleep - blank and dreamless, knowing how much better it would be to wake with him in my arms.

From the back room on the second floor, we stayed along the walls - Chad following my lead - as I carefully avoided the weak and broken floorboards. He remained almost claustrophobically close - hovering on the periphery of my sight.

"Do you think you're dating him?" he pushed when we made it to the main stairs.

Pausing, I shifted, glaring over my shoulder. "I'm in love with him, and he loves me. If you're sticking this close, you're in for a show as the second he's safe, I can't promise I'll be able to stop from really *feeling* it."

Another scrunched up expression. "What are you even - ?"

Grabbing Chad by the front of the hoodie, I shoved him against the front wall. "I hear 'we're alive' sex is the best."

"Whoa, man, I mean...whoa." His hands hovered - not touching me but simply showing me his palms. "If you can bring your boyfriend back to life, maybe leave existentialist fornication for after your psych hold."

I huffed and shoved him back. "Don't screw with me."

A bright light drifted across the window, and we both tensed. It came back, shining directly into the second floor window as a loud voice echoed. "James Madison - come out with your hands up."

"What the hell?" Chad spat.

"It doesn't matter." I pushed him back, running up the stairs. "Stay or go - I don't care, Chad. I'm not leaving without Gray."

"Who the hell is Gray?"

"Theodore."

His eyes widened. I didn't have time to explain. Didn't he say he was going to help me? Why did he just stand there staring at me as if I had gone even crazier than he had thought? He should have realized. I loved Gray with everything I had. Love made men possessed. Protective in their madness, but I wasn't - I wasn't crazy, and as long as I could save Gray, that was all I wanted. To save him. I would do anything to make sure he lived.

"I got this," Chad announced, and he fled down the stairs.

"Whatever," I growled, racing up toward the watch.

Sirens wailed, and fireworks boomed overhead. Lights shined, falling, or maybe I moved too far out of their reach as the shadows loomed on the third floor. The door to the watch grew closer and closer.

And then the fire started.

Chapter Thirty-Five

Burning ash and cinder fell down as the roof crumbled. Screams echoed in the ruined manor, but they weren't Rory's. Down came the eaves. Wallpaper peeled. The rugs - too moldy and damp to catch, caked with debris. Whatever living creatures remained fled as I stumbled through the wreckage. Smoke curled in my lungs, but as the heat built around me, I could only see the one white door. Locked and bound. The last bit of wood between me and Gray.

"Gray!" I called, shoving aside the mess - careful not to get too close to the flames. I had to keep the lines on my body safe. If the fire burned me, it might disrupt the markings. I couldn't risk it. Not after everything. Not after the I.V. and the blood and not knowing what would destroy us. "I'm here! Gray, I'm coming! Hold on!"

As decayed as the rest of the manor was, the door to the widow's watch stood firm. The knob heated, but I had no tattoos on my palms. My fingers remained clean. Still, I wasn't an idiot. Chad's jacket would melt, likely stick to my skin, so I ripped off the hat - wool and damp from the slurry outside which had come and gone and come again throughout December. Jiggling the handle, I cried out, slamming my head against the wood. Locked.

And that was when I heard him. Not exactly a scream. Something bloodless and bone-crushing - a wail of pure agony reverberated through the wood before something slammed up against the wood. Nails clawing. Gray struggled to get out.

"Gray?" I called, beating on the door. I had to get through. He was right there. Right on the other side. Screw a lock. I would kick the door down if I had to. "Gray, answer me! Gray?"

"James?" his voice, soft and panicked, reached me. Pierced my chest and squeezed my heart. How was it possible to love someone so completely? "James, you've got to get out."

Shaking my head, I backed up and ran, slamming my shoulder against the wood, but it stayed solid. "Gray, I'm going to kick the door in. Back away, I don't want to hurt you."

"James! James, don't! They'll get you! Just run!"

As if I could. The first kick did almost nothing. With the second, the hinges creaked, but Gray wailed again. Smoke rose. Sirens wailed. Footsteps thundered, but I couldn't tell where they were coming from - I could barely see anything around the tears as I kicked again - slamming into the doorway only to stumble as it flew open - the lock ripped from the wall.

On the other side, Gray stood. Dark hair tousled, ash covering his face. His eyes bright with tears which streamed down his face. He wore pajamas - soft pants and a plain long-sleeved shirt. Soft. Everything soft and small and slim, and my arms had never wrapped around anything so lovely.

Pulling him from the watch, I buried my face in his ash-covered hair. "Gray..."

His arms wound around me. Hotter, somehow, than the fire which raged behind him and around us. The wood creaked, and the air rushed through with the hungry burning, but none of that mattered. Gray stood in my arms. I had done it.

One-two one-two

No. No - no - no, this wasn't a dream. This was real. I had Gray. She couldn't take him from me.

Then the knife slid into my side. Quick and cold and aching as I collapsed to my knees, Gray carried me down. His eyes shadowed and apathetic to my pain - although the tears kept pouring down his pale face.

"Oh, little bird, that wasn't so hard now, was it?" Dr. Ose murmured, coming up from behind Gray. His fingers trailed over Gray's back as he focused on me. His dark eyes swirled. "Don't worry, Mr. Madison. You won't feel pain much longer."

The man ducked, pressing his lips to Gray who shifted like a sunflower toward the light to kiss him in return. A shadow loomed over him. I should have seen it. Should have known. This wasn't Gray.

"How?" I gasped, pressing firmly against the wound as blood dripped from the knife in Gray's hand. "She took him back. How did you get him?"

Carreau - the master puppeteer - shifted Gray's body, back out of the kiss with the most serene contentment. "There's a reason she never left the watch, James." He had no right to speak with that voice. To make it sound bored and apathetic. "It took so much energy to get all those spirits high

291

enough, but we just knew you'd be the one she'd come down to the first floor for - well, you and the little bird."

"I'm not letting you kill him," I growled.

I struggled, pushing myself up one for the pain to knock me down once more. Carreau cooed, "Oh, poor boy, you can't win." Leaving Ose, he knelt before me, brushing Gray's fingers over my face. "But think - you and Gray get to be together forever. In death, and your bodies, in life. We're so thankful he found you. Perfect little host - so receptive and needy. You were desperate, and even better, you were just my type."

A blur of white flew across the room. Crashing into Ose, the form slammed its head down again and again, crying out more curses than I could have claimed to have known.

"Not. This. Time!" Rory cried, beating his head against Ose's over and over, leaving the man bloodied in the entrance to the watch. Standing, he swirled. The long sleeves of his straitjacket twirling as his bloodied hands hung at his side. "James! Grab him!"

I threw myself forward, wrapping my arms around Gray as Rory slapped the knife away. With a jerk, he shifted my sleeves, forcing the markings on my arms to press against one another. All along my skin, the tattoos burned.

"I'm not a idiot, Carreau," Rory spat into Gray's face. Sparks jumped from my body, and with each beat of my heart, I could see the electricity manifest, growing brighter and brighter as if I would go supernova. "Nobody's getting inside that body, and you're sure as shit coming out of this one."

Struggling, Carreau bellowed. His features - the shadow of his phantom form split, pulling and twisting before combining once more with Gray's face. "I've won, you pathetic worm. Even if Viktor can't take the other one, this body is mine."

Bloodied to an almost featureless pulp, Ose groaned, "Edmond..."

"He's already pulled me through the veil. Unless you want him to burn with me, I'm free," Carreau insisted, but I held firm. The rage and desperation and longing growing hotter and hotter within me until the light blinded me as the world careened so far from what I believed to be true, but hadn't that been the way of it - Crables Manor existed in a dimension unto itself. Monstrous. Impossible. "Ink can't stop me!"

His face peeled, shadow stretching as Gray screamed. The two splitting and pulling back together only to part once more in my arms.

"Rory - the roof," I yelled as I struggled to hold fast.

Rory's eyes drifted up. Wiping blood from his face, he sighed. "Florence?"

One-two one-two

All in black, she came from the watch. Her hair coiled upon her head - loose but firmly held. Her skirt swooshed around her feet. Round and full as her waist was tightly cinched and small. Older than I expected considering her story.

293

Brushing her hands over her skirts, she tilted her head, watching as Carreau and Gray fought against one another. In a low voice, she announced, "That will not do."

In a blast of light, she moved. Her hand grabbed the shadowy visage of Carreau, wrenching him free from my grasp.

As Florence threw Carreau into the flames behind her, the floor buckled and broke beneath us, sending me and Gray down onto the creaking remains of his bedroom floor. All the air rushed from my lungs, but my arms held tight.

Spots. Black and white blocked my sight until Gray shifted, struggling to roll off me. "James - you've got to get up," he urged. "We have to get out of here."

"Gray?" I tentatively reached, cupping his cheek.

His eyes glistened as he pressed into my touch. "Yes, it's me. You did it."

"Had more than a little help."

He laughed. I hadn't even realized how long it had been since I last heard him laugh, but I missed it more than anything. Struggling to my feet, I wrapped an arm around his shoulder as he held his about my waist - pressing his hand against my wound.

"I'm so sorry," he whispered again and again as he half-dragged me down the stairs.

"It wasn't you." Gray nodded, but he apologized once more when I winced as he headed toward the front door. "Police might still be out. We should go out the back."

"Police?"

"Long story."

Shaking his head, Gray opened the door regardless. "I've been in this house long enough. If the police want to complain about trespassing, I'll make my apologies."

"Gray - that's not -" but out we went. A few people mulled about in the street, but the police were gone. Cheyenne hovered on the other side of the tape, and when she saw us, all the blood rushed from her face.

"Oh my god...you weren't lying," she whispered, lifting the tape for us. Her eyes remained wide as she stared at Gray. Her lips parted without any sound until I groaned, and she saw blood dripping down my side. "Oh my god! You're bleeding!"

I tried to reply, but the world went sideways.

"James!" Gray caught me as Cheyenne rushed forward.

"Move," a deep voice commanded, and Cheyenne blubbered before shifting out of the way. "Cheyenne, call 9-1-1. Tell them we need an ambulance outside Crables Manor."

"Professor Haggard -"

"Go!"

Gray held my hand, holding tight to me. "James - hold on. Please."

Whatever mode Professor Haggard went into as he pressed on my wound, he stuttered when he looked up at Gray's face. "You're dead."

Clinging to me, Gray gasped, "What?"

"You're dead. You're Theodore Thompson. You're supposed to be dead."

The pain ebbed away even as the darkness drew nearer, and here his hands lessened in pressure as he panicked. "I might be dying - can we focus on my having not lied to you and Gray being alive after I'm no longer bleeding?"

"Shit! Yes, sorry - but he's - and you..."

The last thing I saw was Professor Haggard shaking his head as he pressed hard, struggling to staunch the bleed even as his entire understanding of life and death crumbled.

Chapter Thirty-Six

Beams of sunlight cascaded, dripping warmth into the clinical white of the room. Monitors beeped, but while the hospital seemed so cold before, soft heat curled around me. Kept me gently cradled. All from a simple touch. A hand curled around mine - the warmth of a body alongside me.

Blinking, I shifted. No pain. A dull ache - maybe - but tubes pulled at my arm. They had me on the good stuff. Snuffling closer to the dark hair leaning against my shoulder, I sighed, almost purring in contentment.

"James?" Gray shifted, rubbing his eyes. "Hm?"

My heart swelled in my chest, almost exploding at the sight of him. Pale face, high cheekbones, bright eyes, and the loose dark lines of his sleep-tousled hair. Blinking away the tears, I bit my lip. I had to keep it together. We did it. No reason to cry - but relief overwhelmed me. Half-laughing, half-crying, I reached for him. Our foreheads pressed together. The soft gusts of his laughing breaths - the wide smile of his face as he pressed close to me. Warm and solid - for all his slim form - there, there in my arms.

"Hi," I whispered.

Pressing a quick kiss to my lips, he laughed - I'd never heard a more beautiful sound. "Hello."

"I missed you." I cupped his face, tracing the sharp angle of his jaw. "I missed you so much. I thought - I thought I wouldn't make it in time..."

He shushed me gently, pressing kisses over my face. "I'm here. I'm not going anywhere, I promise. I'm safe now. We're safe now."

"You don't have to - if you don't want to - I don't want you to feel like you have to be with - "

He silenced me with a kiss. His body pressed against mine. The weight of him drew me back to the warm safety of those scattered sunbeams, and I wanted to be upset. Wanted to comment on the cliche of him kissing me silent, but he was here. Gray was alive and in my arms, and there was nothing that could destroy how much I wanted him to want to be there with me. To love me in the same confusing, all-consuming way I loved him.

In the hope of a softer love. A love which could last - passionate and hot even as it gentled between us. Comfort and confidence in its strength. I wanted that walking down the street hand-in-hand to get groceries sort of love. Side by side on the subway - heads bowed over one phone sort of love. Getting an apartment and arguing cat or dog kind of love.

"I love you," he confessed - his breath warm against my lips. "Believe me, James, I have no intention of ever staying anywhere out of obligation to anyone."

Pulling him into another kiss, I moaned. "I love you too."

"Lovely confession boys, but let's try to keep your heart monitor from going off, James. You're making the nurses nervous," Professor Haggard announced from the door.

Gray blushed - pink rising to his cheeks as he slipped from the bed to a chair beside it. "Apologies, Dr. Haggard."

At that, Professor Haggard sighed. "That will never stop being strange."

"Sorry," Gray repeated. "I'd love to say you'll get used to it, but I'm rather baffled myself."

"I'm glad you're here."

Gray's eyes softened as he took my hand. "Me too."

"Yes - you are both very lucky to be alive - especially the young man who died over fifty years ago," Professor Haggard announced, sliding the door closed behind him. "Now, James - we kept your original hold from your parents because you are eighteen; however, you were stabbed, so we had to reach out to your emergency contact - "

No - oh, no. This was not how I wanted them to find out. My eyes darted around the room, but I couldn't see them, so probably they couldn't see me. My hand which held Gray's tightened. "No - I don't want them here."

"James..." Professor Haggard trailed off, looking exceedingly uncomfortable.

Gray shifted closer to me. "He's awake and not a minor. He doesn't have to see them if he doesn't want to."

"We've informed her that you've been stabbed and about your psych hold as a result of Tom's call," Professor Haggard pressed on, focusing on me as if he couldn't fully bear to confront all the truths Gray represented. "She asked to see you -"

"And I'm sure she'll refuse to pay even a penny the second she realizes I'm in here with my boyfriend," I retorted.

Professor Haggard rubbed the bridge of his nose. "Your student medical insurance covers all of this. I've also taken on any discrepancy as it was my fault you ran off to go to your boyfriend - my brother's son, and stop him from going down his father's footsteps into addiction."

My brain crashed - blue screen of death - blank. "What?"

"Theodore 'Gray' Haggard - my young nephew, who I only recently discovered as he ran away from a foster home after his mother's death - "

"But Rory died in 1984..."

Waving a hand, Haggard huffed, "Grandnephew - god only knows, but I'm adopting the poor kid."

"Wouldn't it be easier if he wasn't related to anybody in particular?" I suggested, and Gray nodded though he seemed rather pleased to be associated with Rory in any way. "Anyway - you're not making me forget. I don't want my mother here. I'm not - " But why wasn't I? She'd have to learn eventually, right? "Fine." I pressed a kiss to the back of Gray's hand. "No point in delaying the inevitable."

Gray's brows furrowed. "James - if you want, I can -"

"No. This is who I am. Either she accepts that, or..." I shrugged.

Professor Haggard adjusted his white jacket with a sigh. "That's - um...a very brave choice. I understand how hard that must be for you, but...James, she's already left."

"Oh."

That didn't matter. My mother hadn't even bothered to hear any sort of explanation from me. She hadn't fought or screamed or anything. I meant so little to her that she came - and what? Saw me and Gray? Immediately knew exactly who I was because as much as I tried to hide it, I mean, Simon knew. Maybe she always suspected. And none of that mattered because I ceased to exist to her at that moment.

It was better this way. Better that she left. All these tears, they were for Gray. Because I had him back. I saved him. He loved me, and I loved him, and nobody else mattered. Not really. Not as much. Because I always knew what would happen when they found out. This wasn't going to be a happily ever after in that way. My parents wouldn't even think twice about it. I meant nothing to them if I wasn't exactly what they had intended me to be, right?

Crawling back into the bed, Gray curled around me, softly whispering, "I'm so sorry. You're going to be fine. I swear - everything will be fine."

"Why?" The question escaped me though I knew exactly why. Professor Haggard opened his mouth to answer, but I couldn't hear the words. I knew Gray would blame himself. Shaking my head, I wiped my tears away. "I don't want to know. Just - did she say she'd be back?"

When the professor shook his head, a weight almost lifted. Abandonment hurt, but for years, I had struggled beneath the weight of would-they-wouldn't-they always knowing deep down this would be the end result. Anyway, compared to everything else, getting disowned hardly rated, right? It was better this way. Better it was over.

Pressing my face into the crook of Gray's neck, I breathed him in - the scent of him curling around me as warm and pure as the sunlight still streaming in - no dimmer for all that had happened.

Epilogue

Sitting on my lap, Gray glowered at his notebook. As he hummed, paging through it, I rested my chin on his shoulder and adjusted my arms wrapped around his waist.

"If I quit and don't get my GED, will you still love me?" Gray grumbled.

I laughed and pressed a kiss to his neck. "What would you do?"

"Telephone psychic. I'd be amazing at it," he asserted even as he shifted to mathematics. "Oh, math, at least you haven't changed."

When the door opened, we both glanced up as Tom entered. I couldn't blame him for his part in getting me held over winter break. Nine times out of ten, he would have saved my life. Still, our relationship hadn't recovered. He worried. I came out, and while Tom might've been the perfect roommate for somebody, we couldn't find a way back to anything more than the most lukewarm of friendships.

With a nod, I shifted back as Gray returned to his studying. "Hey, man."

"Hey, you both coming to dinner with the crew tonight?" Tom asked, tossing his bag on his desk.

I shook my head. "We're meeting Alexander and Chad for dinner. Apparently, Alexander's friends with somebody who knows the chef at this place downtown."

"Are those two dating?"

Gray snorted, holding back a laugh. "We'll probably never know."

"Well, I'll leave you two to it. See ya later, James. Bye, Gray!" and with a little wave, Tom raced off as we both quietly returned the sentiment.

Shutting his notebook, Gray turned in my arms. "If you're not rooming with him next semester, who's the fourth in your suite?"

"Some guy on the football team," I offered with a shrug, nuzzling against his smooth skin. "If you don't get your GED, odds are you can't get into Harvard - which means we can't room together for my junior year."

He groaned, shoving me backward into the mattress as he tossed his notebook onto my nightstand. "What if I want to go to Boston College?"

"We'll get an apartment."

Straddling my hips, he huffed. "And if I decide to go straight to work?"

"We'd probably have an easier time getting an apartment." I tucked a lock of his dark hair behind one of his perfect pale ears. As his brows furrowed, I smiled. "Honestly, Gray, you've got time to decide. Thanks to Dr. Kedves, I've got an internship up here for the summer and housing thanks to Ari."

"He does have a nice house..." Gray pursed his lips. "Maybe I should become a psychiatrist too. Between the hospital and teaching here, he lives a truly comfortable life."

I couldn't resist drawing him down into a kiss. "He's also a trust fund kid, so..."

"Well, damn! So was I. The mistakes I've made," he jokingly lamented though in his eyes, some truth existed behind his words.

Whether by death or choice, we both missed our parents. His father died shortly after his supposed death. We visited the grave every few weeks. My heart had raced at the gravestone beside his father's - I never wanted to see Gray's full name in that way ever again. My parents still hadn't contacted me since the hospital, and my phone plan had 'mysteriously' been cancelled without a word.

Professor Haggard added me to his when he added Gray. For how happy the man always seemed, his life was incredibly empty of people, but he seemed to like it that way. Even with Gray about, he didn't bother to be terribly social outside of comments tossed here and there as he raced around. Even the ring on his left hand served to keep people away rather than as a symbol of any sort of matrimony.

We didn't exactly talk about that. Not with him at least. I had my suspicions, but the way he immediately stepped up to help me and Gray afterward won me over. He had no intention to confide in either of us about Rory, but last time I had seen Zeke, he seemed to think Professor Haggard had had some sort of emotional catharsis. If Haggard cried half as much in joy at Gray being real as Zeke, then he was probably right.

Legs entangled on my dorm room bed, we curled together, breathing the calm - the warmth of contentment which grew more and more familiar. Admittedly, it didn't last long. We were both young and in love, and if we met Alexander and Chad still a bit breathless, nobody could blame us. After years of hiding who I was, my days were so much better than my dreams. We were alive. Together - in love.

www.ingramcontent.com/pod-product-compliance
Lightning Source LLC
Chambersburg PA
CBHW021459240626
47154CB00002B/441